THE KILLING MOON

A. S. FRENCH

NEONOIR BOOKS

ALSO BY A. S. FRENCH

The Astrid Snow series.

Book one: Don't Fear the Reaper.

Book two: The Killing Moon.

Book three: Lost in America.

The Detective Jen Flowers series.

Book one: The Hashtag Killer.

Book two: Serial Killer.

Book three: Night Killer.

Go to www.andrewsfrench.com for more information.

1 AMERICA

The beer chilled her throat, the taste reminding Astrid of the time she threw up over the neighbour's cat. Then she smiled at her companion.

They appeared to be a loving couple, the way they held hands as the candle flickered next to them. But they were the opposite of in love. The sparkle in his face wasn't because of desire but concentration to stop him from screaming. She'd already damaged one of his fingers as she squeezed again.

'You can tell me where the kid is, or I keep doing this.'

'I don't know where she is.' The words struggled to climb over his trembling lips.

'You're Daniel Gideon's lawyer. He kidnapped his daughter from London and smuggled her into the US, and you know nothing about it?'

'He'll kill me if I tell you.'

His skin was like old leather against hers.

'That's better than what I'll do to you.' She pressed hard against his bone. 'You'll be alive, but wish you weren't, pissing blood through a tube for the rest of your miserable existence.'

All her life, Astrid had imagined visiting the city of her childhood dreams. She'd hoped her first visit to the Big Apple would be more relaxing than this. Perhaps she'd have time later for the Bowie pilgrimage she'd been planning.

As she rubbed her skin over the lawyer's weather-beaten flesh, she imagined strolling down Lafayette Street and into Washington Square Park. She took her middle finger and dragged her purple nail across his palm as he told her what she wanted.

'He's keeping her in the penthouse.'

'Which one?'

Astrid let go of his hand. He flexed his fingers and grimaced.

'She's at the place on Dutch Street.' The pain subsided in his eyes, and she watched his relief transforming into the confidence he'd had when he first met her and assumed she was the date arranged for him. 'You won't be able to get inside; his security is too strong.'

'Tell me about it.'

'You need a key card and photo ID to enter the building.'

'You're his attorney; you must have those.'

He nodded. 'I can get you to the elevator, but he has too many guards inside the penthouse.'

'What security does he have?'

He took a napkin and wiped the blood from his hand. 'Gideon always has four men around him, all of them ex-Navy Seals.'

All she had to do was get into that room, which was where the lawyer came in. Astrid grabbed him by the arm.

'You can pay for the taxi there.'

She eased him out of the diner, keeping a firm grip on him through his expensive coat. The New York night airbrushed her face, the bouquet of the city replacing his bitter aftershave: smoke from grilled hotdogs and kebabs, traffic fumes, body odours, perfume wafting from stores and people, the scent of cheap leather goods and plastics from the street vendors, an oily, pissy smell coming up from the subways, garbage piled at the curb, and dusty air.

Astrid squeezed against him in the taxi.

I should think like a local; this is a cab.

It was a twenty-minute drive into Manhattan. On the way to the penthouse, she texted her contact in New York; without his help, she wouldn't be able to get Chloe Gideon out of the city. First, she had to get the kid away from that building. She gave the driver a hundred dollars when they got there.

'Keep the engine running and wait for me.'

Light summer rain cut across her face as they stepped out of the cab. Thunder rumbled overhead as she let go of him, and he stumbled forward. She followed the lawyer inside. The entrance was white and glittered like a disco ball. There were two security guards behind a desk, staring into screens and ignoring her. Another one loitered halfway down the lobby, standing next to an enormous canvas constructed of four identical portraits of Marilyn Monroe. The place stank of wealth and privilege, only obscured by the aroma of the orchids lining the far wall.

The lawyer removed his ID and a key card for the elevator. 'We're here to see Mr Gideon.'

The guard with the face sculptured from cracked concrete checked his details without expression, while the taller one built like a heavyweight boxer scrutinised her. They were granted admission with a grunt and strode from the desk. He swiped his card, and they entered the elevator. Astrid's hair was damp from the rain.

Sweat trickled down his head. 'What will you do when you get inside? They'll all be armed, including Gideon. Being with me won't keep you safe.'

It was a sixty-second ride to the penthouse. She considered his question, but didn't answer it. 'How many apartments are there in the building?'

The lawyer tried to wipe the fear from his face. 'There's fifty.'

'How many where we're going?'

He scratched at his ear. 'Five. He doesn't have the privacy he wants here, but he can't live in his other properties anymore.'

Even with all her research, this was news to Astrid. 'Why not?'

'He owns them in name only.' The lawyer pulled at the top of his shirt as if spilling state secrets. 'Mr Gideon's finances are not as healthy as he makes out in public. Several stock market losses meant he had to sell the other properties apart from this penthouse.'

That was good news to Astrid. Getting the kid away from Gideon wasn't the biggest problem she foresaw; it was what his response would be to losing the girl. If the billionaire were having money problems, then perhaps his focus would be somewhere else once she'd completed this job. And he'd have fewer resources to retaliate with.

The door opened, and they stepped on to the top floor. Rubbing his damaged finger, the lawyer rushed towards Gideon's place. Astrid stopped him with a touch to his shoulder, nodding at the red box on the wall.

'Smash that with your good hand.'

His eyes shrank and his mouth trembled. 'You want me

to break the fire alarm? That won't bother Gideon. He thinks he's invincible.'

Astrid cracked her knuckles. 'Just do it.'

She couldn't tell if the damp on his face was sweat or tears. He did as instructed, and the broken glass fell onto the floor. A high-pitched wailing sped around them, the screech of a banshee telling people to find safety. She pushed him towards the stairs at the end of the corridor. Gideon's place was behind them.

'Everybody get out, now!' Astrid shouted.

The first residents appeared from the apartment opposite, a grey-haired couple in their seventies. 'What's happening?' the woman said.

Her gaze was unfocused, moving randomly around her surroundings, her eyes obscured with cataracts so it was difficult to tell what colour they were. The man looked as if a puff of wind would blow him over. Astrid went to help them towards the fire exit, taking the woman's hand. The skin was cold to the touch, her flesh resembling one of those turtles who live for more than a century. The couple smiled at each other as if this was a regular part of their day.

Astrid thought of all the shared memories they had.

And then you forget them all.

'Come on; you'll be safe once you get downstairs.'

The woman reached for her face. 'We should take the elevator; it's quicker.'

Astrid shook her head. 'It's too dangerous. Use the stairs.'

More doors opened, and other people followed as the shrieking alarm continued.

Astrid handed the woman to the lawyer. 'Help as many as you can.'

It had been two minutes since he'd smashed the box,

and there was still no sign of Gideon and his men. Every other apartment but the one she wanted had emptied.

Just when she was about to bang on Gideon's door, it opened. The first guy out was a couple of inches shorter than her, about five foot ten, with a gut to embarrass Father Christmas.

This will be easier than I thought.

The next bloke out changed her mind. His arms were bigger than her legs, his chest you could row down the Hudson on. The other guard was slow on his feet; the second was alert and ready, searching everywhere for danger. After checking the corridor, he turned to give somebody inside a signal.

Gideon exited next. With dayglow eyes and sculpted cheekbones, he was a man who looked like he couldn't tell the truth to his reflection. His suit was worth more than everything she owned. It didn't matter. It wasn't his wealth she wanted; just the child he'd stolen from her mother, the daughter taken from his estranged wife.

The kid came out behind him, eight-year-old Chloe Gideon, without a care in the world on her face. Astrid froze for a second, her mind drifting back to the niece she hadn't seen for six months: Olivia. The girl she'd put at risk from a serial killer and who Astrid had been stopped from seeing again. Later, when Astrid's sister Courtney had calmed down, she'd relented and let them talk over Skype every night. The memory of it prompted Astrid into action.

'Everybody out!' she shouted again.

The other security followed Chloe from the room, and all six of them strode towards Astrid. The portly bloke at the front was suspicious.

'I can't smell any smoke in here.'

Astrid pointed down. 'It's on the bottom floor and

working its way up.' The guy turned to seek advice from Gideon. It gave her enough movement to stumble forward and bump her shoulder into his. 'Sorry.' She projected her best flustered clumsiness.

Gideon didn't even acknowledge her as he dragged his daughter into the stairwell. 'Let's just get out of here.'

The lawyer had told Astrid there were two exits from the building, including the fire escape leading through the underground car park and into the street. There were twenty flights to descend as the other residents disappeared from her view; the old couple were quicker on their feet than she'd expected.

She hung back a little, trying to get behind Gideon's crew, but the final two were having none of it. They stared at her, and then moved forward. The last of the group coughed as his fingers twitched towards his weapon. He was an ungainly figure, hospital-thin, unsteady on his legs as he grasped at the handrail. She glanced into his haunted eyes, recognising he was the weakest of the four, before kicking his knee. He crumbled on to the stairs and fell into his colleague. It happened so fast the others didn't see it.

As the third guard buckled under the force hitting him in the back of his legs, Astrid swung her elbow and caught him in the throat. The blow knocked him into unconsciousness, and he rolled down like a bowling ball. There was no escaping that.

The four ahead of her turned at once. Gideon was perplexed, his daughter's face full of excitement. The chubby guard fumbled for a gun he no longer had, while the second one froze. The delay was their undoing.

She had the weapon in her hand, the one she'd slipped out of chubby's jacket when she'd bumped into him. She cracked the second guy over the head with it, and he slumped against the rail. Astrid grabbed him to make sure he didn't tumble over. She was tempted to let him, but eased him on to the stairs. Then she spoke to the kid.

'Can you run down these steps, Chloe?'

The kid smiled at her and nodded. She took Chloe's hand and turned to Gideon, who hadn't uttered a noise during the chaos; until now.

'You don't know who you're dealing with, girl.'

Astrid suppressed a laugh. Her girlhood was long behind her, buried deep inside the shadows of her mind. She gripped on to the gun as she spoke.

'You think none of this matters because you'll retake Chloe whenever you want.'

His smile reminded her of Antony Hopkins in *Silence of the Lambs*. Or perhaps it was Anthony Perkins in *Psycho*.

'I don't know who you are, but soon enough, I'll have her back, and you'll be dead.'

He said all the right words, but didn't convince her. She leant in close so only he would hear.

'If she weren't here, I'd have thrown you over the rail by now.' She glared at him. 'You come near her in the future, or if anything bad happens to Chloe or her mother, I'll drop you from a larger height than this. But only after you've suffered, and you'll beg me to end it.' She turned from him and held on to the kid's hand. 'Your mother's waiting for you, Chloe.'

The girl smiled. 'Good. I don't like it here.'

They jogged down the stairwell, past broken and confused security, until hitting the exit at the bottom, then ran around the corner and into the cab.

'885 2nd Avenue,' Astrid said as she got her phone out and dialled a British number. By the time they reached their destination, Chloe had spent a long conversation reconnecting with her mother. Astrid touched the gun in her pocket. She had to get rid of it before getting her flight back to London.

As they stepped out of the cab, she stared at the kid speaking on the phone. Astrid had an hour before she could talk to Olivia.

It had been a good night's work.

2   CHILD'S PLAY

His handsomeness was unnerving; hair shorter and greyer than the last time she'd seen him, but he still possessed the glint in his eye which could disarm anyone's libido.

'Sorry about the extra security. All embassies now have to go through more stringent checks because of the electronic attacks we've had.'

'Attacks from whom?' Astrid thought she'd better show some interest since he was doing her a huge favour.

'Oh, you know, the usual suspects: the Russians, North Koreans, the Chinese, virtually everyone in the Middle East; and probably the Americans, even though we're supposed to be partners with a special relationship.'

'Is the kid going to be okay?'

'We've got Chloe settled into one of the guest rooms upstairs. I've organised her flight home, and spoken to her mother.'

Roger Taylor, working at the British Embassy in New York, offered her a drink. She declined. She hadn't touched a drop of alcohol in six months, not since that last heated confrontation with her sister. Astrid wouldn't be able to relax until Chloe was home in England, but most of the tension had seeped out of her. She stared at the row of bottles behind Taylor and told herself she deserved at least one glass, especially when she saw the unopened bottle peering at her.

'I'll have a double gin and tonic, Roge, if the offer's still open.'

She knew he hated the shortening of his name, but he appeared unmoved as he poured her the measure. The ice clinked as he handed it to her.

'I'm surprised the Agency has you rescuing kidnapped children. I'd have thought such a thing was way below the remit of the great Astrid Snow.'

The glass was cold to her touch as she lifted it to her lips. The gin was bitter and electric; as soon as it slithered down her throat, she understood it wouldn't be the last of the night. He continued to smile at her, and she remembered why she didn't like him. But, he was the only person who could help her get Chloe safely out of the country without her father knowing. He may have lost some of his wealth, but Gideon still had influential friends worldwide.

'I've left the Agency. This is a favour for a friend.'

The last bit was a lie. Astrid only had one friend in the world, and that wasn't Chloe Gideon's mother. The reason she was in New York was to quell the yearning in her heart for the kid she couldn't see.

Whatever this illness is, I don't need a cure for it.

'You've left the Agency? I thought that was impossible.'

'I'm making the impossible possible.'

I should get that printed on a shirt.

She finished the drink and got up to leave; content he'd

get Chloe back to her mother. Now she had an hour to kill before phoning the sister who hated her.

Taylor pushed a photograph across the desk towards her. 'If you're in the business of finding missing children, you could return the favour I'm doing for you with the Gideon kid.'

She peered at the image. Staring at her was a dark-haired teenager who was too thin, but so happy her teeth sparkled out of the picture. The girl held a placard stating NO MORE FRACKING.

Astrid picked up the photo. 'What's this?'

Taylor poured himself a drink, but she refused the offer of another; she'd never leave if she started on a second. There was plenty of time for that back at the hotel after speaking to Olivia.

'That's Alex Sanchez, the seventeen-year-old daughter of a friend of mine. She went missing a week ago.' The colour had drained from his chiselled cheekbones. 'I hoped you might find her for me.'

She handed him the photo and moved towards the exit. 'Maybe she fell down a mine.' She looked at him one last time before leaving. 'Thanks for the help with Chloe, but you don't need me. That's what the police and the FBI are for.'

She'd closed the door before he replied. A female security officer escorted her out of the building, checking to make sure she didn't leave with something she shouldn't.

Astrid sighed as she met the Big Apple's inky cold night. She strode past burger joints, pizza palaces, and outdoor vendors hawking hotdogs. A slight drizzle drifted across the skyline, and she gazed into it. When she was a kid, this was one of the places she'd escape to in her head, her reality constructed from black and white movies, tawdry crime thrillers, and the four-colour magnificence of a Marvel Comic; all while listening to a soundtrack of the Velvet Underground and the New York Dolls mixed in with Chic and Odyssey.

She took a deep breath and wondered when she'd return to England. There was only one thing she wanted to go back for, and her sister had put a halt to that, all apart from the occasional phone call.

Astrid hailed a taxi and headed for the hotel, her mind focusing on Olivia and the conversation they'd have. She thought about that as the car moved through the city.

Talking to children was never something she'd been good at. A deficiency Astrid knew came from her childhood, her discomfort compounded by society's rarely spoken but continually implied idea of the childless woman as a child-hating freak.

As she reached her mid-twenties, she began to feel fiercely maternal towards teenage girls when she encountered them. She understood how to speak to them and knew how to talk to the men who hassled them, but she had no desire to seek any close friendship with other women. Most of the time, she blamed that on her sister; on how Courtney had encouraged their father to hit Astrid and the way Courtney revelled in her hatred of her. Other times, she decided it was because there was something wrong with her; something broken inside her brain, which left her struggling to make an emotional connection with others.

But then she discovered she was an auntie and slowly started to change. It took five years for it to happen, for her to need to see her niece, if only once and from a distance, but she understood she wasn't the person she'd believed herself to be. All of these thoughts consumed her as the taxi drifted through the New York night and reached her destination.

Astrid got out of the car and scanned the surroundings. Her hotel was somewhere between downmarket and further downmarket. She'd considered trying the Chelsea Hotel for the nostalgia, but ended up at the Ritz Excelsior, a name which promised extravagance and comfort, but delivered neither. It was a five-storey building claiming twenty luxury rooms on each floor, but if the place was anything to go by, then luxury had gone downhill in recent years.

A scarred lip and raised eyes greeted her as she entered the hotel. The receptionist's eyebrows were as false as the breasts aimed at Astrid like neutron bombs. *Texas Chainsaw Massacre* shadows cascaded off the walls from the stuffed animal collection consuming most of the place. The carpet was an earthquake of convulsing colours vomited up from an explosion in a crayon factory. She ignored the aroma of dirty laundry and took the stairs.

In her room, she grabbed a towel that had seen better days and ran it through her hair. She kicked her shoes off, pulled her brand new Levis from her legs and dropped them with her jacket and top onto the floor. Once she was dry, she climbed under the covers to get warm. The pitiful-looking radiator hanging off the wall was a redundant artefact.

Astrid scanned the news on her phone. There was no mention of Gideon and the troubles at his building. She wondered if she'd scared him enough not to do anything stupid. An image of Chloe smiling on those stairs, when she knew she was leaving the man she'd never view as her father, settled the pain in Astrid's stomach. Then she saw the clock on the digital screen and it was time.

She wiped the webpage from the screen and dialled the

number in the UK. She listened to the tone connecting across the ocean, the constant hum vibrating inside her heart, and sucked in her breath. When no one picked up after a dozen rings, she stopped and tried again. She went through the same process for fifteen minutes before giving up.

Perhaps they're out. But this is when Courtney told me to call.

Her sister might have gotten confused by the time difference between the countries. She decided to leave it and try again in an hour, reached for the remote and turned on the small TV.

I guess not everything is big in America.

She checked the internet on her phone, set up a 10,000 Maniacs playlist on YouTube and did a Google search for Alex Sanchez. First, she found the accounts of her disappearance; nothing national, only local media stating the basics: the last sight of her was leaving a community venue in her home town of Angel Springs a week ago. There had been no reports or sightings since. The police investigation was ongoing.

They've likely given up on her, but why is Roger Taylor so interested? Does he have a thing with the mother?

Astrid assumed that's what it was. His reputation as a ladies' man had preceded his arrival at MI6. She'd worked with him once on a joint operation between the Agency and MI6, and made it clear from the start she'd tolerate no shenanigans from him. He'd been the perfect gent throughout their assignment.

She dug through Alex's media posts, discovering this wasn't a typical teenage girl posting about clothes or makeup; she was an activist, and a vocal one. The kid talked about gun control, voting rights, social inequality, and feminism. There were photos of her wearing anti-fascism t-shirts and animal rights logos. Alex attracted her fair share of trolls, harassing her online, and some of the comments made Astrid clench her hands into fists.

She switched from her playlist, found Alex's YouTube channel, and watched the latest Sanchez video: Alex on a march against war in the Middle East. Not only was the kid vocal, but she was also intelligent and erudite. When her speech finished, the camera cut to her and other protestors sitting outside a town hall as the police arrived to drag them away.

Astrid scrolled through the other videos, her curiosity engaging with the one titled 21st *Century Feminist*. She increased the volume and hit play: it was impossible to tell where it was filmed, but Alex was inside with a blank wall behind her, no sign of an audience as she spoke.

"When I was a girl, I was sold a lie. I was told the women's movement had achieved rights and equality for us. I was told that through education, I could achieve anything, be free to be me no matter how different I might be from everyone else. There was nothing I couldn't achieve as long as I had drive and ambition; opportunities once inaccessible to women and girls were now available to me. Yet, I noticed the world didn't fit this story. It was dangerous to go out at night on my own as a girl, but boys could go and do as they pleased; if I kissed boys, I'd be condemned, whereas their mates would praise them; and if I kissed girls, I'd be hated or ridiculed. I was told girls should be careful how they dressed, not to be thought easy, but that porn and topless photos were empowering. That what happened to boys was anyone else's fault but their own, but what happened to girls was always a girl's fault. I couldn't even find safety in my home because online harassment of women and girls is a pandemic of abuse and hostility. Remember, my friends, we still have a long way to go to achieve true equality in this world."

Then the video finished. It was at that point Astrid knew she wouldn't be leaving America anytime soon. She forgot about her deadline for calling Olivia and searched through everything she could find about Alex Sanchez. There was an Instagram post of her singing *Back in the USSR* by the Beatles, tweets about her looking forward to a trip to Washington, and a review of the latest Jennifer Lawrence movie. Plus, a single blog entry about her favourite recipes: fish and chips came top. She couldn't wait to go to Britain to taste the real thing.

Astrid picked up her phone, Courtney's number staring at her from the screen. She cleared it and called Taylor. He answered immediately, sounding distracted on the other end until he realised it was her.

'What's your connection to the Sanchez girl?'

He struggled for words, and she imagined him straightening his tie and reaching for the martini somewhere near him.

'I met her mother, Christina, when she was a migrant trying for asylum into the States. I was there as an observer for the British Government, and I helped her and Alex get citizenship. I've felt responsible for them ever since.' He paused, and she heard him take that drink. There was a woman's voice in the background, and then he continued. 'Christina is in a terrible state. I'm worried what she might do, and the local police appear to have pushed it to the bottom of the pile.'

'What can you tell me about the family and the girl?'

He hesitated for a second before clearing his throat. 'They emigrated from Ecuador three years ago. I think the father died there, so there's only the two of them. Christina was a veterinarian, but she's struggled to find work in the US.' She heard him refill his glass and the female laugh in the background. 'Does this mean you'll look for her?' There was a cocktail of desperation and hope mixed into his voice.

'Text me the family address and a phone number if you have one. I'll speak to you once I've seen the mother.' With that, she hung up.

Astrid listened to the rain battering the window and turned on the TV; there was little chance of her getting any sleep now. She'd hire a car and leave early in the morning. She flicked through the channels and settled on an old episode of the *Outer Limits*. The low hum of the minibar slipped into her brain.

'We have control of the vertical,' the screen said as she turned off the light and welcomed the embrace of the gloom around her.

3 ROAD TO RUIN

She woke with a lethargic moan, her throbbing head breaking the silence of the room. Astrid's fingers slipped through spilt bourbon and floating dead ants. Her teeth were like a ticket someone forgot to remove from a vending machine, and there was something stuck between her lips. She pulled it out and stared at a stub for a free packet of wine gums from the local shop, not even a lottery ticket. She had no idea how it had got there. Then she glanced at the empty minibar and recalled a late-night stagger from the hotel to the nearest convenience store.

As hangovers went, it wasn't the worst she'd had. The aching in her skull ebbed and flowed like a low tide; there was a balloon covering her brain, inflating slowly and increasing the pressure. She stepped into the bathroom and threw up, her throat feeling as if a ten-tonne truck was speeding through it. A quick cold shower helped wake her up.

Astrid gathered her things and shuffled downstairs to pay her bill. The hire car she'd booked online arrived ten minutes later. She dumped her bag, with a single change of clothes, into the back seat. It was a budget rental, no-frills and compact. She cranked the radio up, skipped past the stations featuring Shock Jocks, fire and brimstone evangelists, and sleazy politicians to find one blasting out non-stop sixties rock.

New York to Angel Springs took her five hours, her thoughts full of missing and kidnapped girls. She tried not to focus on Olivia too much, promising herself to call Courtney again when she reached her destination.

On approaching the town, she drove alongside a long stretch of water as cars hissed by her window. On the radio, David Bowie sang about Robert Zimmerman as she focused on the research she'd found regarding where Alex and her mother lived, discovering they had a motorhome in a trailer park.

She knew trailer parks were big business in America, especially for those who owned the land, and was curious to see how Alex's mother viewed her new life compared to what they'd left behind.

Billboards lined the ride into town, promoting Angel Springs's religious institutions and services: one proclaimed Hell was real, while another claimed you couldn't hold hands with God if you were masturbating. The thought of sex sent a nostalgic tingle through her body as she tried to remember the last time she was intimate with someone. A large image of a sad-looking Jesus cradling an aborted foetus shook the feeling from her.

When she got to Angel Springs, she headed for the motel she'd found online. She paid for a week, noticing the curious looks she received for her accent, and watched another guest lower his eyes when she peered his way. Then she took her flimsy bag of possessions to her room. It was contemporary and up to date if your idea of a modern hotel was from the 1970s. The bed was too short for her frame, and the furniture was all plastic and ready to end its days on a beach on the other side of the world. Kitsch replicas of Warhol prints and Lichtenstein rip-offs adorned the walls. At least it had free Wi-Fi, and the air conditioning worked.

She threw water on her face, tried to do something with the mess that was her hair and failed, then checked the Sanchez family's residence on her phone. There were a few knowing looks from the staff as she left and climbed into the car.

Then it was time to explore Angel Springs. She drove past bagel shops, museums, theatres, clubs, bars, and at least a dozen churches, two synagogues and a mosque. Outside a church, she observed people singing and dancing while being showered with water from several hoses. It confused her, at first until she realised it was a communal baptism.

Thirty minutes later, after getting lost twice, she found a parking spot and began her search for Christina Sanchez by asking the mailman for directions. Once he'd deciphered Astrid's accent, he pointed her in the right direction. She zipped up her jacket and strode towards it.

Smoke drifted out of a clutch of motorhomes. Outside one of them, someone had set up an antique boom-blaster music player throwing out the tortured tawdry tales of romances gone wrong. Next to that, a grill blazed out fumes of burnt meat and onions on the point of blackened disintegration. A group of women milled around, watching as children kicked stones at each other as if it was the newest Olympic sport. Tiny patches of grass sprouted out through cracked concrete and plastic sheets tossed to the ground in carefree abandonment. Astrid couldn't imagine the stuck-up snobbery of Roger Taylor feeling comfortable in this environment.

She checked the address he'd given her: number sixty-six, Grace Cathedral Square. When she'd ambled through the rusted gateway, there'd been no obvious numbering system on the vehicles, and she'd spent a fruitless ten minutes getting her bearings. Then she saw it scrawled onto a makeshift post box nestling in front of a Winnebago. Sitting on the steps was a young boy with a drawn-on pencil-thin moustache, wearing a baseball cap the wrong way round. Astrid stood close enough for her shadow to swallow him whole.

'Does Mrs Sanchez live here?'

He peered at her as if staring into an eclipse, scrawny hands flapping at his face. 'What sort of accent is that, lady?' The cigarette in his mouth belched out smoke at a frantic rate.

'I'm English.'

His eyes lit up like fireworks. In her short time in America, she'd found the knowledge of her Englishness elicited one of two responses: irrational anger or unusual admiration. She wasn't sure how this kid was going to respond until he did.

'Have you done the Whitechapel Murder Tour? Do you know Alan Moore? Do you like Orange Juice, the band, not the drink? Do you have Keira Knightley's number?'

He spoke as if words were bullets and his mouth was a machine gun. His excitement drew several others to them, both kids and adults, staring at the visitor in their community.

A young girl glared at her. 'Are you the police?'

'I'm looking for Christina Sanchez,' she repeated. 'To help find her daughter.'

A hush went around the group, soon replaced by heated chatter.

'Send her in,' a voice from the motorhome said.

The people parted and the kid gave her a knowing nod. Astrid stepped into the vehicle. It seemed bigger on the inside, like a modern Tardis where the walls appeared to consume less space than they should. A dull sheen of faded red engulfed most of the interior apart from the odd splash of paper covered in roses.

'Who are you?'

Christina Sanchez sat in a velvet armchair which wouldn't have looked out of place in a stately home. A built-in sofa was at her side, resplendent in little cushions adorned with the faces of grinning cats. Rose-hued curtains hung at the windows, and a luxurious carpet filled the floor. Everywhere smelt of fresh peaches and cigarette smoke.

'My name is Astrid Snow, Mrs Sanchez. Roger Taylor asked me to find your daughter, Alex. Didn't he contact you?'

'I haven't seen him for a long time. Are you an English cop?'

'I'm more of a private investigator. Taylor hired me to help you, but if you'd rather I didn't...' She turned as if to leave.

'No. You can stay. Sit over there.'

Christina pointed at the sofa and the grinning cats. Astrid pushed her back against the felines, feeling the hardwood behind them. Outside the window, the crowd still gathered.

'Do you want me to search for your daughter, Mrs Sanchez? Even though it was Roger who asked me, I won't do it without your permission.'

If she said no or revealed Alex had run away, Astrid would leave and never look back. She stared at the other woman's face, noticing the slight tremble in her voice as she clutched at the crucifix around her neck.

'Call me Christina. Is Roger paying you to do this?' There was suspicion in her tone.

'No, Christina. I owe him a favour, and, having watched some of your daughter's videos online, I feel a kindred spirit towards her.'

'A kindred spirit?'

'She reminds me of me when I was younger.'

'You're not like that now, wanting the world to be a better place?'

It was a curious question. 'I thought I wanted an easier life, but here I am thousands of miles from home, away from those I care about, a stranger in a strange land, but still, I want to help you and your daughter.'

Christina Sanchez reached for a cigarette, but then stopped. 'You won't find Alex in this town.'

'Why do you say that?'

'Those videos you enjoyed so much, and Alex's other activities, have angered many. It's easy for those with the Devil in their hearts to hate young girls like her, no matter how strong she is.'

'When did you see her last?'

'Two weeks ago. We argued, she was sitting where you are now, and then she got the bus to school.'

'I thought she'd only been missing a week?'

'Yes, that was the last time anyone saw her. She never returned from school after our disagreement, but she rang here, telling me she was staying with her friend Beth for a few days until I calmed down.'

'What was the argument about?'

Christina breathed heavily, her fingers scratching

against her arms, the unmistakeable actions of a smoker going cold turkey.

'I told her to stop with all these protests, to concentrate on school and make more friends. I said if she didn't, I'd throw her out.' There was a tear in the corner of her eye. 'I didn't mean it, though.' She wiped it away with her sleeve.

'So what happened after that?'

'I saw Beth at the shops, and she said Alex wasn't with her, said she'd joined the Future Youth Project. I didn't know what that was until I asked around.'

'What is it?'

Christina twisted her head to the side, an expression of surprise crisscrossing her face.

'I thought it was another of those social justice groups she was always going on about, but it wasn't.' She smiled now. 'In fact, it was the exact opposite, a religious youth group set up to help Senator Brady get re-elected.'

Astrid sat back and tried to remember where she'd heard that name. Then it came to her; the billboards and posters outside town weren't all promoting religion.

'Senator Bob Brady, the Republican pro-life NRA member?'

Christina nodded. 'I went there, you know, to the compound he has outside his mansion. They said Alex stayed two days, and then left. I told the police. They said they'd checked, but couldn't find anything wrong, but they would say that because the Chief of Police is Bob Brady's cousin. And they claimed they'd looked everywhere and spoken to her friends at school, and they said she told them she was going to run away because she hated it here and hated me, and was going to go somewhere more liberal, like California or New York.' Her sentences rambled on into one long burst, spoken without taking a breath, her eyes misting over and her hands shivering. 'So maybe she did run away after we'd argued.' She stared at Astrid. 'This could be a waste of your time.'

'But she did go to this Future Youth Project?'

'That's what some of them said, but I don't understand that; why would she?'

It didn't make sense to Astrid either. 'Have you got a last name and address for her friend?'

Christina reached into her pocket, removing a small card and handing it to her. 'This is her business card, but her home address is on it.'

Astrid arched her eyebrows. 'She's seventeen and has a business?'

'It's one of those YouTube things all the kids have nowadays. Can you imagine what would have happened if we'd had those when we were younger?'

That was when Astrid realised they were about the same age. And she considered how different her life might have been if the internet, social media and mobile phones had been popular when she'd run away from home the first time.

Perhaps I would have catalogued my home life online immediately instead of waiting so long to report what happened: posted images of the bruises hidden underneath my clothes, made videos of Courtney laughing at me and encouraging Father to talk with his fists. And there could have been a daily blog of Mother's descent into alcoholism.

'What do you think has happened to Alex, Christina?'

She peered at Astrid through saucer-like eyes. 'She didn't like her life and went somewhere else.' Christina Sanchez kept scratching at her arm. 'She'll come back when she finds out the grass isn't always greener on the other side.'

'Can I look in her room?'

Christina stood and walked to the rear, where she opened a door and let Astrid inside. Then she went outside to join the others. Astrid heard voices consoling her.

It was small, barely able to squeeze a single bed and a tiny wardrobe inside. The walls were bare, with faded paper peeling off like dandruff. She looked in the closet, finding only clothes. She checked under the bed, but that was empty. It was a vain hope to find a diary which might outline Alex's secrets and indicate where she was.

Astrid closed the door behind her and stepped outside. Christina was with a group of women, who all went quiet when Astrid approached.

'I'm going to the police station, Christina. I need to tell them I'm working for you as a private investigator into the disappearance of Alex. Is that okay?'

Sanchez nodded while the others placed consoling hands on her arms and shoulders. 'Will you be in touch with Roger?'

Astrid had no desire to speak to Taylor anytime soon, but would have to at some point. 'I'll report to you first,' she said as she left.

She strode from the park, got into the car and asked the GPS on her phone to locate the police station.

Let's see how many locals I can annoy.

4   POLICE AND THIEVES

Astrid spent a frustrating thirty-minute drive trying to find something decent to listen to on the radio, switching between stations without any luck, finding most of them broadcasting heavy religious messages. She settled on one where the male host presented the daily message from the Bible, disbelieving what she heard.

'*You may purchase male or female slaves from the foreigners who live among you. You may also purchase the children of such resident foreigners, including those born in your land. You may treat them as your property, passing them on to your children as a permanent inheritance.*'

She waited for him to explain how the passage from Leviticus related to the modern world, but instead, he segued into some dire tune by Van Morrison. She changed the station, finding one where the hyper-active DJ lamented men's failure to step beyond their fragile masculinity. Her destination approached as a caller spoke about how he couldn't use an umbrella because it was too feminine.

Astrid pulled up outside the police station, wondering

how low umbrella sales were in Angel Springs. She ignored the locals staring at her and pushed the door open.

The building was bright and clean. Uniformed officers strolled around while smartly dressed women pummelled keyboards and answered phones. She gazed at the American flags dotted through the room as she strode to the reception. A young woman with dark glasses peered at her. Astrid gave her details and took a seat to wait for the Police Chief.

She used her phone to browse online as she waited, checking to see if Alex had visited any of her social media websites in the last twenty-four hours, but discovered nothing new on Twitter, Facebook, Instagram or YouTube. If Alex had any other internet presence, her mother hadn't mentioned it.

Astrid scrolled through the latest video comments, wondering if any of the people who'd left obscene and threatening messages might be responsible for Alex's disappearance. There were more than a dozen threats of rape, most of which promised extreme torture first, and plenty of violent threats to Alex and her family. Every single poster had an anonymous name, the worst had cartoon characters as their avatars.

She was making a mental list of the most worrying posts when the man she'd come to see arrived.

Police Chief Roscoe Tanner was ready to blow like a volcano when she saw him. Someone had parked in his spot, and when he found out who it was, he'd throw them into the worst cell available. Only as he described the vehicle to the woman at reception did Astrid realise it was her car he was raving about. She didn't mention it as she was ushered into his office and introduced herself while he removed his hat.

His ebony-lined eyes were subdued and sunken, sharp tufts of hair exploding from his head as if a rocket had gone off in a fireworks shop. There was grit in his teeth, and he struggled to remove it as he stared right through her.

'You've come from England to find the Sanchez girl?'

He didn't pronounce it as England, but as Eeengland, with a hefty emphasis on the E. She didn't correct him on his misinformation.

'Would it be possible for you to update me on your attempts to locate Alex?'

She tried the sweetest voice she could muster, but her charm didn't work on him. Astrid waited for him to deny her any information, surprised when he smiled at her.

'Do you have a PI licence for this state, Ms Snow?'

'I'm working for the British Embassy in New York, Chief Tanner. Would you like me to give you their phone number?'

His grin turned crooked. 'Teenagers disappear all the time, and then turn up a few days later.' The smile vanished as he scrutinised her. 'Christina's going to a lot of trouble for nothing.' He must have expected her to protest, but she kept quiet. Neither of them spoke for a minute as she glanced around the room at the photos of former US presidents lining the walls.

The silence eventually proved too fragile for him. He wiped the sweat from his eyes and glared at her. 'Giraffe, get in here,' he shouted.

Within an instant, the tallest woman Astrid had ever seen - she was at least six foot six - ducked her head to avoid banging it on the frame of the door and stumbled into the room.

'Yes, Chief?'

Tanner gestured her over to him and whispered in her

ear as she bent down. She glanced at Astrid as she listened to him. Then he lifted his head so Astrid could hear.

'Take Ms Snow to the booking desk and give her an update on the Alex Sanchez case.'

He bared his teeth at her like a rattlesnake without the rattle. The tallest policewoman in the world peered down at Astrid in anticipation. She got up and followed the officer out, nodding her appreciation to Tanner, who ignored her.

They moved down a long corridor and turned into a room with a table and two chairs. The policewoman squeezed into one while Astrid sat opposite. She stared at her badge, seeing the name as Crowley and not Giraffe.

Crowley noticed where she was looking. Her smile was the warmest welcome Astrid had received so far in the town. 'It's one of the many nicknames they have for me. But you can call me Grace.'

'What can you tell me about the disappearance of Alex Sanchez, Grace?'

Crowley frowned. 'I'm sorry, Ms Snow; I can't tell you anything. The Chief wants me to keep you here until he leaves.'

Astrid removed her phone and dialled Taylor's number. While she waited for him to pick up, she returned that smile to Crowley.

'What work do they give you, Grace?'

'Traffic reports mainly. I don't get out of the station much.'

'How long have you been a police officer?'

'Five years. I graduated top of the class.'

Astrid was wondering if that was supposed to be a joke when Taylor answered. She didn't stand on ceremony. 'Do you still have contacts at the State Department?'

His voice was liquid Valium. 'Of course I do. Have you made any progress finding Alex?'

She ignored his question. 'Get in touch with your friends and convince them to pass this message to whoever's in charge of overseeing the police in Angel Springs.' Astrid turned her head and spoke in hushed tones to Taylor before finishing the call. She smiled again at Grace. 'Do they have a car which is comfortable for you to drive?'

'Some of the newer unmarked vehicles have extra adjustable seats.'

'Have you ever worked out of uniform?'

'No.' Confusion reigned across her face.

'What's it like living in small-town America?'

'Angel Springs is more of a small city than a small town. We're surrounded by hills and home to some of the north-east's most beautiful gorges and water springs, amazing places to go swimming. The lake is forty miles of clear pristine water and a boon for sailing enthusiasts, with several parks along the shoreline.'

It was as if she'd stepped straight out of the tourist brochure. 'Do you sell many umbrellas?'

Crowleys eye's narrowed as her brows creased. 'What?'

Astrid shook her head. 'Forget it.' She placed her hands on the table. 'Is there much for kids to do here?'

Officer Crowley smiled with lips wide enough to swallow the sun. 'There are loads of things going on in Angel Springs for all age groups, but we have a growing student population, and there's a heap of activities for young people around that. You'd find it difficult getting bored here.'

She said it with such enthusiasm, Astrid doubted the truth of it. 'I grew up in London, and I can tell you sometimes having too much to do is just as bad as being bored.'

'You mean like having too many dangerous oppor-tunities?'

Astrid grinned. 'Always.'

'Giraffffe!' The Chief roared from the bowels of the police station. 'Get in here and bring that Brit with you.'

They must have heard his voice on the other side of town. Astrid found the walk back to his office more pleasurable than the previous one. Tanner's face was redder than a sunburnt orange when they got there. She watched him struggle to calm his breathing. She spoke before he exploded.

'I want to see your file on Alex Sanchez, plus I need to borrow Officer Crowley for a few days, out of uniform, and one of those new cars the department has. Is that okay, Chief?'

He couldn't look at Astrid; whoever Taylor had spoken to had left more than a flea in his ear. Tanner shouted at Crowley.

'You've got three days.'

As they went, Grace gazed at her in admiration. 'I'll get a copy of the file.'

She left Astrid standing in the middle of the room. Several officers tried not to stare at her. The tension was palpable, and she wondered what it would take to make them break.

Grace returned in a few minutes, clutching the paper and a set of keys. 'We need to go out back for the car.'

'I'm sorry,' Astrid said as they got outside.

'What for?' Grace gave her the sweetest of smiles.

'Once this is over, you're probably going to be in trouble because of me.'

They stepped on to the pavement, strode down the side

of the police station and into the rear where the cars were. Grace moved towards the shiniest vehicle.

'You don't have to apologise for anything; they can't make my working life any worse than it already is. At least now I get to do some interesting police work. I should be thanking you.' She opened the driver's door and adjusted the seat, lowering and pushing it back. She slid in as Astrid got into the passenger's side. 'Where do you want to go first, Ms Snow?'

'Let's head to your place so you can change clothes and talk me through that report. And call me Astrid.'

They travelled through the town, over dusty roads, past cavorting dogs, with Astrid paying close attention to the locals and their local ways. The street baptism had dispersed, with drops of water lingering along the road and pavements. The re-elect Bob Brady posters grew in frequency the further they went.

She nodded towards the giant image of Brady's grinning face on a roadside banner. 'What are your thoughts on him?'

Grace frowned. 'We're not allowed to discuss politics while on duty.'

'I was told Alex had joined one of his youth groups.'

'That's the information we have as well.'

'Don't you think it's rather unlikely, considering her history of protest and activism against everything he stands for?'

Grace drove down a long, narrow alley, and then turned at the end. She parked next to a row of dumpsters. 'Teenagers are always changing their minds about stuff, usually over the most trivial things. I know I did at her age. What about you?'

They got out together. 'Sure,' Astrid said, 'that's when I knew I preferred girls to boys.'

She watched Crowley turn her head to the side as she clutched the report to her chest. She clambered up a set of rickety steps and opened the door to a decent-sized house. Astrid followed her in.

'Can I get you a drink?' Grace shouted from somewhere inside.

'I'll have the sweetest hot tea you've got,' Astrid said from the living room.

She stared at the floral patterned curtains and decided they were the worst thing she'd seen in her life, until she gazed at the carpet covered in tiny illustrations of cats. She wanted to get off it as soon as possible in case it corrupted her shoes.

The other furniture included a pea-green three-piece suite, a large TV on a stand too small for it, and a coffee table. More impressive was the bookcase: Jacques Derrida next to Kant, Nietzsche brushing spines with Germaine Greer, Simone de Beauvoir sharing space with Hannah Arendt. On the bottom row, it looked like the complete works of Agatha Christie.

Grace appeared in the doorway. 'This was my gran's house. I haven't gotten around to changing the furniture and décor since she passed.'

'What about the books?'

'They were all hers, but I love to read, as well.'

Astrid reached down and picked out *The Murder of Roger Ackroyd*.

'This is one of the first things I ever read. Christie was a genius.' She was seven when she discovered how untrustworthy authors could be, but it was two years before that she realised the same about people. She put the book back and glanced at the stack of records and CDs piled in the corner: most of it was jazz from the 1950s, with the odd sixties American rock album dropped in for good measure. 'Is the music your gran's as well?'

'No, that's all mine.' She picked out one by Thelonious Monk. 'I've loved jazz since I was a little girl.' Astrid put a finger in her mouth and pretended to throw up. Grace shook her head. 'You obviously have no taste. Come through to the kitchen, and we'll have our drinks and read this together.'

She held the police report in one hand and the CD in the other. Astrid followed her into the room, hoping she wouldn't play the disc. As she considered how not to offend her host, she scrutinised a kitchen stuffed with garish ornaments: a six-piece set of tiny chefs stood next to a row of grinning pigs near the window, while a dozen or so novelty salt and pepper pots lined the shelf above the cooker. She took a seat at the table and glanced at the plate of chocolate biscuits in the middle. An aroma of sugar and cocoa drifted off them.

'They smell freshly baked.'

'Tuck in,' Grace said. 'I can cook a meal later. Just tell me what you want.'

Astrid couldn't remember the last time someone had cooked for her. 'That would be great; thank you.'

She grabbed a biscuit and bit into it, savouring how the chocolate melted in her mouth as Grace pushed a large, steaming mug of coffee towards her. Astrid warmed her hands on the mug while staring at the photos dotted around the kitchen. Grace was in every one of them at various ages, always holding on to an older woman Astrid assumed was her grandmother.

Astrid read through the report. There wasn't much in it

which differed from what Christina Sanchez had told her. What she was interested in was what wasn't in it. She sipped at the drink and finished scanning the text.

'What are the statistics for missing kids here?'

Grace pushed the papers to one side. 'We get perhaps four or five a year. Most of those eventually return because they wanted to sample the bright lights of a big city, but find it's too much for them and hightail it home.'

'What about the ones who disappear but are never reported or recorded?'

Grace looked sheepish. 'How do you know about those?'

Astrid twirled another biscuit through her fingers, rich on the one side, impoverished on the other. 'I've lived on the streets, been to plenty of places where things are seen differently dependent upon whose interests are affected the most, and it works the same everywhere. The authorities can only do so much, and when resources are lacking, or the motivation is missing, certain people fall way down the list of priorities. Does Tanner have any children?'

'He's got two daughters, thirteen and fourteen years old.'

'I guarantee he'd get the National Guard out here in an instant if one of those disappeared.' Grace nodded in agreement. 'How many kids do you think go missing from communities similar to where Alex lives?'

'There's been a few this year, more than usual.'

'What number are we talking about?'

Grace held out her hands. 'Perhaps five or six.'

'Why haven't the authorities done anything about that?'

'The Chief and the Mayor usually put them down as runaways because, well, you know...'

Astrid knew what she meant. 'Because why would any

kid want to live somewhere like that?' She finished her drink and stood. 'Can you get a list of those names and dates of when they were last seen?'

'I'll try,' Grace said. 'The Chief doesn't usually keep official records if the families don't report their child missing.'

'Okay, that's a start. Now I need you to take me to this youth group Alex supposedly joined.'

'We might have a problem getting in; they don't like strangers inside their compound.'

Astrid devoured another biscuit. 'Well, that's fine, because you're not a stranger, Officer Crowley. So go and get changed.'

Grace did as instructed as Astrid considered how far the corruption went in this picturesque religious town.

5 YOUNG AMERICANS

Once they were back in the car and on their way, Astrid asked Grace what the locals thought of Alex's political activism.

'Most people ignored her.' Grace headed into the country. 'As far as I know, she didn't have anyone her age supporting her, which is why she travelled into New York to join up with other protestors and demonstrations.'

They entered the rolling countryside. 'From what little I've seen of the town and its people, I'm assuming she didn't fit in with the consensus.' They drove past a Christians for Brady billboard as Grace nodded. 'So did she encounter any problems here because of her activism?'

Grace put her foot down. 'Some were more aggressive towards her, calling her names, SJW, that sort of thing. Alex took it in her stride; she wouldn't let anybody intimidate her.'

'Did she ever get in trouble with the police?'

Grace shook her head. 'As I said, I don't think she started or participated in any demonstrations in Angel Springs.'

'What about any other activities, problems at school, or petty crime?'

'Not that I'm aware of.'

They drove past dilapidated farmhouses, which looked like they hadn't been lived in for years, down by the edge of a great lake and into a large wooded area. Astrid rolled the window down to take in the country air, breathing in fresh flowers. The greens outnumbered the yellows and purples as they left the town behind them, and it wasn't long before they reached the first sign for the Future Youth Project.

She pointed at it.

'What do you know about this?'

'Not a lot. What they promote isn't my cup of tea.' Grace scratched at her throat. 'Senator Brady funds the organisation. I think someone on his staff thought it would be a good idea to have the youth vote behind him.'

'How old do you have to be to vote in America?'

'The legal voting age in the US is eighteen, but voter registration and pre-registration rules and ages are different in every state. You can pre-register at sixteen here.'

'Brady wants to get them in early?'

Grace shrugged. Astrid remembered how disinterested she had been with politics at that age, how all she'd cared about was getting away from those who hurt her. Things only changed when the Agency recruited her. Then she paid attention to what her employers wanted her to do and how those assignments impacted the world.

She wondered what her current worldview was as they stopped outside a walled compound. It reminded her of an old Soviet Block training camp, which became a Russian troll factory. Someone had painted an inviting inscription at the top across the wooden railing: *Working for the Future.*

Astrid got out of the car and grimaced at the soullessness of the whole thing. Even the mass of flowering trees either side and around the walls couldn't inject any beauty into its sparse and utilitarian façade; she'd seen the outside of prison blocks which looked better.

'We stand here in our torpor and deliver destruction of all human emotion.'

'What?' Grace said.

'Nothing,' Astrid replied. 'Just something I wrote in my youth.'

'You're a writer?' Grace pressed the buzzer at the gate.

'I dabbled in my past life.' Before Courtney ridiculed her for it, and her father beat it out of her. Then her diaries disappeared the day she went to the law and accused him of beating her for a decade to the same police who employed him. The courage it took her to look into their faces and detail every time he hit her was something that changed Astrid forever. It wasn't just a family she lost then, but all her fear.

She thought, once she escaped the clutches of the Agency, she might return to her writing, but missing children seemed to be monopolising all of her time.

Grace was about to speak when a shadow appeared from behind the compound. A spotty youth wearing oversized blue glasses stood at the gate. He gazed at the tall policewoman, and then turned his head to Astrid.

'What do you want, girls?' He must have been all of sixteen.

Astrid watched Grace bristle as she showed him her badge. 'Let us inside, kid.'

The boy didn't budge. Astrid walked up to the gate separating him from her. 'I like your gegs.'

'What?'

'Your specs; they make you look smart, intelligent even. Are you the brains of the outfit?'

He stared at her as if she was from another planet. 'Are you English?' he said after much-scrunched concentration.

'Born and bred in the land of Albion.' Astrid tried to sound like a member of the Royal Family.

He scrutinised her even more before lifting his finger to his ear when it vibrated. 'You can come in.' He opened the gates.

'We'll need the car,' Grace said as she returned to it. She drove into the compound while Astrid followed the boy inside.

All she thought about as they headed towards the buildings were similar facilities she'd seen on the news over the years; Waco and various other cults that'd come to an unpleasant end. Brady's impressive mansion stood magnificent in the sun, while to the side were several fabricated huts and cabins, which she assumed housed the Future Youth Project. A dozen or so poles lined the path, with the American flag fluttering from all of them.

Grace parked the car and joined Astrid as a group of teenagers with complexions as grey as their clothes greeted them. They projected fake smiles and perfect white teeth. The kids led them through the grounds, past the manicured bushes and water fountain, and into the mansion.

'Senator Brady lets us use this for all of our meetings and events,' one of the teenagers stated.

They strode down a large corridor adorned with the heads of many dead animals and the smell of something disagreeable. The teenagers must have noticed Astrid wrinkling her nose in discomfort.

'We had to have the whole carpet industrially cleaned recently,' one of their guides said as they ushered Astrid and

Grace into a vast library. Globe lamps hung from the ceiling and seemed as out of place as Astrid felt. She recognised Senator Bob Brady's bulbous features from the billboards and posters as he strode towards them with his hand out.

'Officer Crowley,' he bellowed, 'Roscoe said you'd be coming.'

Everything about him screamed wealth and power. His head was perched at an angle, looking away from Astrid, but she knew he was analysing every part of her, likely based on what Tanner had told him. He wore black leather shoes shined to within an inch of their life, a navy blue suit that must have been tailored for him. He smelt of cologne freshly shipped from Paris while his smile was sculpted into his cheekbones. Grace gave Astrid a quick look and shook his hand.

'Senator.'

He held on to her fingers for too long before turning to Astrid. 'And this must be our British visitor, Miz Snow, is it?' He thrust his hand towards her. She gripped his flesh as if squeezing coal into diamonds. He quickly let go. 'I hear you're a bit of a shamus, travelling over land and sea to find one of our errant children.'

She couldn't tell if he was messing with her or not. 'Thank you for letting us into your facility.'

'No problem, little lady. Perhaps you could introduce me to the Queen someday.' He barked out a laugh which made the windows tremble. 'So, ladies, how can I help you?'

He looked like someone who smiled for twenty hours a day, maybe more if he got a good night's sleep. She'd seen it before with politicians, when the face worked through reflex only, while inside the head, their real thoughts crept far too close to the outside world. He would turn the smile on without thinking, and she guessed it was a rare time when he let his guard down. That's what she aimed for.

'Can you tell us what Alex Sanchez did while she was here with you, Senator?'

He had the look of a waiter who knew he wasn't about to get a tip. 'I never met the girl, Miz Snow. Didn't the police tell you that?' He scowled at Grace. 'I was at a funeral when she was here.'

He'd lost the initial spark from his face as Astrid scrutinised the shade behind his eyes. 'A funeral?'

Brady moved to the side and poured himself a long glass of ice water. He didn't offer any to them as the temperature increased, and Astrid imagined she'd swallowed the sun in the last twenty seconds. Heat swept through her chest as she assumed Brady had sent some secret signal to his teenage minions for one of them to turn the heating up in the room. He bit into a piece of ice, and it cracked at the same time as Astrid flexed her fingers.

'Yes, Miz Snow; I was attending the funeral of a great man when that girl was allegedly here.' He peered at her and rolled the ice between his lips. 'As a general rule of thumb, the younger you die, the better the turnout for a funeral. The dream is to expire at the age of ninety-nine with no one at the crematorium apart from a couple of stragglers who have turned up for the wrong person.' He swallowed the cube and grinned at her. 'How many do you think will see you off into the next world, Miz Snow?'

She couldn't decide if it was a veiled threat or not; she hadn't spent enough time with the man to understand his motives yet. 'Hopefully, that'll be long into the future.'

He pulled in his chiselled cheekbones in mock horror. 'Of course, of course, Miz Snow. But the older I get, the more I find myself thinking about the end of my days. It's one of the reasons I'm determined to do my best for this town and the people of America. And why I'm fighting to get so many youngsters involved in the running of this great country. I want them to have a better upbringing than I did.'

Astrid was surprised by the implication. 'This isn't your family home?'

His laugh was hearty and genuine. 'I grew up inside a log cabin, surrounded by trees and creatures that skittered and ran and flew. I was fourteen when I first visited the city, overwhelmed by the size of it. Running water and a toilet that flushed were gifts from the gods to me. Before then, my only entertainment came from reading, which morphed into developing my puppet shows with characters from my favourite books.' He glanced around the library. 'It wasn't isolated where I lived; other cabins and families were working the woods and the river, and there was a school with kids my age. It wasn't long before I was the King of the Puppets for my peers, thrilling and scaring them with tales from the fiction which kept me up at night. The Three Little Pigs metamorphosed into three strangers terrorising the community; Little Red Riding Hood became every child in the school terrified by the Head Teacher. I was slapped on the wrist and made to write a thousand lines when they caught me performing that one.'

The Senator was a man who enjoyed talking. Every time he opened his mouth, even if it was only giving directions, a story flopped out: there was a beginning, middle and end; the beginning being the flowery salutation he greeted you with, whereas the end always left you wanting more. But she didn't want more of his story; she needed to know what happened to Alex.

'Is there anyone here, in your organisation, who can tell

us about Alex's movements with your youth project on that day?'

He picked up a small silver bell and shook his fingers to ring it. Two of the grey squad from earlier scampered into the room.

'Take these ladies to see Glen.'

With those instructions, he turned without any other acknowledgement of their presence or any goodbye and marched out. The twins stared at Astrid and Grace through glassy eyes.

'Who's Glen?' Astrid said as they returned the way they come. They were shown outside and around the corner to a rusted metal hut which, their guides told them, was the group's educational facility. Inside was Glen, the organisation's Strategic Youth Leader.

He wore a skinny tie over a plaid shirt, a painfully short haircut sculpted into a head that reminded her of a wonky apple. He didn't hold out his hand as he instructed the dozen or so students to close their books. Astrid noted the *Pray Your Gay Away* title on their reading material as the learners scuttled out of the classroom, and she and Grace stepped in.

'Senator Brady told us you were the man to speak to regarding Alex Sanchez's recent visit here.'

He pressed the book to his chest. His lips parted like a cobra, ready to strike. 'She was only here for a day. This wasn't the place for her.'

Grace took out the copy of the police report. 'I thought she stayed for two nights?'

'No, ma'am; it was only one day, no nights. She caused too much trouble that first day.'

Astrid watched the darkness creep across his face. 'What kind of trouble?'

He picked up a pencil from the desk and tapped on the wood with it. 'She kept on saying how we were all wrong, that the Senator was a bad man, and she was here to convert us into the right way of thinking.' Glen shook his head and looked dismayed. 'She shouted all the time, screaming that fracking was evil and we weren't doing enough to protect the planet.'

Astrid pictured Alex and imagined the scene as she scanned the classroom. 'How did she end up here?'

He dropped the pencil onto the desk, where it rolled away and tumbled to the floor. Astrid picked it up and put it in her jacket.

'I think one of her friends at school nominated her. Every volunteer has to be nominated by a reliable person before they get invited.

'What do you mean by reliable?' Astrid said.

He grinned at her through perfect white teeth. 'Someone who has good, conservative Christian American values.'

'I'm just a poor English girl, Glen; perhaps you can explain to me what it is you do here with the Future Youth Project.'

She reached out for his hand, unsurprised he flinched when her skin touched his. He stepped back and rubbed at his forehead.

'We promote American values.' He glanced at Grace. 'The Future Youth Project is committed to ensuring young Americans will understand and find inspiration in the ideas of individual freedom, a strong national defence, free enterprise, and traditional American life.' Astrid resisted the urge to engage him in conversation regarding those views; they were only necessary to her locating Alex. 'We do this through education and training while developing ongoing community projects which help the most impoverished.'

It sounded grand. 'Did you spend any time with Alex?'

He shook his head. 'I only saw her for a few minutes when the others told me how disruptive she was. A few of us had to talk her into leaving. This wasn't the right place for her.'

Grace continued making notes. 'And you have no idea where she went after here?'

'No, ma'am.'

Astrid turned and left before she slapped the smile from him. Grace was two steps behind her.

'Well, that was a waste of time.' They returned to the car.

'It was quite the opposite, Officer Crowley.'

'What do you mean?'

The gates opened for them, and they left the youth of America behind.

'Did you see the look on his face when I mentioned Alex? I thought he was going to wet his pants. He lied, and he let it slip when he said Alex caused too much trouble that first day. The first day implies more than one, and he didn't realise what he'd said. How come your report says she was here for two nights, but he claims it was only one day?'

'I don't know. There's no name attributed to that in the report.'

'We need to find out who said it and speak to this friend who nominated Alex to come here.' They drove on, leaving the country and heading into town. 'Drop me off at my room so I can take a quick shower. Then we'll meet in the bar across the road with the information you get from the police station.'

'No problem,' Grace said.

Astrid didn't doubt she'd break through the lies they'd heard; a bunch of callow youths and a corpulent politician wouldn't hold out for too long once she applied the right kind of pressure. There was just one thing she couldn't fathom out.

Why would Alex go there in the first place?

6 50FT QUEENIE

Grace drove to the motel. The weather had transformed into a swirl of elements pummelling the town, with bits of dirt hovering everywhere. As Astrid got out of the car, dust spun in the air, turning the sky into a wave of tiny particles which bit at her face. Thunder arrived like the prelude to a death metal opera; heavy rumbling flooded every side of them. At first, it was a crack, with a vicious assault to the ears, but then came a rolling sound which dissipated into the surrounding hills.

Astrid shielded her eyes from the worst of the conditions. 'What happened to the sun?'

'We get freaky weather all the time now.' Grace closed the door, but left the window open. 'Some people say it's to do with climate change; others blame the fracking which started last year on the other side of the woods. Or it's the spirits of the miners who died over the years.'

Grace drove away, and Astrid thought of the ghosts from her past. She strode into the building, shaking grit from her hair and mouth, the taste of it making her cough on to the floor. The thunder continued outside, the roar of it ringing in her ears as her ghosts shrank into the shadows lurking inside her skull. The receptionist with droopy eyes lowered her head and stared at the ground, chewing like a dog snapping at a wasp. Astrid pulled thick wads of dust from her hair as she headed upstairs, the key in her hand and looking forward to a long shower.

She only had one change of clothes with her, wondering if it would be sufficient if the local weather were to be this stormy for the next few days. That thought occupied her as she wiped nature from her face. The grit in her eyes irritated her enough to lose concentration, placing the key in the door and pushing on it before she realised it was unlocked. Her vision was clear enough to see the mess in the room, her bag upturned and emptied, and the contents of the drawers scattered on the floor.

Then someone shoved her in the back.

Astrid hit the bed chin first, her face buried in the sheets as the blade snapped into the covers and grazed her cheek. Her elbow sprang upwards and found her attacker. The intruder lurched into the table against the wall, crashing down and rolling on to the carpet. She pushed up and twisted to meet him, blood sliding down her cheeks as the weapon came at her again. She dodged to one side and threw her arm into his neck. He coughed and spat through his black mask and hit the wall. She moved forward and grabbed the knife from him, was about to press it against his face when something struck her on the rear of the skull. Cheap porcelain shattered against her head, bits of a doll-like female figurine flying into the air and flopping to the floor.

'Fuck!'

Astrid jumped on to the bed, pressing into the wall. As she readied for the next assault, her attackers fled the room.

She stumbled after them, a fog drifting over her eyes which was worse than the dust storm outside.

They staggered down the stairs as she grasped at the wall, their feet bouncing off the steps as her fingers found tattered paper and wrinkled paint. By the time she reached the bottom, they'd gone. The receptionist was nowhere as Astrid lurched through the door and onto the street. A thick haze had replaced the dust as she struggled to see anything around her. The air was quiet, the thunder having dissipated, and the only sound was the thump of her heart vibrating inside her head. She rubbed at the back of her skull, picking tiny bits of porcelain from her flesh and staring at them, a nervous laugh crawling from her throat at the sight of a ceramic hand with spots of her blood on it.

She dropped it on to the ground and considered her options. Pain and irritation prompted her to go after them, even though she had no idea which direction they'd gone. Common sense told her she was more vulnerable than they were and would be disadvantaged if she headed into the vapour covering most of the street.

A burning smell hung in the air, with a taste of electricity on her tongue. She bit her lip as spots formed before her gaze. She'd had a concussion before, and this was starting to feel like that. Astrid clutched at the ache at the back of her head and staggered into the hotel, where she slumped into a chair and removed her phone. Then she rang the number Grace had given her earlier as she struggled to keep her eyes open.

THE PARAMEDICS ARRIVED before Grace did. They were attending to the bump on Astrid's skull as Officer

Crowley burst in. The receptionist had returned and looked sheepish as she sat in the corner, biting her nails.

'I don't know how they got in,' she cried.

'What happened?' Grace said.

Astrid touched the back of her head. 'Two people attacked me in my room. They didn't break in; they either had a key or picked the lock. They ransacked the place, but there's nothing of mine missing.'

Once she'd dug her nails into her arm to make sure she stayed awake, Astrid had checked her meagre things before the paramedics arrived. Then she returned downstairs and waited, as the receptionist repeatedly apologised for something she said wasn't her fault.

Grace removed her hand and took out her notebook. 'Did you see who they were?'

Astrid went to shake her head, but it hurt too much. 'The one with the knife wore a mask. I didn't notice who smacked me.'

Grace turned to the nervous receptionist. 'What did you see?'

A scruffy white cat jumped on to her lap, and she clung to it like a shield. 'I didn't see nuthin,' I swear.'

'The swelling should go down in a couple of days, and the cut on your cheek is only a nick,' the paramedic said to Astrid. 'Are you sure you feel okay, no dizziness or blurred vision?'

'I can't see what's going on around here, but I'll be fine,' she replied. 'Once I find somewhere else to stay.'

Grace picked up Astrid's bag. 'You'll stop with me while you're in town; no arguments.'

Astrid followed her out. The weather had returned to normal, and she was thankful for that small mercy. She grinned through the constant vibration bouncing through her head.

'But, Officer Crowley, what will the neighbours say?'

Grace ignored Astrid's question as she started the car. 'Do you think they were waiting in your room for you?'

'I'm not sure. Perhaps they were burglars, and they lashed out as a reaction.'

'Why would someone go through your stuff? Have you got anything worth stealing?'

'It's amateur hour scare tactics, that's all. Somebody wants me out of this town.' She removed the fingers from the back of her neck. 'Maybe the locals still think they're fighting the Revolutionary War, and they just don't like the English.'

Grace drove away. 'You could be right, and they might have been petty criminals thinking they've got an easy mark since you're new in town.'

Astrid gritted her teeth as the car bounced over a pothole.

'I guess anything is possible.' She glanced at the pretty streets with their clean shops and impressive architecture. The earlier storm appeared to have left no lasting damage. 'Did you find out who recommended Alex to the Future Youth Project?'

'Her name is Beth Sharp, Alex's friend and a student at the same college. I have an address for her.'

Astrid suddenly felt better. 'Wasn't she the last person to see Alex?' Grace nodded. 'Before we go to yours, let's speak to her. I want to find out why she helped Alex get into that group.'

Grace made a left turn, the momentum of which threw Astrid's shoulder into the policewoman. There was a brief smile between them before she righted herself.

'She'll be coming out of school in about fifteen minutes; we can meet her outside. As long as you feel up to it.'

'I'm fine.' Astrid touched the scar forming on her cheek. The paramedics had cleaned the blood away, but she could still smell it.

'You look great, don't worry.' Grace's laugh was nervous and light.

'Why, thank you, Officer. I hope you write that down in your report.'

They laughed together, a natural, comfortable thing as if they'd known each other for years.

'Speaking of reports,' Grace said, 'I checked to see who'd made the statement regarding Alex spending two days at the youth group.'

'And what did you find?'

'The original report, the one I photocopied this morning, was altered; it's been replaced. Now it says she only stayed there until the afternoon on one day. There's no name next to the statement, even on the original. If I hadn't copied it, we wouldn't have known this.'

'You know you can't trust anyone in your station, Grace?'

'I guess so.'

She sped down the road, and Astrid saw the sign for the Lincoln Parks School ahead. They had ten minutes before the school got out. She flexed her fingers and let the aches and pains settle into her body. The two attackers had caught her by surprise, but she chastised herself for such a slow response and for being too casual as she went to her room. She'd taken the small town of Angel Springs for granted, but she wouldn't anymore.

Astrid peered out of the window, fascinated by the uniformed guards patrolling the school. It was impossible not to see the guns strapped to their sides. Grace parked opposite in front of the park. She reached into the glove compartment and removed a bright orange swag of chocolate treats.

'I need a regular sugar intake during the day.'

Astrid looked her up and down, scrutinising her large frame in the car. 'Too many sweets will stunt your growth.'

Grace chuckled and offered the bag to Astrid, who declined. 'That's what I thought, so I've eaten stuff like this all my life, but it didn't work.'

'Maybe you should have switched to fags?'

The policewoman narrowed her eyes as she bit through a handful of chocolates. 'What?'

'It's a British slang word for cigarettes. Kids in Britain were told smoking would stunt your growth.' She glanced at the armed security again. 'I guess it's one of the many cultural differences between our countries. When I was at school, the worst thing that could happen to you was detention or other kids itching for a scrap or a bit of name-calling. You might get grief for having the wrong hairstyle or for liking dodgy music, but that was about it.' She searched for any good memories of her schooldays, but knew it was a fruitless exercise. 'I can't imagine what it must be like attending school and thinking you could get shot as you're sitting down to learn about geometry or human biology.'

Grace slipped the sweets back into their resting place and laid one hand on the dashboard. 'Touch wood, but so far, thankfully, Angel Springs has never had a school shooting.'

'Do you think that's because of the armed security?'

She shook her head. 'I doubt it. I guess we've been lucky the town hasn't produced any kids with those kinds of disturbed minds.'

'I have some experience of dealing with sociopaths and those with lives fuelled by violent criminal fantasies.'

Grace's wide eyes added to her unique allure. 'Tell me more, Ms Snow.'

Astrid ignored the throbbing at the back of her skull. 'Some people crave recognition, some of which is driven by violent fantasies that start at an early age. The majority of these focus on inflicting pain on others, more often than not as a release for their own perceived pain or as a form of revenge against supposed injustices. The fantasies typically intensify over several years before they're acted on. With time, the mental images become more detailed, often reinforced by a distorted sense of what is just or moral, such as the need to avenge a perceived offence or the belief in a divine right to decide the fate of others.'

Grace scratched at her leg. 'They sound like politicians.'

Astrid laughed. 'Several studies have shown high-level functioning sociopaths often gravitate to high-pressure jobs in government or industry, which I suppose is better than becoming murderers.'

'I'm guessing most of these will be men.'

'More than ninety per cent, I'd say. Murderous sociopathic or psychopathic women are rare, but not unknown. According to a study published in the *International Journal of Women's Health*, female psychopaths are more likely to flirt and use their sexuality to manipulate people. They're more likely to be verbally aggressive and mean, and less likely to attack people violently. On the other hand, psychopathic men are more physically aggressive and more likely to commit fraud; this is perhaps why there are many more men in prisons.'

A mischievous grin crossed Grace's face. 'Do you flirt to manipulate people, Ms Snow?'

Considering what she'd gone through, Astrid felt good and smiled. 'Why, Officer Crowley, what are you implying?'

Grace licked her lips and swallowed the sweet. 'Is it nurture or nature that creates society's killers?'

'There's no easy answer, but it's a mixture of both.' Astrid inspected the guards talking to each other as they prepared for the kids to come out. 'At a young age, violent offenders are often pessimistic about their future and have low self-esteem. Many have been harassed, bullied or rejected by classmates, suspended from school, or pressured by teachers. Someone with a less balanced psyche and in the wrong environment can then snap into the sort of destructive criminal behaviour sometimes seen in American schools.'

'I know guns aren't legal in Britain, but don't you see similar actions from damaged kids?'

Astrid pushed her childhood memories into the shadows. 'Yes, but not on the scale you have. There are examples of violent conduct, of knife attacks, but the incidences are low. I've no doubt things would be worse if firearms were easily available back home.'

'Did you carry a gun when you worked for the British government?'

'Only when I had to, and it wasn't the British government I worked for.'

Grace pulled a face of mock disappointment. 'Don't shatter my illusions, Astrid. I had visions of you travelling the world like a female James Bond, driving the coolest cars and wearing the most expensive clothes.'

'You mean a chain-smoking, heavy-drinking, Benzedrine-popping womanising hero who indulges in her vices to silence the demons brought on by her dark profession as a government-sanctioned killer?'

'Well, since you put it like that.'

They laughed together in stereo.

'I'll tell you some stories to curl your hair later.' A group of adults with younger children gathered outside the school. 'Do you have any other family, Grace?'

She turned her head from Astrid and let out a deep sigh. 'There's only me. My parents died when I was ten, and my gran took me in.'

Astrid recognised the sorrow in Grace's face, wondering what her life would have been like if her parents had died when she was young. She didn't have any aunts or uncles, so she'd have ended up in foster care, but that was preferable to the reality. She still would have had Courtney to deal with. She pushed the image of her sister from her mind.

'Do you want a family?'

Grace raised a hand to her lips, appearing to want to chew on her nails before thinking better of it. She dropped it on to her leg instead.

'I thought about it a lot after Gran died and I was on my own. I'd dreamed about having a sister or brother, and as I got older, with only Gran around, getting married and having kids seemed the best way for me to make sure I was never alone. Plus, all the other girls in school were always talking about having children, so it felt natural for me to feel the same.'

'Society expects us to become mothers.'

'I've never felt that outside influences are pressurising me. Some women don't feel maternal, there's no control over that, but it kicked in for me as I got older.' She peered out of the window, staring at the adults arriving for their kids. 'But this job isn't conducive for meeting the right person or for raising children.' She glanced at herself in the mirror. 'I'm probably getting too old for it anyway.'

Astrid laughed. 'How old are you?'

'I'm thirty this year.'

'Plenty of people become parents into their thirties and beyond. You've got loads of time.'

'What about you? Do you have any kids?'

'No. I guess I'm one of those people with no interest in becoming a parent, but I do have a niece I'm trying to get close to.'

Grace didn't reply, nodding towards the school where a portly security guard was marching to the front.

Inside her head, Astrid was back at school, listening to her sister telling her how all the other kids hated her and how even the teachers disliked her. Not for the first time, she worried about Courtney guiding Olivia through her childhood. Her concern for her niece only increased her determination to find Alex Sanchez as soon as possible.

To find her before it was too late.

If it wasn't already.

7 SEVENTEEN

Astrid stuck her fingers into her ears as the bell signalling the end of the school day shrieked.

'I always hated going home after school.'

Her father wouldn't be there when she got in, but it only added to her stress having to wait for him. And then there was Courtney tormenting her with those comments her sister practised to perfection. She stopped looking at her mother for help once the smell of alcohol became Gloria Snow's favourite perfume.

Grace pursed her lips. 'Most kids hate school. I did.'

Astrid observed her partner struggle to get comfortable in the car. 'Did you get a lot of grief because of your height?'

Students filtered out of the building.

'Yeah, it was a constant deluge of name-calling, as much from the teachers as the children. I think the adults thought they were funny, but the kids went straight for the jugular.' She gazed out of the window. 'It prepared me for working in the police, so I can't complain. I guess you were the most popular girl in school.'

Astrid detected a hint of sorrow in Grace's voice.

'No, I was a loner, but I loved learning, and it kept me from my family.' Astrid stepped out of the car, Grace following her. 'Do you know what this kid looks like?'

Astrid's mobile vibrated as the throng escaping into the world increased in front of them.

'I've sent you the photo,' Grace said as she watched the kids.

Astrid peered at the image on her phone, staring at a portrait of an average-looking teenage girl with a face covered in mascara and lipstick purple enough to have been stolen from Prince's cosmetic bag.

'Hey, Tall Paul, whatcha doing ere?'

A gang of girls gravitated towards Grace, pointing and giggling at her. 'Lanky Skanky,' they shouted in unison. The school security did nothing while the teachers slithered back into the building. Astrid searched for any sight of Beth Sharp as Grace showed the kids her police badge. It elicited a mixture of responses, from bemused stares to WE DON'T GIVE A FUCK glares.

The mouthiest of the girls strode up, flaming red hair, flaring her perfect teeth and flicking her fake eyelashes.

'Couldn't they get a uniform to fit ya, Giraffe?'

She tried to hide her reaction, but Astrid saw Grace cringe at that word.

'Do any of you know where Beth Sharp is?'

The ruby-headed girl stood with her hip jutted to the side, one arm draped across her body, clasping the elbow opposite. Her head lolled down to her shoulder, casting her long hair on to the faded Diana Ross t-shirt which clung to her like a second skin.

'We don't talk to the cops, even giant ones.'

The girl gang burst out into fits of laughter, exhibiting teenage angst and bravado. Astrid moved to Grace's side and scrutinised the red-headed ringleader, a delinquent already in the making with eyes like burnt cigarettes. Astrid was about to say something when she spotted Sharp leaving the school and moving down the steps. She had kohl-encircled eyes sunk into deathly pale cheeks, hair bursting from her skull, and was dressed entirely in black.

The mouthy red-headed girl saw her too. 'Run, Beth; a pig and a giraffe are coming for ya.'

The mob started whooping and hollering a combination of animal noises. Sharp twisted her head to the side, gazing straight at Grace. She was off and running before Astrid could react. The kid pushed through the crowd as the rest of the school joined in with the carnival atmosphere.

The last thing Astrid wanted was to run after a teenage girl, but she set off anyway. Grace surprised her again, not so much a giraffe in her movements, but travelling as fast as a gazelle. She parted the teenagers, about to lay her hands on Sharp when the kid took a quick turn around the corner and, unable to halt her momentum, Grace stumbled into a woman walking her dogs. When Astrid reached them, the dog-walker stood cursing the police officer who was trying to make her excuses.

She helped Grace up as the disgruntled animal lover skulked away. 'Did you see where she went?'

If Sharp had slipped into the shadows, she'd be impossible to find. Grace dusted herself down and nodded beyond Astrid.

'She ducked into the first building on the right down that street. They used to be apartments, but the place was condemned six months ago.'

'Okay, partner, let's see if we can locate her.'

Astrid moved out, with Grace hobbling behind her as they approached the dilapidated concrete. The door was hanging off its hinges, the wind pushing it back and forward, so it creaked worse than Grace's knees. Astrid made her way in, with no concerns for her safety, finding a corridor draped in debris, rat shit and dust. A set of metallic boxes covered in rust, unused post boxes for twenty apartments, clung to the wall on her left. Beyond them were a broken elevator and stairs. Damp covered everything, and the building stank of a year's worth of garbage.

'You won't need that,' Astrid said as Grace reached for her weapon. 'Not for this kid; she's scared of her own shadow.'

They moved up the first flight, curious eyes checking every nook and cranny for signs of danger.

'Five flights with ten apartments on each floor, from what I remember,' said Grace. 'You want to search through fifty places and all the corridors and maintenance rooms? We'll be here all day.'

'This should be enough; unless she can stick to walls like Spider-man.'

Astrid pointed to the space where the stairs should have been, which was only a black hole. They inched towards it, staring up at the inaccessible floors above them.

'I guess that's one of the reasons they condemned the building,' Grace said. 'You want to go through each room together?'

'No, that'll take too long. You check the five on the right; I'll do the ones opposite.'

She was inside the first apartment before Grace replied. A quick analysis told her it was three rooms: the main one with a small kitchen, then the bathroom and bedroom. The furniture was cracked and broken, a moth-eaten sofa sitting in the middle of the room as if someone had tried to drag it outside and given up halfway through. Paint peeled off the walls, and flies circled everything; it stank of damp and rotten vegetables. The kid wasn't there; neither was she in the other rooms.

Astrid stepped out of the flat as Grace exited the one opposite, shaking their heads at each other. They got the same results from the following three apartments on each side. Two rooms left, and if the kid wasn't there, she must have grown wings.

Apartment Five had a similar layout as the others, filled with the identical stink of garbage and dirty feet. Astrid didn't have to check the rooms: Beth Sharp sat with her back to the far wall, knees pulled up to her chest, eyes shrunk into her head. She was scared, but it wasn't of Astrid.

Astrid relaxed her shoulders and lowered her tone. 'Who's threatened you, Beth?' The girl shivered and tried to crawl even further into her skin. Her jaw quivered, her mouth opened, but no sounds came out. She lifted a hand to her face, and it trembled as she wiped at her eyes. 'You can trust me, kid; I'm not here to hurt you.'

Astrid hadn't moved, standing a few feet away. Sharp dropped her arms to her side, her tremors subsiding but always present.

'They punish kids like me.'

The words crawled out of her mouth, terror vibrating off every syllable.

'I want to help you, Beth. But you'll have to help me to do that.'

She bent her knees to get down to the girl's eye level. Beth may have been seventeen, but she seemed a lot younger crouched amongst the shadows and the debris of the building. It was cold, but sweat slithered from her forehead and into her eyes. Astrid removed a tissue from her pocket and handed it to the girl. Beth took it in her shivering fingers and wiped at her brow.

'Thanks.'

Her voice trembled. Astrid questioned if she should leave her alone until she overcame her fear, and then remembered Alex probably wouldn't last long if someone had abducted her and she was still alive.

'Is this connected to Alex Sanchez's disappearance, Beth?'

She nodded. 'Yes.'

Astrid pushed on. 'How did you get her to go to the compound?'

There was a noise in the corridor, but Astrid didn't take her eyes from the girl.

'Glen wanted her there, said she needed punishing. Alex needed to expose them for what they are, for what they're doing, so I said I'd get her inside.' She lifted her trembling fingers to her mouth and bit her nails. 'Glen and I grew up as neighbours, and we used to, you know, go out together.' She chewed on one finger until there was no nail left. 'And it's my fault what happened to her.'

Something deep inside Astrid wanted to take hold of the kid and tell her not to worry, that it wasn't her fault, that everything would be okay. But she was incapable of breaking through the emotional wall she'd constructed around herself for so many years.

'Okay, let's get you out of here.' There was another loud bang from the corridor. Astrid turned to the door, for the first time noticing the sleeping bag behind it and the opened food tins and fresh rubbish. 'Have you been staying here, Beth?'

She thought the kid was going to strip the flesh from her

fingers as she pushed her hands further between those shiv-ering lips.

Beth nodded. 'Yes.'

All those years living on the streets flashed through Astrid's head. 'Why?'

She took her fingers from her mouth and wiped her eyes. 'It's safer here sometimes. I can't trust my dad.'

Astrid stared at Beth and saw herself reflected in the kid, remembered the fists and the belt and all the other objects he hit her with. She rubbed at the bruise on the back of her neck and the cut on her face, new injuries to replace the old ones. There were others on her body, acquired long after she'd left her family behind, and each one of those told a tale of triumph over adversity, but it was the scars from her childhood which she could never erase.

She was fighting off those memories when the voices came from the other side of the door.

'Little piggy, little piggy, let us in, or we'll blow the house down.'

Astrid scanned the room for a weapon as Beth sank so far into the sofa she nearly disappeared into it. The door swung open, and three blokes swaggered inside: bundles of toxic masculinity clutching onto baseball bats. Behind them in the corridor, Grace was out cold on the floor.

'You've assaulted a police officer.' Astrid flexed her fingers. The back of her skull throbbed, and she imagined the cut on her cheek leaking warm blood down her face.

'You can't believe how difficult it was to reach up and give her a little love tap on the head.' The middle one spoke, his arms and chest puffed out as a sign of leadership. She guessed all of them to be in their mid-twenties and of low IQ. Apart from the leader. He scanned the room for other bodies, his gaze darting around as if he'd done this before and was calculating for logistics and danger. 'Give us the girl.'

Astrid stared at him. 'Was it a dishonourable discharge?'

His eyes shrank to pinpricks, but it didn't camouflage the hate vibrating inside him. 'What?'

'Did you get a dishonourable discharge from the military? I wasn't talking about one of your nightly emissions from that.'

She pointed at his groin. His two companions hovered at his sides, bats twitching in their hands. Astrid noticed their jerky movements even though she focused on him. When they'd entered the apartment, she'd moved from opposite Beth to behind the end of the sofa. Now they couldn't jump her together, which was why she knew they'd have to come at her from either side.

His grimace turned into a grin. 'You need to give us the girl, English; then we'll leave you alone.'

'Beth must be important for you to attack a police officer.'

The girl buried her head into a cushion at the sound of her name.

'You've got it all wrong, English; we saw you drag her here, so we followed you in. The cop was already on the floor when we arrived to rescue her from you.'

As he spoke, the other two inched their way around the sides. Astrid had to work out which one would be the quicker. She moved to her left, close to the kitchen and the utensils that had gathered rust for months.

'So, that's how you're going to try and explain this when I beat the three of you senseless?'

She observed the movement of his eyes and the tiny flick of the head to his attack dogs. It was quick, but not as speedy as her as she sprang to her left and grabbed the grease-stained frying pan from the counter. She brought it around in one swing and smashed the baseball bat from the thug's hand; it went flying through the air and landed over the sofa. As it sailed across the room, she thrust her knee into his groin, following through to crack against his chin as he tumbled down.

As he hit the ground, she turned to meet the goon coming from the other side; he was big, but he wasn't fast. She put her free hand into the top of the couch, pushed up and leapt over the cowering girl below. Astrid landed and grabbed the discarded club before the attacker and his leader could react. She threw the wood with precision, catching the second thug between the eyes before he could change direction. Bat and skull cracked as one, sending out a long howl from the man as he grasped at his head. He collapsed and joined his compatriot in a heap.

Astrid peered at the leader. 'It's just us now.'

He glanced down at his fallen compatriots, and then stared at her. 'I survived Afghanistan and Iraq.' His glare cut through Astrid. 'I don't need anyone else to deal with you.'

He climbed onto the end of the sofa, towering above the timid girl below who tried to find safety behind a dirty cushion. Astrid backed away from him, towards the window. She couldn't endanger the girl. In the doorway, Grace's legs twitched.

'Why do you want Beth?' she said to him. 'She didn't tell us anything.'

His perfect white teeth shone brighter than a shooting star. 'I'm just protecting America from foreign degenerates like you.'

He strode across the sofa, his feet moving past Beth as she squeezed into the frame of the furniture. Astrid had her back against the cold of the glass, watching him stride towards her. If he moved to the right, he could squeeze the life from the trembling girl's throat. Astrid couldn't do anything until he got off that couch.

He reached the end, one foot on it, the other next to Beth's face.

'What are you waiting for, Mr Dishonourable Discharge?'

He launched himself at her, foot aimed at her guts, hand swinging down towards her head. She ducked, his shoe missing her hair by inches. She rolled on to the floor underneath him and bounced off the sofa. As he landed and fell into the window, she had her arm around his neck and was pulling on his throat. He was taller and stronger than her, but she had leverage, and a calmer mind. Astrid pressed against the back of his knee as she dragged harder against his neck. His hands flailed at his sides, trying to grab at her and failing. He gasped and choked as she squeezed the life from him.

'Let me go, you English bitch.'

'Are you sure they didn't kick you out of the military because you're useless?'

He struggled, but it was no use. He couldn't get an advantage as oxygen seeped from his lungs.

'Are you going to kill him?' The girl was off the sofa and staring at Astrid.

'Do you want me to?'

'Not while I'm watching.' Grace had recovered and was standing behind her.

Astrid gave one last squeeze and dropped him to the floor when he was unconscious.

She turned to Grace. 'How much of that did you see?'

Grace rubbed at the back of her head. 'Enough to know never to get on the wrong side of you.'

Beth Sharp shivered on the sofa as Astrid held out her hand. 'You're safe now, kid.'

The girl took Astrid's help and got off the couch, trembling as she looked at the thugs sprawled on the floor. 'Thank you.'

Astrid let go and turned to Grace. 'Are you going to arrest these three?'

Grace strode past her and flipped the thug leader over and on to his back with her foot. She let out a long sigh. 'This will open up a whole can of worms.' She restrained the bloke.

'How come?'

'Because, my new English friend, this is Jed Fowler, nephew to the esteemed Senator Bob Brady.'

Grace cuffed Fowler's friends as Astrid wondered if she'd made things better or worse.

8 LOSING MY RELIGION

Grace frogmarched Fowler and his mates out of the building while Astrid talked to Beth.

'You can't stay here; will you go home?'

The kid stood on the street corner, her eyes darting everywhere, fingers pulling at her hair as if it was an alien infestation on her head. 'No, that's just as bad.'

'You keep an eye on these three losers while I get the car,' Grace said.

Astrid watched her leave and wondered how she could help the kid standing next to her. Beth tried not to stare at the thugs in their handcuffs, but her unease as they stumbled past was obvious. Astrid moved back into the doorway of the building for some privacy but was still able to see her attackers cooling their heels on the kerb. She removed her phone and called the only local number she had apart from Grace's. Christina Sanchez answered on the second ring.

'Do you have good news for me?'

She sounded as if she was underwater. Astrid told her everything she'd learnt so far about her daughter's disappearance, including the danger she thought Alex's friend was in.

'I know what to do next, but I need a safe place for Beth until this is over. Can she stop with you?'

There was silence, and then Christina spoke to somebody in Spanish. 'She can't stay here, but someone in the community will look after her. Bring her to me.'

Astrid thanked her and ended the call. Grace was at the unmarked police car, bundling the three thugs into the back.

'Are you coming to the station with me?'

'Not right now.' Astrid glanced at Beth. 'I have to take her somewhere safe. Can you get a taxi for the two of us to your place?' Grace arched her eyebrows. 'And I need the keys to your house and your car.'

Grace had the phone in her hand. 'Is there anything else you'd like? The winning lottery ticket or the secret to my heart?'

Astrid tried to stop her lips from curling up, but failed miserably. 'Ask me about the second one next time I see you.'

Grace pulled her to the side, Astrid enjoying the feel of the other woman's fingers on her arm. 'What are you going to do? You'll need to give a statement about what happened here.' She peered over Astrid's shoulder at the scared teenage girl. 'And she'll be safe at the station.'

'I'm not sure about that. We know someone there altered the original report about Alex's disappearance.' She nodded at her attackers. 'Do you think they'll be charged?'

Grace shrugged. 'It seems unlikely considering who Fowler's uncle is. I didn't see anything, so it will be their word against yours, but we can't just let them get away with this.'

'I agree. At least keep them for a while and find me the details about the other kids who've gone missing in the last six months. I'm sure there's a connection between those three idiots and Alex Sanchez.'

'And what will you be doing while I'm there?'

'I'll get Beth safe, and then I'm heading out to the compound to have another word with Glen.'

'I doubt they'll let you back in, and even if they do, how do you know he'll be there?'

The taxi arrived as Astrid spoke. 'I won't be asking to get in. There'll be somewhere around that perimeter where I'll be able to sneak through or over, and Glen will be there until at least eight o'clock because I saw his teaching timetable on the wall earlier.' She took the girl to the taxi.

'You better keep me updated at all times.' Grace shouted as Astrid and the kid climbed into the car.

THEY COMPLETED the journey in silence. Beth kept scratching her leg and squirming in her seatbelt until Astrid changed the radio station and found the Ramones singing about slugs and snails chasing them. The girl smiled for the first time since Astrid had found her.

When they were inside Crowley's home, Astrid explained to her where they were going.

'Do you know why Senator Brady's nephew is interested in you?'

Beth shook her head. 'I've never seen him or the others before today.'

Astrid stood opposite her. 'Those three were there for you, not me or Grace; do you understand that?'

The shaking returned to her hands. 'Yes, but I don't

know why. I haven't done anything.'

Astrid stared at the girl, unsure if she was keeping something from her or not. Working for the Agency had taught her many skills, including the ability to spot when most people were lying. Perhaps Beth's fear was masking the tell-tale signs of deception many gave away without realising it.

'Christina Sanchez will keep you safe until I call you, do you understand?'

Beth blinked, and then nodded. Astrid transferred numbers between their phones before fetching water from the kitchen for the teenager; the kid downed it as if she'd just returned from the desert. Her head twitched as she clasped the glass to her face, glancing at the collection of porcelain figures on the shelves. She brushed water from her lips as she stared at Astrid.

'Do you live here?'

'I'm staying for a bit. I'll be going back to England once I find Alex.'

Even though the kid had denied knowing why those three were searching for her, Astrid sensed she was hiding something. She was about to ask another question when Beth strode out of the kitchen and into the living room. Astrid followed her, finding the teenager thumbing through Grace's collection of books.

She had a copy of *The Golden Compass* in her hands. 'My dad thinks reading is a waste of time.'

'Where's your mother?'

The girl reached into her pocket and retrieved a piece of gum. She unwrapped it and slipped it into her mouth, chewing as she spoke.

'She ran off with the woman who worked in the library.' Beth peered up and scrutinised the marks on the ceiling. 'Perhaps that's why my dad hates me reading.'

Astrid felt sorry for her, but couldn't let that stop her from pushing for more information about what happened.

'In that building, you said some people in the town are hurting kids.' The girl's black-rimmed eyes narrowed. 'Is Jed Fowler one of them?'

Beth's mouth was shut, but her expression told the answer. Astrid decided not to push her any further. It was time to get her into a safe place, so they left for the Sanchez motorhome.

Alex's mother was waiting for them when they got there. Astrid explained what had happened at the derelict building.

She checked her phone as the scared teenager walked towards Christina. It was six o'clock; she had two hours to find a way into the complex and into position while Glen was inside that cabin. She got into the car and drove out of town.

━━━━━━━

ASTRID LEFT the car far enough from the Senator's youth project so no one would stumble upon it and get suspicious. She rubbed at the ache in her head as she strode through the woods and around the perimeter fence.

She stopped next to a tree to get her bearings. The smell of grass and vegetation irritated her. Astrid wanted to be back in the comforting grey of the city, to breathe the smoke and pollution of that urban jungle. She set off again and dreamt of London's concrete beauty.

She'd only been walking twenty minutes when she came across a gap in the metal fence surrounding the compound. As she examined it, there was a movement behind her. She twisted around to see a grey-haired old man gazing at her. He put his fingers to his lips before slipping away into the woods.

Astrid forgot about him and stepped through the gap, hoping there'd be no guard dogs. The mansion was up ahead, past some pig pens, a large barn, and the educational facility where she expected to find Glen. According to the timetable she'd seen earlier, there were five minutes to go before the end of the latest 'Pray your Gay Away' session. She kept a close eye on her surroundings as she approached the pigs roaming in the mud. They squeaked and whined as she got there, but not loud enough to alert anyone. The grounds lacked security as she edged around the side of the barn, peering inside, expecting to see farming equipment but finding it empty.

She crept through the shadows and towards the light of the portable cabin. She ducked her head and glanced through the window. Glen was there, at the front of the class, talking to a dozen young people. They gazed at him, a mixture of adoration and awe gripping their faces. He was full of manic glee, hands waving like a windmill when he reached the height of his speech. When he finished, they all stood and clapped. Astrid hadn't heard what he said, but knew it couldn't have been good.

The youngsters started to file out as she pondered how to get him alone. He stayed behind to collect his papers and switch off his presentation. She was about to move to the door when one of the youngsters returned, a beautiful blonde-haired young man with the deepest, bluest eyes.

She sighed inwardly at the annoyance of it, watching the teenager approach Glen. The lad knelt, and Glen caressed his cheekbones. Astrid removed her phone and set the video to record. She hadn't known what to expect when she got inside the grounds, but it wasn't this. The boy unzipped Glen's trousers and acted as if he hadn't eaten all day.

It was over in a couple of minutes, and she stopped the recording. The lad wiped his mouth, leaving with a smile on his face. Glen's grin was bigger as he put away his teaching materials. Astrid watched the boy go before entering the cabin. She coughed to get Glen's attention. He turned to stare at her in surprise, shaking his head and baring his teeth.

'Security won't be so gentle when they throw you off the grounds this time.'

She moved towards him, holding her phone out and playing the video she'd just made. Astrid increased the volume; the moans and groans coming from the screen were the only sounds there. When it finished, they stared at each other in silence, a pause so pregnant she thought a herd of midwives would come charging into the room at any second, ready for him to give birth to his fear and embarrassment.

'It doesn't matter.' All the joy evaporated from his face. 'Security will have that from you as soon as I call them.' He took his phone out.

'Can they get this from me before I upload the video to the internet?'

He glared at her. 'What do you want?'

She moved towards the window, making sure no one was watching from outside as she had. 'Tell me about Alex Sanchez and what happened to her here. And I'll know if you're lying, so don't bother.'

Glen's shoulders slumped, and he wiped the sweat from his forehead. He flopped into a seat and pulled at the top of his shirt.

'It wasn't my idea; it was the Senator who wanted her

here.'

'Why?'

Astrid moved close enough to record his voice without him knowing. A confession acquired under duress wouldn't hold up in any court, but she wasn't there to get evidence for a prosecution; she would be judge and jury in this search for Alex Sanchez.

He trembled as he spoke. 'She was proving to be too much trouble, with all her activist videos and social media posts, especially with the elections coming up next year. So the Senator needed something done about her.'

'So what did you do?'

He pulled at the top of his shirt again, a river of sweat swimming down his head.

'I got Beth to tell Alex I had to talk to her, to sort out a truce, but I knew she'd want to come here and record some of what we do, to expose us. But we turned the tables on her. She wasn't as clever as she thought she was.'

Astrid calmed the rage building inside her. She hoped his use of the past tense when speaking about Alex was his poor grammar and nothing else.

She pushed her head into his face. 'Tell me what happened, or I'll post the clip.'

She pulled away to let him speak.

'I'll show you.' He grabbed his phone and searched through his files. When he found what he wanted, he gave it to her. 'Just watch that video.'

She hesitated. She'd witnessed many terrible things, had instigated many terrible things in her life, but she wasn't sure she needed to see this. It was a momentary pause; then she hit the play button.

The screen was black, the sounds of people shouting through the darkness. A light flickered on to it, and Alex's face appeared in view, her eyes large and lips a vivid purple, defiance and assertiveness shining out of her. Then the voices rose, and the taunts rang out.

'Libtard, libtard, libtard,' they screamed.

The camera swung round to catch the people shouting, a dozen or so of them, with faces covered by masks of a disgraced president.

'Pig her up, pig her up,' they bawled.

Someone handcuffed her wrists as she fought back, but there were too many. Large hands placed a thick metal necklace around her throat, with a long steel rod at the end. An unknown assailant pulled her across the room. Astrid guessed it was the empty barn she'd walked past earlier.

Alex tried to talk, but the chain squeezed against her skin was too tight. Astrid watched her grasping it, her fingers scratching at the metal. Astrid's hand strained against the plastic of the phone.

The group of masked lunatics tore the clothes from Alex's squirming body, her legs trembling as they pinned her to the ground and stripped her naked before pouring water all over her. Then they covered her in white feathers.

Astrid forced herself to keep watching, fire burning through her veins as she glanced at Glen. She dug her nails into her palms.

Alex was dragged outside, bare feet stumbling through the mud as the chain pulled at her. The screen went dark again until light erupted from the torches surrounding Alex. Glen and his comrades had tried to terrify her. Still, the defiance seeped from her through the phone and into the spot where Astrid was contemplating razing everything to the ground.

The pigs screamed as the people chanted. 'Pig her up, pig her up.'

She watched as Alex was hauled to the enclosure and thrown in with the squealing animals. They trampled around and over her legs and arms.

Astrid stopped the video.

'You wanted to terrify her into submission, to drag her down to your level; did it work?'

Glen shook his head. 'No. We locked her inside the basement, and then did the same thing all over again the next day. We gave her no food, no drink, left her naked and covered in shit, wet and freezing, but still, she spat in our faces.'

Astrid smiled at the thought of it. 'She was here for two days?'

'That's all I know.'

'Then what happened?'

Glen sank into the chair. 'Some of the Senator's men came and took her away, to clean her up and give her new clothes. I don't know anything else after that.'

Astrid kept his phone and dropped it into her pocket. 'Does anybody else have a copy of this?'

'No, that's the only one.'

She headed for the exit, turning to look at him. 'If it isn't, your video will be all over the internet, do you understand?'

His head shivered as he nodded. 'Yes.'

Astrid had her hand on the door and was about to leave. 'These men you said took Alex away, was one of them Jed Fowler?'

The fear in his eyes was the only answer she needed. She left and returned the way she come, moving alongside the barn where they'd held Alex, past the pigs, through the gap in the fence and back to the car. She texted Grace as she headed for the woods.

Do you still have Fowler at the station?

She'd rather have some time with him alone, but this would have to do. The reply shattered even that option.

We had to let him and the others go. They said you attacked them when they tried to rescue the girl. There are no witnesses to who hit me.

Astrid was through the fence when she finished reading the message. She replied as she ran back to the car.

Do you have an address for Fowler?

Grace texted the details. The phone rang twenty seconds later, the ringtone of *Lust For Life* making Astrid smile as she kept on running and answered it at the same time.

'What happened, Astrid?'

'Give me a minute, and I'll tell you.'

It took fewer than sixty seconds before she was inside the car and telling Grace everything she'd gotten from Glen.

'Those fuckers!' Astrid grinned as Grace continued to swear. She calmed down after releasing her anger. 'I'm still at the station. Meet me at my place, and we can discuss what to do next.'

Astrid saw the time on the dashboard. She had more than three hours left of her first day utilising Grace Crowley's many skills, but this was something she had to do alone.

'Okay, I'll see you there later.'

She ended the call and double-checked the information she had open on the webpage. She entered it into the GPS and headed in the opposite direction to Grace's house. Now she had a date with one of those fuckers.

9 HOUSE OF PAIN

Astrid left the forest and drove north, the video of Alex on a loop in her head. Jed Fowler would pay for what had happened, and so would Senator Brady. First, she had to find the teenage girl, and Fowler was her best lead.

The information on her phone told her where to go. The car ducked through the edge of town, past the old industrial heartland and through the other side. There was no decent music on the radio, so she ran through a random collection of tunes in her head, everything from *Tomorrow Never Knows* by the Beatles to *You Can't Tie a Good Girl Down* by the Crystals.

She ignored the texts from Grace asking where she was, concentrated on the road and put her foot down. The night was empty, apart from the occasional stray dog scampering in and out of the headlights.

Astrid drove past the abandoned warehouses and turned down a narrow lane. The terrain bounced underneath her as she imagined David Bowie singing about scars that couldn't be seen. She increased the volume in her head in an effort to drown out the cruelty thrown at Alex on that video. She hadn't seen any of the people who'd hurled the abuse, but she recognised the hate and the anger. Regardless of what Glen had told her, the whole thing was more than a desperate attempt at humiliating a teenage girl. Alex's attackers had enjoyed what they did, sucking in pleasure from the violence they dished out. And they repeated it on a second day.

The music screamed in her skull, the ache of her life jumping around like crickets on a hotplate. Her knuckles turned white as she clenched the wheel and pushed on to the accelerator. She stared at herself in the mirror, not recognising the person peering back. The trees whisked by outside as she gritted her teeth, biting down on her lip as she realised what was emerging from her memories.

The voices came first: her sister, Courtney, reeling off a list of insults designed only for Astrid.

'You're a joke without a punchline, Sis. We're all laughing at you because you're stupid and ugly. No wonder Dad has to discipline you to put you right.'

Then she disappeared to be replaced by him: Lawrence, Astrid's father. His violence was physical, rarely verbal. The belt was his favourite weapon, but he would use his hands if he had to. She continued to drive as her arms and legs ached, blows ricocheting through the years and landing on her flesh. He struck her while Courtney whispered in her ears.

'You can't save this girl; you can't help any of them. You'll get them all killed, just like you nearly did with Olivia. How can you think to be around her when all you bring is terror and death?'

In desperation, Astrid switched on the radio and found a soft, warm female voice telling her how everything in the world was good, no matter how terrible it might appear to be. And then, the presenter increased her tone and changed tack.

'*But now is the time to be extra vigilant. American culture and Christianity are under threat by insidious forces pretending to be loyal to this Great Nation. Those who oppose true Christian American values, and you know who they are, are waiting for you to drop your guard, and they'll swarm through our town and replace us.*'

The voice paused for breath, and Astrid wondered if she was listening to an updated radio version of *The Invasion of the Body Snatchers*.

'*In all of our years, we've faced all kinds of struggles. The only time we faced an existential battle like this was in the Civil War and the Revolution when the Nation began. We are on the verge of losing it as we could have lost it in the Civil War. You must vote to retain Senator Bob Brady as our representative in the Washington swamp.*

The DJ stopped talking and played some song about nails in the feet and hands as symbols of love. Astrid shook her head, thankful when the music drove her memories and anger into the shadows. She knew her past would return at some point, it always did, but she couldn't do what she was about to without controlling her rage.

She pulled the car up five hundred yards from the house, far enough not to announce her arrival. She got out and slipped into the darkness surrounding the trees. The ground was damp from the recent rain, nature clutching at her feet as she trudged through it.

A giant shadow loomed ahead, the outline of Fowler's place grasping out for her. When she moved from the gloom, she was impressed by its size, staring at her like the house from *Psycho*. It was far too big for one person, yet the data she scanned on her phone said there was only a single occupant.

From the outside, she saw it had two floors and an attic, which had an ornately decorated window straight from HP Lovecraft's demented mind. A set of steps led to the entrance, but she wasn't going that way because it was too exposed. A light hung at the front, with others over the windows on either side of the door. She avoided that and moved back into the shade, creeping to the rear. No sign of any vehicles told her he probably wasn't home, which was fine; she'd give him a warm welcome when he returned.

Astrid pushed through the bushes at the side. Her shoes squelched in the undergrowth as she clambered up the small hill leading to the rear of the building. The smell of the countryside was everywhere as she crept up to the back of the house.

She reached into her jacket and removed the knife borrowed from Grace's kitchen. Astrid had unlatched the window in less than a minute and clambered inside.

The floor squeaked as she stepped into the lounge. Moonlight flickered through the gap she'd climbed through, casting a light shade of illumination around her. Dozens of faces stared down at her, fixed into permanent glares at whoever it was that had killed them. Stuffed animals covered the walls: foxes, bears, deer, and even a lion over the grand, unlit fire near the entrance. She wondered if those dead eyes judged her as she stepped past them or if they encouraged her to punish the man she searched for.

Astrid moved into the corridor, convinced Fowler wasn't in the house, but still cautious as she went. There was a smaller room ahead, empty apart from a large TV and gaming system and one of those chairs which transformed into a portable bed with a flick of a lever. Behind her was a decent sized kitchen, so clean and sparkling she assumed it hadn't been used in a while. She gave it a quick scan and turned to go upstairs, stopping when feeling a draught from underneath the steps. A long piece of dark material, thick cotton, was tacked to the side. She ran her hand across it, the texture making her skin tingle as it billowed slightly from the wind coming through the wood. She dug her fingers into it and ripped it free with a tug, leaving it on the floor and revealing a padlocked entrance.

Have you something to hide, Fowler?

She reached into her jacket for the knife again. If he'd installed a digital security system, she might have had trouble hacking into it, but the rusty lock was no match for her. She was through the door and heading inside in no time at all.

The room smelt of leather and sweat as she searched for a light switch, finding one on the wall. When she flicked it on, she realised what was generating those unpleasant aromas. Astrid moved down the stairs into the basement and the torture chamber she'd entered. There was a raised bed with a coffin-shaped cage underneath, bondage chairs, manacles, chains and paddles. Restraints dangled from the ceiling. She peered at the equipment, staring at the cage and calculating it was too small for an average-sized adult. Images raced through her mind, terrible things which made her heart beat faster. She dug her nails into her palms and pushed the sight from her head.

She dodged the stains on the floor and moved towards the computer on the desk. It was switched on, with the screen littered with files, the majority of them video clips. She leant over it, found the latest one dated two days ago, and played it. A naked Jed Fowler hung from the rafters, needles sticking out of his chest as a masked dominatrix added some more. Blood trickled down his flesh, a smile creeping over his face. Next to him, an obese bloke in a gimp suit far too small for his bulk dragged a heavy whip across the dangling man's skin. She watched it for twenty seconds before turning it off.

'This town is full of secrets, and now you've discovered mine.'

Fowler's voice came from behind her, a tremor in his tone. She turned to see him halfway down the stairs, and the gun pointed at her head. She recognised the weapon, a Glock 17 9mm short recoil-operated, locked-breech semi-automatic pistol. The irony of an Austrian-made revolver being one of the most popular in the United States brought a smile to her face.

'You must keep a copy of 50 *Shades of Grey* next to your *Bible*, Fowler.'

He moved down to the bottom of the stairs, his hand never wavering as he gripped the weapon. 'Everything that happens in this room is between consenting adults.'

She turned from him, fingers still on the keyboard and moving to another random video on the computer. Astrid pressed play. His breath warmed the back of her neck, the chill of the barrel close to her face. Fowler's digital version was strapped to a table as two masked individuals pulled large kitchen knives across his chest.

'You enjoy this pain?' she said without facing him.

The sharp silver crisscrossed his flesh like a warped game of noughts and crosses. In the clip, the others, one man and a woman from their body shapes, went about their work in complete silence. Small sighs of pleasure escaped from the mouth of their willing victim.

'It calms my mind.' Astrid twisted to see him, the weapon brushing against her cheek as she did. His eyes peered right through her. 'You look like someone who might enjoy the occasional stab of pain, English.'

'Is this where you brought Alex Sanchez?'

The gun was inches from her face, his finger trembling on the trigger. He stepped backwards and let out a hefty sigh.

'I don't mess with kids, lady. This place is for my friends and me.'

'Does your uncle, the Senator, know about this hobby of yours?'

She watched the sweat trickle down his forehead. He grinned like a kid caught in the cookie jar.

'What do you think?' He used his free hand to wipe at his cheek. 'Uncle Bob's not so bad; it's those fanatics who follow him and drive his election campaign you've got to be careful of.'

'So, what happened to Alex? I know you and your thugs had her after Glen did his best to break the kid.'

He shrugged. 'She took a shower, and we gave her clean clothes. That was job done as far as the senator was concerned; she'd learnt a lesson, and we had leverage over her. We threw her out of the gates and into the woods. I haven't seen her since.'

Fowler lowered the gun and slipped it into his pocket; the video continued behind Astrid. She stared at his expression, remembering all those times she'd spent with people lying to her, recognising the traits which gave their deception away. Her training focused on reading a liar's intentions via their face, on blushing cheeks, a nervous laugh, and darting eyes; micro-expressions which could reveal the truth. Yet the more she worked with suspects, the more elusive any reliable cues appeared to be. The problem was the wide variety of human behaviour. With familiarity, you might be able to spot someone's tics whenever they lied, but others would act very differently; there was no universal dictionary of body language. Experience had taught her it was more about the words offered than how people used them, which is why she scrutinised what he'd said.

Fowler had smiled when talking about teaching Alex a lesson and grimaced when remembering she was thrown into the woods when they'd finished with her. Hurting kids wasn't his thing. He wanted to experience pain, not dish it out, which was why he'd put the gun away. They'd let Alex go, but what happened to her then?

'I believe you, Fowler.'

He flashed white teeth at her. 'So, what do we do now?'

Astrid glanced around the room, readjusting her evaluation of him. She flicked at the leather restraints as she strode towards him, brushing off those childhood memories of parental beatings. She'd gotten over the terror several years ago; an incident with a sadomasochistic killer deep in a Bavarian forest had wiped that particular fear from her mind.

'What state was Alex in when you let her go?'

Did they break her or not?

He relaxed his body, arms by his side, as he leant into a bench covered with instruments of torture. She watched as his hand lingered over a pair of pliers, noticing the glint of expectation in his eyes.

Perhaps he wants me to hurt him.

Astrid had entered the house, assuming she'd have to use pain to get him to talk, realising now that would be a waste of time. She hoped he'd volunteer the information she wanted.

'Uncle Bob watched the whole thing on a video feed.' Disgust crept across his face. 'He doesn't like being close to violence and was convinced we'd broken the kid, but I wasn't sure. There was still a flash of defiance behind her eyes when she stumbled into the woods.'

Good for Alex.

Astrid moved towards the stairs, hands on the railing as she analysed him. 'You know anything about the other kids who've gone missing from this town?'

He shook his head. 'Most of them are runaways, I'd guess. There are loads of shitty places people get stuck in around here and not many prospects if you don't have the right connections.' There was sadness in his voice. 'I wanted to run away when I was a kid, but I wasn't brave enough. I joined the army, but I still couldn't escape.' He shook his head. 'Some of them always find their way back here.'

Against her better judgement, Astrid pitied him. 'You missed your chance to get away, so you're stuck here.'

'I'm a coward, a follower, not a leader. I've made my choice, and now I have to make the best of it.'

'Why did you come after me in that abandoned building?'

He held up his hands. 'That was the Senator's orders. I don't think he likes you for some reason.'

'What did he tell you to do?'

'We had to scare you a little.'

'Your job was to run me out of town?'

'I guess so.'

'You weren't after the girl?'

Fowler shook his head. 'I'd never seen her before. The tall cop was a surprise as well.'

Astrid recalled Grace on the floor after one of them hit her, the temperature rising inside her veins. She resisted the urge to thump him and turned away.

She left him behind, exiting the basement and passing

the sad eyes of the stuffed animals lining the corridor as she headed for the front door. A cold wind bit her face as she stepped into the night. The phone vibrated in her pocket. She was inside the car, sheltering against the elements, when she answered it.

'Where are you, Astrid? I've been trying to get in touch for ages.'

'It was turned off, Grace. Stealth was my priority.'

'So where are you?' Her voice rose with tension.

'I've just left Fowler's place. They let Alex go once they had the video of her.'

'You're only a couple of miles from the river. I'm sending you the directions to meet me there.'

'What's wrong?'

'A body's been found by the side of the water, an unidentified teenage girl. I'm on my way there now.'

The phone went dead before Astrid replied. The digital clock in the car said there were five minutes to midnight.

10   CRY ME A RIVER

It took Astrid ten minutes to find it, red and blue lights showing her the way, the silver of the moon dancing off the surface of the river. It was the start of her second day with Grace as she watched her move through the uniformed police and crime scene investigators.

She approached Grace, who was talking to a woman who bore a striking resemblance to the silent movie actress Louise Brooks and wore a long coat over an expensive suit and trousers. At her feet lay a body concealed by a thin layer of plastic.

'Astrid Snow, this is Dr Briana Jones, the town's Coroner.'

Moonlight cut through the trees, tiny pinpricks of it dancing in the indentations of the plastic below them. Astrid knelt, her hand hovering over the sheet, before pulling it back. Blood covered the forehead and down to the eyes. She flicked the flies away and peered at the kid who wasn't Alex. She wanted to let out a sigh of relief, but she didn't; it might not have been Alex, but it was still a teenage girl.

It was still somebody's daughter.

Astrid's bones creaked as she stood. 'Who is this, Grace?'

'Katie Spencer, aged fifteen, reported having run away from her care home a month ago.' Sadness drifted out of her.

Astrid turned to Jones. 'What happened, Doc?'

Dr Briana Jones bent down more gracefully than Astrid had, pulling back the sheet. She slipped plastic gloves on to her hands, reaching to move the red-stained hair from Katie Spencer's eyes.

'The girl suffered a blow to the rear of her head, which could have come from a fall or an attack. Her lungs are filled with water, indicating she died from drowning after she fell into the river.' She stared at Grace. 'You might find this interesting.' She lifted Katie's right sleeve to show the cut marks covering her wrist and arm. 'It's the same on the other arm, down both of her legs, and across her stomach.'

'Are they self-inflicted?' Astrid said.

'On the first appearance, I'd say yes, but I need to examine them properly at the lab. Some of the cuts are old, more than a year, while others are fresh, within the last few days.'

Astrid tugged at her jacket, memories slashing into her.

'What are you doing here, Crowley?'

It was a woman's voice sounding like nails dragged across glass. Astrid glanced at its owner, an attractive green-eyed woman with dark hair pulled so tightly from her head her skin might burst at any second. Next to her was a scowling man built like a marine. She'd seen them before, at the police station, when speaking to Tanner.

Dr Jones curled her lips at them. 'Detectives Cope and Wylie; it's always a pleasure.'

They ignored the Coroner. 'This is our case, Crowley;

you and she shouldn't be here.' Detective Julie Cope nodded at Astrid.

Detective Peter Wylie glared at them. 'So leave before you end up in our report.'

Astrid returned his glower with a smile, turning to Cope and letting her gaze linger on the female copper longer than it should have.

'We're here because we thought this was the missing girl I'm searching for. Your Police Chief gave me three days with Grace to find Alex Sanchez, and since there are only two days left, we won't waste any more of your time or ours.'

She strode from them, through the scattered vegetation and back to the car. Grace and Dr Jones followed her to the vehicle.

'You need to tell me everything that happened at Fowler's,' Grace said as she caught up with Astrid.

Astrid watched as Dr Jones removed a packet of cigarettes from her pocket and offered them to her. She shook her head as Jones slid one out and lit it.

'I'm amazed at how many medical professionals I've met over the years that smoke or drink too much.'

Dr Jones's green eyes sparkled as she pulled her coat against the chill of the night. 'It's because we know how fragile life is, and we want to enjoy it before we slip into the darkness.'

Astrid had known her for fewer than ten minutes, but already she liked her. 'I thought most in this town were deeply religious and waiting to be greeted into the next world?'

'It fluctuates dependent upon mood.' Jones blew smoke into the air, and Astrid's lungs grasped at it like a drowning woman reaching for safety. 'Sometimes, when people come to the morgue to identify a body, in their grief, they ask me if I believe in God and an afterlife.'

'How do you deal with that, Doc?' Curiosity gripped Astrid.

The Coroner sucked on the cigarette. 'Whose God, I could ask, yours or mine or a universal benevolent entity? Is there a benefactor God and another God responsible for visiting suffering in the world? Are they asking me this in the pursuit of validation of their beliefs, or perhaps looking for an external comfort in the most difficult of times?'

'But you don't say any of those things, do you?'

Jones blew warm smoke into the cold night air. 'You're right, Astrid, I don't.' The end of the cigarette sizzled in the dark. 'I look them in the eyes and determine if they're trying to catch me out or not, and then if I decide they're genuine, I tell them yes, I believe in God. If I can provide even a small degree of comfort in a difficult time, I will.'

Astrid admired the woman, but she didn't want to push her too much about her personal beliefs, so she changed tack. 'Is your name a homage to a dead Rolling Stone?'

Dr Jones rolled the poison stick around in her mouth, succulent ruby lipstick glistening in the twilight. 'He had those large, haunted eyes my mother loved. It says Brian on my birth certificate, but people have always called me Bri, so I pronounce it a different way now, so it sounds like French cheese.' She blew an elegant collection of smoke circles into the air. 'I could have named myself Indiana, but I wanted something less geographical on my driving licence.'

Astrid lapped in the second-hand fumes. 'Don't you get a lot of grief in this community?'

'Don't judge the town and its citizens on first impressions, Ms Snow. Most of them are decent people, good

Christians, doing their utmost for themselves and those around them. A few fundamentalists who've attached themselves to Senator Brady's coattails are not representative of who we are.'

'What about the teenagers who've gone missing over the years?'

Dr Jones finished her cigarette and flicked its slumbering embers into the gloom. 'We're a small community with limited resources and funding. The authorities are not perfect, but we do our best. Some of those kids come back, and some are runaways desperate to be anywhere else.' She glanced over as her colleagues removed Katie Spencer's body from the ground.

'And what about the others, Dr Jones; what happens to them?'

'We try to find them, Ms Snow, and we keep our fingers crossed at all times.'

'So, what do you think happened here?'

The Coroner watched her colleagues take the teenager's remains away. 'It looks like an accident to me. The girl probably slipped somewhere in the mud and knocked her head on something hard. I'm sure the officers will find evidence of that once they've searched along the bank. Then poor Katie likely fell into the river, unconscious while the water filled her lungs.'

'You don't think someone hit her, and then threw her in the river?' Astrid pictured the terrible event in her mind.

'It's possible, of course, but I need to examine the wound in the lab to determine what amount of pressure was applied to her skull and at what angle. The Forensic Investigators have to do their work before I can present a conclusion.'

Astrid considered her words and gazed over the vast

area around her; any bit of it could be part of a larger crime scene. 'I look forward to reading your report, Doctor.'

The two women pulled apart and went their separate ways. Briana Jones's comments echoed inside Astrid's head as she watched the Coroner return to her colleagues. Grace was at her shoulder as the wind increased.

'What happened with Fowler?' Astrid brushed a stray hair from her face and recounted everything from his house. 'And you believe what he said?'

They strode towards their respective cars.

'I do for now.' She unlocked the car and opened the door. 'At least he confirmed that Senator Brady is more involved in what happened to Alex than he let on. We need to have another conversation with him soon.'

She was conscious that having Grace with her wasn't going to last long, which meant getting access to certain people might evaporate quickly. She climbed into the car and followed Grace back to her place.

———

IT WAS one o'clock in the morning when she took the glass of bourbon from Grace's hand as she sipped at her drink.

'We should rest and start again refreshed in a few hours.'

Astrid shook her head, knowing she wouldn't get much sleep any time soon. 'What did you make of the crime scene?'

'It looked as if Katie drowned further up the river from where they found her. There were no signs on that side she or anyone else had been on the ground there. But, the Forensic team had only just started searching the area when I got there.'

'Who found Spencer's body?'

Grace finished her drink and poured herself another. Astrid noticed that this one, unlike the last, was a double. She drank half of it before replying.

'It was one of the town's oldest residents, Manny Burns. He lives in a ramshackle place on the edge of the woods. He was walking his dogs when he discovered her. He doesn't have a phone, either a cell or a landline, in his cabin, so he had to go to Brady's compound and get them to ring the police.'

It appears as if the Senator's fingers are everywhere in this town.

'Burns isn't a suspect?'

Grace shook her glass, so the ice rattled against the sides. 'I'm sure Cope and Wylie will grill him all night but, even if it wasn't an accident, I can't see him involved in anything criminal. He's lived here for seventy years without any brush with the law; not even a parking ticket.' She bit through an ice cube. 'Manny isn't a murderer.'

'Is he tall with shaggy grey hair?'

'That sounds like him.'

'I saw him when I broke into the Senator's compound, wandering in the woods. If he lives close by and walks his dogs there regularly, perhaps he noticed Alex when they let her go.'

Grace finished her drink with a gulp. 'I guess it's worth having a word with him.'

Astrid ran her finger around the top of the glass. 'And ask him about Katie Spencer at the same time.'

'You think they might be connected?'

'One teenager disappears, while another suffers an apparent accidental death close to where the first girl was last seen. That's very coincidental, and I don't believe in coincidences. Did you get the list of missing kids from your station?'

Grace stood and grabbed her laptop. She flipped the lid open and went online. 'I emailed everything to myself just in case things disappear again.'

'Are you allowed to do that?' Astrid would have been detained and interrogated for a week if she'd done something similar while at the Agency.

'It's my work email, so it's okay. I can copy the data into my Cloud account.'

Grace appeared to be unconcerned about any potential reprimands she might receive from her employers. She handed the computer to Astrid, who scanned the details.

'This is all the info for children up to the age of eighteen reported missing for the last two years; is that as far back as the police records go?'

'Only online; there are more paper-based ones stacked in the basement. I thought this would do us for now.'

Astrid wiped a piece of dust from the screen. 'This doesn't include those classed as runaways or kids who've disappeared from the town, but haven't been officially reported as missing?'

'No. I'd have to search through a lot of other paperwork to get even close to those numbers.'

Astrid noticed the tiredness in Grace's voice as she opened another browser window and searched for missing persons data across the United States. She twisted the screen towards Grace.

'Around two thousand children go missing every day in the US. That's eight hundred thousand a year.' She did a quick calculation in her head. 'That's roughly nought point three per cent of the population. How many people live in Angel Springs?'

'I think the last census was just over thirty thousand.'

'On this data, you've got twelve kids reported missing over twenty months, one every two months. Twelve out of thirty thousand is...' Astrid scrunched her eyes into an unpleasant position. 'That's a lot less than nought point three per cent of the population.'

'And your point is?' Grace said.

Astrid pushed her drink away without finishing it. 'Well, we're ignoring many factors here to do a swift analysis of the statistics, including separating the data by age groups and population density, but I'd expect higher numbers for a place this size, even with runaways and kids who eventually return.'

'I'm still not sure what you're getting at, Astrid.'

'What I'm saying is, I think your town has a lot more kids missing than you realise or that people would like to admit. I'd guess those numbers we don't have, those kids who are missing even from your unrecorded data, probably come from communities or homes where there isn't someone to report them missing, or they don't care.'

She remembered the local push for Senator Brady's re-election and all the advertising dotted through the town. 'And in some places, certain crimes, or possible crimes, go unreported so as not to promote a negative perception of the town. A few missing teenagers is hardly unusual in a place the size of Angel Springs.'

Grace slumped against the wall, ashen-faced and grey. 'But, if your numbers are correct, we'd be looking at... at...'

'Around one hundred a year,' Astrid said. 'Which is ridiculous because any town would know if a hundred kids a year were vanishing from their communities, right?'

'I'd hope so,' said Grace.

'And that's why all those other factors we're not

including come into it.' She ran the numbers through her head. 'If we say teenagers make up around fifteen per cent of the population, it still leaves many missing kids. Plus, it's easier to disappear without anyone noticing if you're living in a big city. Still, you've got to admit that, regardless of the size of the population and the spread of geography, two thousand missing kids a day is a hell of a lot for any country.'

Grace grimaced. 'It doesn't bear thinking about.'

Silence engulfed the room. Astrid stared at her new partner. 'But we have to, Grace. I think there's more at stake here than Alex Sanchez.'

'What do you mean?'

'Sometimes, some of the most violent crimes go unnoticed, even to law enforcement, because the perpetrators are clever enough to keep their actions from the public eye. Take Katie Spencer's death, for example.'

Grace narrowed her eyes. 'You'll have to explain it to me because I'm confused now.'

'If the person who found her body, this old man, had taken her to his place and buried her or disposed of her remains in some other way, we'd never have known. And since she's a runaway who few people appear concerned about, including your colleagues, it probably would have stayed like that forever.'

Grace scowled at her. 'I told you, Manny's not a killer.'

Astrid shrugged off her partner's annoyance. 'At some point, Grace, you'll have to tell me why you're so convinced about his innocence, but that's not what I'm getting at. All I'm saying is that if a criminal is clever enough and has the means, they can keep their crimes undiscovered. And in this modern age, with virtually all knowledge easily accessible online, more and more criminals understand how forensic countermeasures work.'

'You believe we'll never find Alex because her killer has concealed her body somewhere?'

Astrid didn't want to think that and wouldn't admit it. 'I'm so tired, Grace, I don't know what I'm saying.'

Grace went to the window, closed the curtains, and then locked the door. 'I'll take the sofa, and you have the bed.'

Astrid grabbed a cushion and dropped it on to the end of the couch. 'You'll barely fit on this, Grace; there's no way you'd get any sleep on here. I find it hard to believe you even have a bed you can stretch out on in comfort.'

Grace moved towards her bedroom. 'Okay, you've convinced me, and I had the bed custom made. It cost me a fortune.' She checked her watch. 'I'll set the alarm for seven; then we'll go and interview Manny.'

'Sweet dreams, partner.' Astrid flopped on to the sofa.

Officer Crowley's hand was on her bedroom door when she spoke. 'You think more kids have gone missing, don't you, and nobody knows about them.'

Astrid shut her eyes and prepared to switch her mind off. 'Someone knows about them, Grace; someone always does.'

11 SHE'S LOST CONTROL

She got to sleep around four o'clock, only to wake three hours later covered in sweat and with the image of her father gazing at her. When Astrid swept the daze from her eyes and her mind, Grace was standing over her.

'I think you were having a nightmare. I heard you from my room.'

Astrid crawled from the sofa, bones aching as her brain struggled to deal with the interrupted sleep. 'I'm sorry if I woke you, Grace.' She pushed her arms into her sides in an attempt to control the trembling.

Why was this happening now?

She'd shoved those memories into the shadows a long time ago. She stumbled into the bathroom and buried her head in the sink, submerging herself into the running water, letting the chill return her to the present. When she lifted up, she'd missed Grace speaking to her.

'What?'

She dried her face. Her teeth were held together by grit, the back of her throat resembling sandpaper. She spread a thick line of toothpaste on to her finger and used it to cleanse her mouth before spitting it into the sink. An aroma of mint surrounded her as she returned to the lounge.

Grace stared at her. 'I said I was up anyway, so there's no need to apologise. Do you want to go out for breakfast, or I'll make eggs and toast?'

Astrid stretched her shoulders. 'I'll watch you cook, and we'll discuss tactics for today.'

'Great; let's crack on.'

She slid into a chair as Grace sprayed oil into a pan. She smelt at her armpit, narrowing her eyes as she watched the food fry.

'I'll need a shower and a change of clothes.'

'No problem, partner. How do you like your toast?' Grace dropped bread into the toaster.

'Well done without being burnt. Do you know if those Detectives, Cope and Wylie, took Burns in for questioning?' Astrid reached for a glass of orange juice. It was cold against her lips and sent a shiver through her throat.

'Knowing them, I'd guess he'll still be at the station. They'll make him wait before interviewing him.' A dark shadow crossed her face. 'Do you want to go there and speak to him before they do?'

'You could arrange that?'

'If we can avoid those two. I think Tanner is wary of you, which means he'll be wary of me while we're together.'

Astrid enjoyed the smell of the fried eggs. 'Cope and Wylie didn't seem too enamoured about seeing us at the crime scene. How well do you know them?'

'Down by the river was the first time they've acknowledged my existence.' Grace couldn't hide the disappointment in her voice. 'When the other officers talk about them, she seems to have many admirers, while everyone avoids him. He's a bit intense, from what I gather. Do you want to see Manny before they do?'

Astrid considered the idea as she finished her juice. 'No; let them soften him up first. We'll speak to him when he goes home.' She wouldn't feel awake until after a shower. 'We'll stop off at the station on the way there after breakfast.'

Grace poked at the yellow of the eggs. 'What do you need there?'

'If you can find out what time he's due to be released, we'll follow him home.'

Grace flipped at the food in the pan. 'Why not talk to him there?'

'If Manny is guilty, he might give something away on his journey home.' Astrid's stomach grumbled. 'Maybe he'll visit someone of interest.'

A large frown consumed Grace's face as she fiddled with her phone. 'I told you before: there's no way he could hurt anyone, let alone a kid.'

'I heard what you said, and I don't doubt your belief in him, but let's not take anything for granted. We'll watch what he does after the interrogation, and then speak to him.'

The bread popped out of the toaster as Grace finished the eggs and placed them on to plates. She handed two slices of toast to Astrid before sending a text. The reply was instantaneous.

'The desk sergeant says our suspect will be out in an hour.'

Astrid grabbed a slice of toast before heading to the shower. 'That leaves me plenty of time to get ready.'

FIFTY MINUTES LATER, they were in the car and sitting outside the police station. Grace pushed the seat as far back as it could go to stretch her legs.

'I wonder how hard they were on Manny.'

Astrid sensed a connection between her and the old man. 'Why don't you think this guy could be a suspect in our case; or for the death of Katie Spencer?'

Grace lifted her hands on to the steering wheel, gripping the thick plastic as if she wanted to snap it in half. Astrid watched her regain control and steady her breathing.

'When I was eight, Manny saved my life.' She peered through the windscreen at her colleagues entering the station. 'I was all alone in those woods, no idea how I got there when I fell down a well. I was there for hours, only the rats and the damp to keep me company. The town sent out a search party, but he found me, him and his dogs. He threw a rope down and pulled me out. I knew then what I know now: he couldn't hurt any kids.'

'It must have been terrible for you.'

Grace let go of the wheel and rubbed her fingers across her knuckles. There was something in her eyes, a glimpse of a shadow, which Astrid recognised from her own past: a trauma not fully addressed.

'After the first few hours, it wasn't so bad.' She raised one finger to her lips and bit on the nail. 'I think it did me good.'

Astrid stared at her. 'Falling down the well did you some good?'

'I was average sized when I fell, but I started shooting up in height the following year. Gran was an evolutionary biologist, and she always joked I only grew so tall because my brain was telling me if I fell down another large hole, I'd be able to climb my way out of it.'

Astrid enjoyed seeing Grace happy, even though she wasn't sure how forced it was. The car's digital clock hit eight, and Burns stepped out of the station on time. He glanced around as if aware someone was watching him before turning towards the beaten-up truck in the parking lot.

'Shall we follow him?' Grace said.

Astrid had considered what her options were on this second day of a new partnership, the places she needed to be and the people she had to talk to. Following Burns was a long shot to finding Alex, but there was something about Katie Spencer's death that nagged at the back of her head. She was about to reply when there was a loud rap of knuckles on the car.

Grace opened the window and spoke to the teenager staring at them. 'What do you want, Heath?'

The kid pulled at the top of his shirt. 'The Senator sent this for you.' He handed her an envelope. 'He said there's no need for a reply.'

With that, he scuttled off down the street. Grace handed it to Astrid.

'It's addressed to you.'

She ripped it open and removed the card. 'I've been invited to a fundraising gathering at Brady's mansion tomorrow night; me and a plus one. Do you have a party dress?'

'You want to go?' Grace twisted her face in surprise.

'Why not?' Astrid ran her fingers across the card's gloss and examined the golden ink that spelt her name. 'It'll give me a chance to slip away and poke around inside that place. It's better than having to break in.'

Grace squashed her lips together and shook her head.

'He'll be up to something; there's always an ulterior motive with Brady.'

'Great; we'll be able to turn his arrogance against him.'

Grace watched Manny drive away. 'What now?'

Astrid stared at the truck, wondering if trailing the old man was the priority, quickly deciding it wasn't. 'We'll speak to Burns later. Where's the Coroner's office?'

'It's inside our biggest hospital. I'll text Dr Jones to let her know we're coming.'

Grace started the engine and turned the car in the opposite direction.

Astrid stared at the invitation to Brady's party as they drove. This was one of the few places she'd been to across the world where the streets didn't feature the homeless and the destitute.

'Angel Springs appears not to suffer from the social ills most towns do. I know I haven't been here long, but I've seen little of drug addiction or beggars.'

But don't forget the missing kids.

'We have several charities who supply food and shelter for those who can't afford it, most of which are funded by various churches.'

'If a society can't provide the fundamentals of life to all of its population, regardless of circumstances, then it doesn't deserve to call itself civilised.'

'Did you read that somewhere?'

Astrid shook her head. 'Just something I learnt from being homeless.'

She gave a summary of her time as a dispossessed runaway. Grace parked the car outside the hospital, and they got out.

'It must have been hard for you, living like that.'

'It was less dangerous than where I'd spent the first fourteen years of my life.'

She left those words hanging in the air and climbed up the steps. The sign for the Coroner's office pointed around the corner, past the ambulance bay and the section for paediatrics. Grace's phone vibrated with a new message.

'Dr Jones is in the morgue.'

They marched inside together. The hallway was spacious and modern; everything which could shine did. Astrid took deep breaths as they strode through the corridor. As a young girl, she'd spent too many hours in such places, holding her pain inside as she watched her father convince nurses and doctors his younger daughter was the most accident-prone child in the world.

They followed the signs down a long corridor. A bored security guard sat outside the entrance to the morgue. He lifted his sunken eyes and nodded to Grace as they approached and went through the door.

There was a space with coolers for storing bodies and the autopsy suite for examinations. At the far end, Briana Jones was stuffing her mouth with a bacon sandwich as she stood over a fresh corpse. As they got closer, the smell of exposed brains and congealed blood drifted over them.

'Hit and run victim,' the Coroner said as she wiped her fingers on her coat and shook Astrid's hand. Behind her was a board where she'd written notes.

'Did you manage to complete Katie Spencer's autopsy?' Grace said.

Jones raised her eyebrows. 'Of course I did. Do you want to see her?' Astrid nodded. 'Well, follow me, ladies.' She led them to the coolers, stopping two rows in and pulling the first drawer towards her. The girl's face looked less traumatic than the last time Astrid had seen it. 'As I said at the scene, Ms Spencer died from a massive inhalation of water. The blow to her head would have rendered her unconscious when she hit the surface. There are no signs of foul play.'

Astrid's gaze lingered on the teenager's pale features. 'Have the police checked to see where Katie's point of entry into the river was?'

Jones shrugged. 'The river is five miles long. I don't think they'll bother now they know it was an accident.'

'Or someone made it look like an accident,' said Astrid. She addressed the Doctor. 'What did you determine about her wounds?'

'Self-inflicted over a few years, I'd say.' Dr Jones seemed confident in her opinion. Astrid turned to Grace. 'You said Katie ran away from her home two months ago.'

'That's what they told social services,' Grace replied.

'So where has she been all this time?'

Astrid moved from the kid's body and Dr Jones closed the drawer. Grace caught up with her as she headed for the door.

'Maybe she's been living in the woods, camping or in one of the caves.'

'There are caves?'

'This was a mining town a long time ago, and some of the entrances are still there, even though they've been condemned, and we've warned people not to go near them. That doesn't stop some.'

'Thanks for your help, Doc,' Astrid shouted before they left.

'Do you think someone was keeping Katie against her will, maybe out in the woods?'

They were nearly out of the hospital when Astrid

stopped and faced her partner. 'Why were those two Detectives there if it was only an accident?'

Grace pondered the question. 'It might have been reported as a homicide at first, so they would have gone straight there until they knew better.'

'Yes, but Jones knew immediately, and she would have told them it wasn't murder. They were already at the scene before we got there. I saw them speaking to Burns as we made our way up.'

They left the building and headed for the car.

'So why do you think they were there?'

Astrid considered the question. 'I don't know, but we should find out.'

12 KIDS IN AMERICA

She got Grace to stop at the convenience store after they left the hospital. There was something she needed before they arrived at the place Katie Spencer had run from. Astrid ignored the stares from red-faced blokes and women who looked half-awake, stepping into the store while Grace waited in the car. A soundless TV played on the wall, beaming out Bob Brady's face. She thought of the party invite and considered buying something to take for him. She grabbed a packet of Twinkies as she searched for the main reason she was there, spotting them behind the counter. She paid with the last of her change before slipping everything into her jacket.

'You didn't get me a present?'

'Why, Officer, we hardly know each other.' They set off for the home. 'Do you know this place?'

Crowley shook her head. 'I'd guess it's no better or worse than most of the care homes in town.'

They arrived just before ten o'clock. As Astrid got out of the car, groups of kids loitered around the building, appearing half-bored and suspicious of any adults. They narrowed their eyes and peered at Astrid and Grace as if they were alien invaders.

Astrid stared at them and tried not to remember what she was doing at their age. 'Why aren't they at school?'

Grace pursed her lips. 'Too disruptive, I guess. Most of the schools in Angel Springs take a hard line with students who misbehave, and if the kids are sent home, they're supposed to stay off the streets during school hours.'

Most of them continued their activities and ignored the adults. As Astrid strode up the stairs, she noticed the girl with the black-rimmed eyes wearing a t-shirt she recognised. They stared straight through each other, Astrid feeling as if she'd stepped back in time. She shook her mother's voice from her head as invisible scars returned to irritate her.

The kid turned away as they went inside the building.

It was a cheerless place, even though someone had tried their best to brighten everything up, scattering random coloured posters over the walls. Dotted in between were displays showing the rules and regulations of the estab-lishment.

- Do not steal.
- Do not lie.
- Do not swear.
- Do not fight.
- Do not back talk to adults.
- Do not enter other people's bedrooms without permission.
- Always knock on the bathroom door before entering, wash hands after using, flush toilet, and put toilet seat down.
- Always pick up your toys or anything you were using and put them back.

- Do not eat in your bedroom or any other room
  other than the kitchen and dining room area
  without permission. Always put your dishes
  away.
- No cell phone or computers in the bedroom
  after bedtime.

ASTRID READ through them in her head, the echo of them returning her to the family home and her father's words.

'You'll do as you're told, child. Listen to me and follow the rules. If you don't, you know what will happen.'

But even when she followed the rules, the inevitable still arrived. A new voice dragged her into the present.

'Can I help?'

The receptionist was as perky as the walls, teeth glittering through a set of braces. Grace placed her badge on the desk.

'Can we speak to the person in charge?'

The playful smile dissolved in an instant. The receptionist reached for a phone, pressed one number, and then whispered down the line. 'Miss Conway will be out to see you soon, if you'd take a seat.' She pointed over Grace's shoulder.

Astrid followed the direction and sat down. Kids sauntered in and out of the building with barely a smile between them. There were times during her childhood, before running away for the last time, when she'd longed to live in a place like this; wished for anywhere but the family home. She wondered how much her life would have changed if someone had spotted the abuse she suffered. All it would have taken was a teacher, or nurse, or doctor, or any adult to recognise what was happening and to believe her, and the whole of her existence would have been different.

And what would have happened to those I've helped since then? I saved children and adults while working for the Agency. Would someone else have been there for them, or would they have suffered or died because I wasn't there? Would my trauma have been transferred to others? My past informs my present, for better or worse.

Grace's voice brought her out of the internal dialogue. 'Do you believe Katie Spencer's death is connected to Alex's disappearance?'

It had been a constant question since the discovery of Katie's body. 'In towns like this, there's always going to be links between missing kids.'

Grace nodded, but Astrid didn't think she looked too convinced. In truth, there were no further leads for Alex beyond her ordeal at Bob Brady's youth compound.

A young woman with permed hair and a glittering smile bounced towards them. 'Hi there, I'm Bella Conway. What can I do for you today?'

Grace stood and shook her hand. 'Do you have somewhere private to talk?'

Conway grimaced. 'Oh no, we don't do anything behind closed doors here; everything is out in the open.'

Adults and kids wandered around them, shooting cursory glances at the intruders in their midst.

Grace stepped in closer. 'This is about Katie Spencer, Miss Conway.'

Conway's shoulders slumped. 'Ah, Katie; everyone here knows of her unfortunate accident.' She glanced at her staff and the children. 'We've encouraged people to speak up and not hide their feelings.' She was a walking, talking advert for positivity, regardless of the situation. 'We can't allow negativity to invade our community.'

'Did Katie have many friends here?' Astrid said.

Conway beamed at them and answered the question by not answering it. 'We never interfere in the private lives of our residents.' She spoke as if talking about hotel guests. 'The residential programme we provide is live-in out-of-home care placement. Our staff are trained to work with children and young people whose specific needs are best addressed in a highly structured environment. These placements are time-limited and offer a higher level of structure and supervision than those provided in the home. We offer guidance and organisation which they can't often get anywhere else, even in school.'

She grinned like a maniacal cat. 'And everyone gets along famously.' It was like listening to the speaking clock. 'We provide activities and events which contribute to cementing the links between residents and staff.' Pride filled her eyes as she spoke. 'Like most places, there is the odd teething problem, but I can confidently say we are the best-run facility of this kind in the area, and perhaps across the whole of the United States.'

'So why did she run away?' Grace said.

Astrid watched Conway's hackles rise above her head. 'Some children are beyond help, no matter what you try and do for them.'

Astrid peered at her, hearing the words, but they came from her mother's mouth. 'You're saying Katie ran away because she was unhappy?'

Isn't that why all kids run away?

Conway glanced at the ceiling, a slight tremble in her lips not interfering with her constant smile.

'I guess she must have been, but I don't know why. She

never displayed any signs of unhappiness and, as far as I'm aware, never spoke to anyone here about any problems she might have had.' She regained her composure. 'Katie had her own room and possessions with everything she needed here.'

'You reported her missing to the police?'

Conway stuck out her shoulders and chest. 'No, we report any prolonged absences to social services first, and then they pass it on to the police.' She glanced at Grace. 'I'm sure Officer Crowley is aware of this.'

Astrid moved towards her. 'Can we see where she stayed, look at her possessions?' She wanted to examine the place the girl was supposedly happy in.

'I'm sorry, no; not without official clearance. We have a duty of care to uphold for all our residents.'

Astrid brushed past Conway as Grace was about to speak.

'It's a shame you didn't think about that when Katie was alive.' She stormed out of the door with her hackles rising, scratching at her palm as a trickle of blood appeared on her skin.

Grace followed her outside. 'Well, that was a waste of time.'

'Perhaps, perhaps not.' Astrid strode towards the kid with the dark eyes she'd noticed earlier; she guessed her age to be about fourteen.

The girl turned from her phone and glared at Astrid. 'What?' She chewed gum and blew a giant pink bubble at the adults. Then she sucked it back into her mouth and the air smelt of strawberries. Astrid extinguished the negativity she'd acquired from Conway and spoke to the teenager.

'You call yourself Polly, even though it's not your given name. All you think about is leaving here when you're sixteen, but you don't need to wait until then. You can start your new life anytime you want, and I'll tell you how to do it.'

She reached into her jacket, finding what she'd bought from the store and throwing it at the startled girl. The kid caught it without blinking an eye, still chewing as if it was about to go out of fashion.

'I don't talk to cops.'

Astrid pointed to the building opposite. 'We're going there if you'd like to eat. I'll buy you whatever you want.' She stepped down and turned to the girl before she left. 'And I'm the farthest thing from a copper you're ever likely to meet. I hate them as much as you do.'

She crossed the road with Grace scampering in her wake. Astrid was inside the waffle house before her friend caught up with her. She smiled at the waitress and grabbed the menu as Grace scowled. They took the largest booth available. Grace grimaced as she twisted her hips.

'You can't give that kid a packet of cigarettes.'

'Apparently, I can.'

'I can arrest you for that.'

Astrid held out her wrists in supplication. 'You can cuff me anytime, Officer Crowley.'

Grace scratched at her throat and coughed. 'And what's this about hating the police?'

The blood was drying on her palm as Astrid rubbed at it. 'Well, there are one or two good ones, but most authority figures shouldn't be trusted.'

'And why are you encouraging her to run away from the care home?'

'I'm doing nothing of the sort.'

She scanned the list of food and ignored Grace's blazing eyes. She decided what she wanted and peered out the window, watching the kid isolate herself from the others. The girl examined the packet of cigarettes before gazing across the road.

'I heard what you said to her, don't deny it.'

Astrid smiled at Grace before turning her warmth towards the approaching server. 'Can you give us a couple of minutes? We should have another joining us soon.'

The waitress shrugged and turned to serve someone else. The place smelt of toffee sauce and melted chocolate.

'You think the kid will come here after what you promised her?'

Grace's annoyance wasn't going away. Astrid scrutinised the girl through the window.

'How old is she, fifteen at the most?'

Grace crossed her arms and sulked. 'Probably.'

'I'd been living on the street for a year at that age, escaping from parents I wouldn't wish on my worst enemy. I'd never got along with my sister, but what happened with our father, what he did to me and how he ended up in prison made it worse.'

'Your sister didn't believe you?'

The anger disappeared from Grace's face. Astrid flicked a piece of dirt from her arm.

'Courtney? She encouraged him to beat me. Sometimes she'd watch, making sure I saw her grinning at me.'

Grace's eyes and mouth froze wide open. 'My God, Astrid, that's terrible. I'm so sorry.' She reached a hand across the table, but Astrid didn't take it. 'Did your mother know what was going on?'

Astrid picked up a salt cellar and poured some of its contents into her palm. 'She knew and didn't care, comfortably numb cradling a bottle of rum.' She rubbed the grains between her fingers, the salt stinging the small cut in her skin, before dropping them onto the table. 'So I sought refuge outside the family and found a collective that I thought was like me, but that was another mistake.'

'What do you mean a collective like you?'

'A London gang with high ideals of honour, but who were only criminals. They taught me a lot of valuable things, and I quickly became their cybercrime expert. I hacked into government websites, big business and international corporations, and discovered loopholes that allowed me to enter celebrities' and politicians' private files.

'I thought I was doing something good for the world, righting wrongs and helping people; redistributing money and resources to those who needed it the most.' She laughed at the absurdity of the teenage version of herself, believing she was a modern Robin Hood. 'That was until I realised the gang were only using me for their criminal ventures. I was planning my second escape from those who controlled me when I ended up in prison at seventeen, and was then offered another way to live.'

Grace stayed silent, picking at the menu and avoiding her partner's gaze.

Astrid didn't suppress the memories; there were some good times with Ramon and his gang. But things changed when she left them behind and learnt how to control her life: only then, when she could help herself, was she able to help others.

But now, as a stranger in Angel Springs, could she find a missing teenager?

G race placed the menu on the table.
'You became a spy?'

Astrid pushed her shoulder into the booth, surprised at how the conversation had turned to her life.

'That sounds so glamorous.' The laugh hurt her throat. 'It's not how you see it in the movies. The Agency is the clandestine government organisation the public doesn't know exists; they have no official designation compared to the other intelligence services. Imagine your CIA, but even more secretive and not answering to the customary laws of the nation.'

The waitress brought a jug of water over, and Grace poured a glass for each of them.

'So, you're not Jane Bond, 007 then?'

Astrid sipped at the drink, hoping to remove the bitter taste in her mouth, but failing. 'Hardly. The Agency deals with internal and external security threats to Great Britain and is accountable only to itself.' A decade and a half of memories tumbled through her head, laid out like chapters on a DVD. She could separate them by date, country, target, outcome, and any number of other fields. 'I was part of an organisation which handled things never intended for the public or the courts. Every nation has an Agency, whether they admit it or not.'

Grace's eyes widened. 'Surely there's some government oversight. Otherwise, they could do whatever they wanted outside the law.'

Astrid brushed the last of the salt from her palm. 'And that's exactly why they were created. The British government wanted an organisation to operate outside the law and deal with those threats things like freedom and rights would only hamper.' A sad smile drifted across her face. 'And once you're in the Agency, the only way out is inside a wooden box. But I thought different.'

'What do you mean?'

'Think about it, Grace. If you're an official organisation allowed to operate above and beyond the law, those in charge are never going to allow you to leave and tell the truth about its actions. There is no retiring from the Agency, no option for a pension and an early departure; you work for them until you're physically or emotionally incapable of doing it anymore. Any kickback against this, any revolt or insurrection, only leads to confinement where no one will ever find you. But I choose a different path once I'd had enough.'

Grace watched Polly through the window as the girl crossed the street. 'What are you going to say to her?'

'I don't want her to run away.' She smiled at Grace. 'You should give her a foster home for at least a month to see how it goes.'

Grace's mouth hit the floor as the waitress arrived, and Polly entered. The server was bright-eyed and full of beans, taking their orders in super quick time. Grace was still shell shocked, so Astrid ordered the same for both of them: bacon, eggs and toast with coffee. The kid got the same plus two stacks of waffles covered in syrup. Then there was silence for several seconds, only broken by the girl slapping her hand on to the table.

'What do you want from me?' She continued talking before any reply. 'I know why you came to the home, and you were asking about Katie. I don't know anything about her or what happened to her, and even if I did, what makes you think I'd tell you two?'

Astrid watched the kid's lips hammering away at ninety miles a minute, imagining seeing a different version of herself.

'We don't want anything from you, Polly; I promise. But we can offer you a way out of that home.' She glanced at Grace, noticing the irritation still lingering behind her eyes.

The first stack of waffles arrived as the kid glared at Astrid. The smell of syrup and sugar wafted in the air between them. Polly picked up a fork and dived in, devouring two of them before she spoke.

'How do you know my name? Nobody calls me that here.'

Astrid pointed at the figure printed on the kid's shirt. 'Because I grew up listening to her music when I was your age, and I assumed if you're going to have a picture of Poly Styrene on your chest, it's because you identify with her as I did.' She grinned. 'Then I guessed your name.'

The kid did a lousy job of wiping her face with the back of her hand. 'You're the only person I've met who knows who she was.' She leant in closer to Astrid. 'You don't look old enough to have been around when punk was out.'

Astrid laughed as the waitress brought the rest of the order. 'Thanks; I'll take that as a complement.' She scooped a forkful of scrambled eggs between her lips, following the kid's example and talking with her mouth full. 'You're right, Polly; I'm not that old, but I did discover X-Ray Spex and lots of other music when I was about your age, and it helped me get through some difficult times. Grace and I would like to help you if we can.'

The girl finished the first plate of waffles and shovelled a large slice of bacon into her mouth, scrutinising both of them as she did.

'Are you two a couple?'

Grace pulled at the collar of her shirt and stammered an answer. 'We're partners on a case.'

'That's a shame.' She grinned at them. 'You look like you'd make a great couple.' She stared at Astrid. 'You're English?'

Astrid nodded. 'I came to America to find a kid, a lot younger than you, who'd been abducted by her father.'

Polly chomped on the bacon, her eyes as wide as her mouth. 'And did you do that; did you find her?'

'I did, but now I'm searching for someone else, a girl about your age, name of Alex Sanchez.'

Polly never lifted her head from the table. 'I know her; everyone did.'

'Did?' Grace sat forward. 'Why do you say that about her?'

Polly slurped at her coffee. 'Because she's missing, and there's no happy ending in this town if a kid goes missing. Just ask Katie Spencer.'

'Didn't she run away because she was unhappy in the care home?'

The kid spat shards of bacon over the table. 'Lady, nobody runs away from there because it's bad. Ms Conway might be a bit hippy-dippy, but she makes sure all the kids are looked after and safe. I lived in two other places before this one, and they were like the Wild West in comparison.' She put her fork down and peered at Astrid. 'Every kid in there wants to be with a family who loves them, I'm not gonna deny that, but Conway's place is the best we're gonna get unless the impossible happens.'

'What do you mean by that?' Grace said.

Polly twisted her face towards her. 'Who's gonna want a fourteen-year-old whose parents are locked up because they're druggies? Especially when they look like me.'

A combination of sadness and gravity dragged her shoulders down. She peered at Grace as Astrid watched the girl pour her soul into the Police Officer. The teenager's eyes shifted to the side, glazed with a layer of grief. As she blinked, sorrow dripped from her eyelids and slid down her cheeks. Polly bit her lip as Astrid glanced at Grace, knowing the kid had done her job for her.

'If the care home is such a safe place to live, why would Katie run away?' Astrid said.

The teenager started on the second plate of waffles. 'That's the point; she wouldn't. And she didn't have anywhere to run to. It doesn't make any sense.'

Astrid summoned her most welcoming tone of voice. 'Polly, how would you like to live with Officer Crowley for a while?'

The girl sat back, wide-eyed and with bacon hanging from her lips.

'What?'

'At least to see how the two of you get on.' Polly gulped her food and rubbed at her eyes. 'A month should give you plenty of time to educate Officer Crowley on what good music is, because what she has at home is sorely lacking.'

'Hey,' Grace said to her in mock horror. At that moment, Astrid knew she'd convinced one of them.

But what about the girl?

'You want me to be a cop's kid?' The shadows around her eyes darkened even further.

'I'd like you to have a decent life.' Astrid gazed through Polly's expression and into her heart. 'You might feel safe across the road, but you'll probably never be loved. Don't make the same mistakes I did.'

Astrid stood to leave. Apart from breaking into the foster home to search Katie's room, she'd done all she could. A nagging hunch at the back of her head told her there must be a connection between Alex and Katie, but she couldn't see what it was. She looked at Polly, and then Grace, wondering if her interference would make things better or worse for them.

'I know where Katie used to hang out,' Polly said.

Astrid and Grace glanced at each other.

'Where was that?' Astrid said.

The kid finished the last bit of syrup from the plate and licked her lips. 'All us misfits hang out at the Valhalla.'

Graces eyes and mouth widened at the same time. 'The bar on the river? You're too young to go there.'

Polly's laugh was like water springing from a burst pipe, rising from her chest as she sprayed bits of pancake all over the floor.

'Don't worry, Grandma; the kids don't booze there. We only go for the music or the company.'

Astrid flicked a stray piece of food from her leg. 'Is there a band on tonight?'

'Only the best,' the kid replied. 'A group of angry girls called Riversludge. They'll be on stage at nine.' She gazed at Grace. 'They're far too noisy for those with delicate ears.'

Astrid smiled. 'Will you be there?'

Polly cleaned away the last bits of the food from her plate. 'I never miss their shows.'

Grace nodded to the care home across the road. 'And they allow you to stay out so late?'

The kid stood, pushed past the tall woman and shook her head, studying Astrid as she went.

'And you want me to live with her? She won't last a month with me.' The door rattled behind her.

Astrid turned to see Grace staring daggers at her.

'So what do you say, partner? You'll need someone to look after you once I've left town, and the kid seems the perfect candidate for that.'

She waited for the rant to start.

14 A FOREST

The temperature increased inside the car as they drove to Manny's place. Grace glared at Astrid in the mirror.

'Why would you tell her that? What makes you think I want to foster anyone? What gives you the right? I've only known you for two days, and you do this? You're giving the girl false hope.'

Her face smouldered like the surface of Venus, her eyes darting from the road, and then to Astrid. They bounced through the woods and towards Senator Brady's youth centre before Grace took a sharp turn away from it, cutting onto a path that didn't do Astrid's back any good.

'Pull over,' she shouted as Grace's irritation transferred to her driving.

She scowled at Astrid before stopping. The wheels skidded through the dirt and grass, braking inches from a huge tree; only the seatbelt prevented Astrid from thumping into the front of the vehicle. It cut into her ribs, and she grimaced. She undid it and turned to speak to Grace, but the tall woman was out of the car in a flash, slamming the door behind her. Astrid was more circumspect, slipping from the seat and doing her best to avoid the mud on the ground.

'Did you do this so you could manipulate the kid?' Steam slipped out of Grace's ears. 'How is she going to feel, you getting her hopes up, and then letting her down?'

Astrid waited for her to calm down. Branches crunched underfoot as she moved towards her, scaring squirrels across the woodland floor.

'How far away is the well?'

Grace scrunched up her eyes. 'What?'

'The well you fell into; is it near here?'

'If we walk to Manny's, we'll go past it. Why?'

'Have you been back since the incident?' She was being hard on Grace, with this and the girl; she knew it, but she also accepted it needed broaching sooner rather than later. When Grace mentioned what had happened in her childhood, Astrid recognised her repressed emotions. 'Can you show me where it is?'

'I'll take you there.'

They marched through the trees for about half a mile, the river rumbling somewhere in the distance, until Astrid saw the danger sign up ahead.

'They never sealed it?'

'I don't think they can. It connects to the town's water supply.' The anger had drifted out of Grace, the fear only noticeable by the tremble at the edge of her mouth. 'What are you going to do about Polly? You've made her a promise you can't keep.'

Astrid took a deep breath, ready to give the speech she'd prepared on the bumpy journey into the forest.

'You told me you wanted to have a family, Grace, but you didn't have the time, or your job was too dangerous, or you didn't think you'd find the right person to be a parent with. You don't have to worry about any of those things; you've got a ready-made teenager to try out for a few weeks. There's no need for maternity leave or the messy business of getting pregnant, shuffling around for nine months, and then changing nappies. You can have two weeks, four at the most, to test out motherhood. If you don't like it, then at least you tried, and you'll know either way.'

Grace stared at her, eyes as big as the moon, mouth as wide as the ocean. 'Looking after a kid isn't like picking clothes from a shop. You can't treat the girl as if she's a commodity or a puppy you get for Christmas. And you can't use me as some kind of parenting experiment because of what went wrong in your life.'

Astrid let Grace's frustration wash over her. 'This isn't about me. Maybe I made a mistake and took you for granted, but perhaps this isn't about you either. That girl calling herself Polly needs some guidance and affection, and I think you'd be great for that.'

'You're unbelievable, do you know that? Even if what you said is true, and I'm not saying it is, why this kid? Why not any of the others desperate for a foster home?'

Astrid shrugged. 'She was there, in the right place at the right time, and why not her? Someone has to teach you what good music is.' She didn't wait for Grace's protestations, strode past her, ignored the warning sign, and leant over the top of the well. An aroma of dirty water and fresh mud rushed up from the bottom. 'What's the likelihood Alex might be down there?'

Grace grabbed her by the shoulder and pulled her back. 'This isn't a game.'

'What do you think happened to Katie Spencer?'

Grace let go of her. 'She fell into the river and banged her head. It was an accident.'

'Perhaps she did, perhaps she didn't.' Astrid moved past her and around the other side. 'But that doesn't explain where she's been for two months, or those cuts on her body. That doesn't explain why she ran from a place where she was supposedly safe.'

Grace stepped across from her, placing her hands on the crumbling concrete top of the well. Astrid watched her avert her gaze from the drop below and stare at her.

'What are you saying?'

'Someone is taking kids and imprisoning them somewhere in this town, torturing them and worse. Katie managed to escape, only to fall into the river and hit her head. Whoever is doing this might also have taken Alex.'

'You're guessing.'

'Some of it is supposition, but I see the pattern, Grace. I recognise it because I've seen it before.'

'Is this what you did with the Agency?'

'Partly. Serial killers, kidnappers, sadists were all part of the scumbag melting pot I dealt with. The consistent thing in every one of those cases was that someone always knew what was going on. They knew something, big or small, which could have ended the case early and saved lives. It will be no different in this town; nothing ever happens in isolation.'

'And you think Manny could be the person who knows something about the abductions?'

'Let's hope so.' She peered into the well one last time before turning to her partner. 'What aren't you telling me, Grace?'

A single word tumbled out of her shivering lips. 'What?'

'About your accident here, between these trees, and

inside this well. I know when people are keeping things from me.' Astrid moved closer to her. 'The best purveyors of deception can hide things for a time, but even they give it away eventually. And, with all due respect, Grace, you're not the best at keeping secrets. Something more happened here than you falling down this well.' She was close enough to see Grace's laboured breathing. 'You don't have to tell me, but since you mentioned it, I've seen something invisible weighing on your heart, and if you let it drag you further down, it will interfere with you doing your job.' She touched Grace's arm. 'And I need you at your best to help me find Alex and discover what happened to Katie Spencer.'

She hated laying on the guilt, pushing Grace too far, but believed it would be for the best for both of them. She watched Grace struggle to breathe and scratch at the first bit of free skin she found on her arm. Her voice was hoarse as if the words refused to leave her mouth, and she only got them out by a force of will.

'I've never told anyone the truth, not even Grandma.' She scrutinised Astrid. 'How did you know?'

She let go of Grace. 'I've got so many secrets buried deep inside me; it's sometimes easy to spot them in others.'

The only noise was the whisper of the wind and the flapping of wings far above their heads. Astrid waited for her to speak.

'I said I didn't remember how I got here, but that was a lie.' She stepped towards the well, her fingers hovering over the concrete. 'I was with a group of older girls that day, and they led me here.' She placed her hand on the edge as Astrid joined her.

'They brought you here against your will?'

Grace shook her head. 'It wasn't a kidnapping or

anything like that. One of the girls said fairies lived in the well, and they granted you a magical wish for anything you wanted.'

'So you went with them.'

'My parents had died in a car crash six months earlier.' She brushed her fingers across the stone. 'It was my chance to bring them back.'

'I thought they passed away when you were older?'

'No, that's just another lie I tell myself and everyone else. I was in the rear of the car, unhappy to be strapped in. Somehow I got out of the seatbelt and tried to crawl into the front. My mother turned to stop me, catching my father's hand as she did so. I'm not sure what happened next, but we ended up on the other side of the road, heading straight into an oncoming truck.' She scratched at her arm again. 'The doctors said I was lucky to be alive, but I didn't feel lucky.'

Astrid reached out to her. 'I'm sorry, Grace.' It wasn't just for Grace's suffering, but for her part in resurrecting those memories.

'I'd forgotten or suppressed most of it until now.' She took Astrid's hand. 'But you were right. It's been killing me slowly ever since that day, and I'm glad to tell someone about it finally.'

'You came here hoping to bring your parents back, but what did those girls do to you?'

Grace dipped her head into the well for a brief second before arching upwards. 'I told them I was there to be reunited with my parents. So they laughed at me and said the only way I'd be with them again is if I joined them in the next world. Then they picked me up and dropped me in there.' She pulled away from the well, turned her back on it, and stared in the opposite direction. 'I was so ashamed, I never told anyone, but Manny knew. He saw everything they did.'

'Why didn't he tell the police or someone else?'

'Who would believe him, the town outcast against a group of kids whose parents were all upstanding citizens of Angel Springs?'

Astrid moved from the well and stood next to Grace. 'Do you want to go back? I can do this on my own.'

Grace shook her head. 'No, Astrid; we're a partnership now, and we'll do everything together while that lasts.'

'Then let's go and find your saviour.'

'What if he isn't in or he refuses to speak to us?'

'Then we pay another visit to Alex's mother. Christina didn't tell us everything, of that I'm sure. How far is this place?'

'A few more minutes on this path.'

She saw the cabin up ahead. Grace went to step off the path until Astrid pulled her back.

'Stay on the Yellow Brick Road, Dorothy.'

'There's the cabin.' Grace pointed towards it. 'It'll be quicker if we cut through the trees.'

'Quicker and more painful.' Astrid raised her head. 'Have you seen the cameras above us?'

Grace twisted her neck up. 'Are they on? I can't see any lights on them. And why can't we go through the wood?'

It was Astrid's turn to point into the woods. 'Look at the ground on either side of this path.'

Grace did. 'Okay; there are leaves and branches every-where. It'll be tricky, but we can get through them.'

'Not if you want to stay healthy. Look closer and you'll see the bits of metal poking through.'

'Debris?'

'Traps and wires. Your former saviour only wants

people approaching him along this path. Has he always been this paranoid?'

Grace knelt for a better look at the cluster of leaves, standing to answer the question. 'I haven't spoken to him since the day he saved me. I don't know what goes through his mind. He keeps to himself and rarely ventures into town.'

It took a few seconds for that information to sink into Astrid. 'You haven't spoken to him since he pulled you out of the well?'

A breathless sigh escaped from Grace's lips. 'My grandma didn't want me to. There was talk Manny had dropped me in the well so he could play at being the hero.'

'So what did you say?'

'That it was all my fault and I'd stumbled and fallen. And then he saved me. But you know how people are. There were rumours it was his doing, no matter what I said.' She wiped the sweat from her chin. 'Then it reached the point where even if I'd wanted to tell the truth about the girls, nobody would have believed me. Those that hated Manny would still have blamed him. I saw him, occasionally, on the periphery of the town, but there was never the opportunity to speak to him, to thank him properly.'

'And what about when you grew up?'

The sigh was heavier, more noticeable. 'Years had gone by. I thought it was too late by then. I was embarrassed, I think.'

The porch and the front door were in front of them. Astrid scanned the rest of the surroundings.

'Well, it appears you might finally get that chance to thank him.'

She stared at the cabin, noticing the dilapidated wood

and the smoke drifting from the chimney. Grace nodded at it. 'It looks like he's home.'

She moved up the steps and on to the porch, raising her hand, ready to knock. Astrid watched her hesitate, recognising the nervousness of someone about to revisit their past.

'Do you want me to do it?'

'Hello,' Grace shouted. 'Is anybody here?' Astrid stepped next to her and banged her fist on the faded wood. Grace frowned before turning to the door. 'Manny, it's Grace Crowley; Officer Grace Crowley. Is it okay for me to come inside?'

They waited for an answer, but none arrived. Grace turned to Astrid.

'Maybe he's hurt.'

Then something howled, and a shiver ran down Astrid's spine.

15 HOUNDS OF LOVE

Astrid pushed the door open. Grace's hand rested on her gun as they went inside. It was the smell that hit them first as the stench of bleach hung in the air. The only illumination was from the open door and the flickering fire in the far corner.

'Where is he?' Astrid waited for the howl to come again, relieved when it didn't.

'I can't find a light switch,' Grace said in a half-whisper.

'I don't think there's any electricity in here.'

Astrid removed the phone from her pocket and turned on the torch. She swept it in front of her, catching glimpses of tattered furniture, bunches of newspapers and a pile of crumbling bricks on the carpet. Jam jars brimming with nuts, bolts and screws sat stacked on top of each other on a bench in the corner.

A large shadow moved on Astrid's right. She stepped back from it as it growled. The growl grew into stereo, two pairs of red eyes flashing into life, porcelain-white teeth baring their fangs.

'You shouldn't have come here, Gracie.' The voice came

from the space in front of them, drifting between the dogs. 'Now, they'll get you as well.'

Astrid heard the striking of a match as he lit candles at his side. His long elephant-grey hair cascaded on to his shoulders, the shaky light shadowing his aquiline features: Manny Burns wearing mismatched hunting clothes and patterned slippers at least a size too big. Two bored-looking Alsatians flanked him. He stood with the help of a giant silver cane gripped in his hand. The dogs took a step forward with him. His face was so grim it could haunt a house; the blue of his eyes piercing Astrid's gaze. Grace gave him that warm smile that had so enchanted Astrid.

'You're not in trouble, Manny.'

'Your friend won't be able to help you, Gracie.' One wave of his fingers and the dogs slipped into the background. He reached down and flicked a switch, a cluster of small light bulbs springing into life through the room like fireflies dancing on the wind. 'Please, take a seat.' He sat in a large chair.

Grace strode over and threw her arms around him. Astrid stiffened her back, expecting the dogs to charge out of the dark, happy when they didn't. She took the seat closest to her. When Grace pulled from Manny, Astrid scrutinised him some more. The flesh hung off his face like snake skin, while the remains of his teeth were as yellow as rotten mustard. Grace gazed at him as if he was a long-lost friend.

Which, I suppose he is. He'd saved her life, and she'd never had the chance to thank him until now.

But they weren't there for reminisces or Grace's childhood; they were there for Alex and Katie, and who knew how many others? She kept her eyes on the dogs and inched forward. 'Who do you think is coming for you, Mr Burns?'

'Call me Manny, Ms...?'

She smiled at him. 'Astrid.'

'Someone is always coming for me, Astrid. When I was a kid, it was my father and his belt. Then it was the other kids at school, followed by the older teenagers where I lived. The Viet Cong came for me next, not that I blamed them; I shouldn't have been there. When I returned home, the government came for me, then forgot about me, and then came for me again. Now, it's those who don't want me here anymore, who don't want me in this town.'

'Is that anyone specific, Manny?'

He shuffled in his chair. 'It's those who don't want me watching them.'

Grace placed her hand on his arm. 'Did you see what happened to the girl who drowned in the river?'

His eyes shrank a little, and Astrid noticed the added tremble in his fingers. 'She came up out of the earth, and she ran, ran as if the Devil chased her. That's why she didn't watch the ground properly and fell into the water. By the time I got there, the current had taken her downstream.' He stared at Grace, a lifetime of struggle and sadness flowing from his gaze.

She let go of him. 'What did they say to you at the station?'

He stroked the head of the closer dog. 'They had nothing but claimed they did, saying my DNA was on the girl. I just sat there and let them ramble on. They were trying to tire me out; too stupid to know I haven't had more than two hours of sleep a night for more than forty years. They threatened me, and then released me.'

Grace dug her nails into her palms. 'What did they threaten you with?'

He sputtered out a throaty laugh. 'Something vague and unknowing.'

Astrid pulled Grace to her. 'Why would Cope and Wylie try and force a confession out of him if it was an accidental death?'

Grace shrugged. 'Perhaps it hadn't been confirmed by Dr Jones when they spoke to Manny.'

'Do those Detectives have reputations for framing people?'

'I don't know. There were problems with some officers before I joined the police, but I haven't heard anything since then.'

Astrid turned to Manny. 'What do you mean when you say Katie came up from the ground?'

He peered at her. 'There are tunnels all over this place, some of which are hundreds of years old. Most have connections to the mines. Kids are always going down them, messing about and causing trouble. I've heard the noises; sometimes they mess around too much and bring parts of the walls down.'

'Can you show us where this was?'

He nodded. 'I can, but don't you want to hear about the other girl as well, the one those fanatics hurt?'

Astrid glanced at Grace. 'Do you mean Alex Sanchez?'

His hands trembled as both dogs whimpered. With more light now, Astrid checked the rest of the room as he reached for a bottle of clear liquid she assumed wasn't water. Debris cluttered the cabin: broken boxes crammed with dusty photographs, rusted tools, yellowing newspapers, moth-eaten clothes, orphaned single shoes, and cracked crockery.

'The girl wandered into here, looking for a phone. I

don't have one, but I gave her something to eat. I also told her the quickest way from the woods and into town.'

'Did Alex say anything to you about what had happened to her or where she was going?' Grace said.

'She explained what those bastards did to her.' He gritted his teeth. 'I always knew they were up to no good inside Brady's little cult. She still had bits of feathers stuck to her. I asked if she wanted me to go to the police with her, but she refused. She's a brave girl, stronger than I could ever be, but after she got cleaned up and I gave her a drink, I think the shock finally hit her.'

'Why do you say that?'

'Just before she left, she went into a bit of a daze and kept on repeating the same thing.'

Astrid stepped towards him. 'What was that?'

'She kept saying she was going to make him pay.'

'Who was she going to make pay? Was it Senator Brady?'

Before he could reply, the dogs stepped forward and growled. He held on to them. 'There are people outside.'

Tension rippled through Astrid. 'Do the cameras work?'

He shook his head. 'Not for years.'

Someone howled in pain as she went to the window, taking a quick scan of the area. Grace was moving towards the door when Astrid stopped her.

'There are at least four of them, including whoever stepped into one of the traps. You keep an eye on them while I check the back of the house, but don't go outside.'

The dogs stared at her with glowing eyes. There was enough light for her to see where she was going, avoiding the tray of dog food and water on the floor. Old newspapers and records lay scattered everywhere, and she picked her way through them.

When she got to the back, an unusual sight waited outside: rows of electrical equipment were piled together like a wall. Rusted refrigerators bumped shoulders with washing machines, big-screen TVs, freezers, tumble dryers and cookers. She wondered if they'd make a good defence against the four men approaching the cabin, carrying rifles. She returned to the living room, wishing she had a weapon and immediately seeing that wish come true.

'Do you know how to use one of these?' Manny held a shotgun towards her. The dogs were panting as if expecting to be fed.

She took the firearm from him. 'Point, aim and pull the trigger.'

Grace held a revolver. 'How do we know these are hostiles?'

'Why else would they be here?' Astrid said.

They both looked at Manny, who shrugged. Grace moved closer to the window.

'I can show them my police badge.'

A bullet smashed through the glass and into the wall before Astrid replied. She pulled Grace to the floor as the dogs barked. Manny stood there grinning as if he'd been waiting for this all his life. Astrid examined the escape maps unfolding inside her head as more bullets crashed through the cabin. There were only two ways inside, and they had a clear sight of both those approaches. Then she glanced up.

Unless they come through the roof.

'Grace, take Manny and the dogs to the back. Get your line of fire through the windows on either side of the door. Shoot anyone who tries to come in uninvited. I'll cover the front.'

Astrid moved towards the window. She pushed her shoulder against the wall and slithered up to peer through the glass as Grace helped Manny into the back. The bloke who'd stood in the trap was gone, with no sign of anybody amongst the trees.

When gunfire erupted at the rear, she lifted the shotgun as the dogs howled. She knew she shouldn't leave her post, but Grace's scream drew her from the window.

In that instant, the front door burst open, and a man swivelled towards her. He pointed the gun at her face as she brought the shotgun up and smacked the weapon away. She dropped her hand and blasted him through the foot. He shrieked as he crumbled, just as two others rushed inside

Astrid crouched as the bullets whizzed through the spot where she'd been; then more bounced off the chair as she ducked behind it. She rolled into the skirting board, gun pointed up in anticipation, but all that came was the sound of snarling and frenzied animals pouncing. The screams followed from two different sets of lungs as one of them managed to get a shot away. The dogs barked as she imagined those sharp white teeth biting through human flesh.

As the noise grew, something crashed into the back wall before everything spun around her. A shot was fired, a man screamed, and bones were crushed and broken. The stink of fresh blood swallowed the space above her as she peered over the sofa: one of the dogs was bending over an intruder and ripping out his throat. The bloke she'd blasted in the foot was missing, a trail of blood leading out of the front door. The other dog and attacker were also absent.

Astrid pushed herself up, the ringing continuing in her ears as she reached for her face. Red dripped from her forehead, and she placed her fingers on the wound. She wasn't sure what had happened, perhaps a stray bullet had grazed her before she found cover, but the pain wouldn't stop her.

Her feet were unsteady, her body unable to stand correctly before the attacker hit her in the side.

They tumbled over and rolled through dust and dirt. A steam train bowled through her head as he punched her hard in the ribs; the agony was great, but she was used to it. A tall bloke loomed over her, a lopsided grin on his face not distracting her from his right ear flapping away from his head. He was going to kick her in the stomach when she moved to the side and swung her hand around. The trousers he wore were light enough for her to dig her nails into his leg and tear at his flesh. He howled in unison with the dog.

Astrid reached up to punch him in the groin, but he brought the pistol down and cracked it across her cheek. Her jaw twisted into an unnatural angle as she stumbled into the wall. The runaway train of pain in her skull had split into a hundred different carriages, and every one of them sped through her blood and bones. She watched him raise the gun and aim it between her eyes. She waited for the aching to end and thought of all the people she'd let down, focusing on an image of Olivia as he grinned with his finger on the trigger.

Then the dog leapt at his throat.

Man and beast crashed to the floor next to her as she rolled away, unable to do anything but watch the hound chew through his flesh.

When he stopped moving, she pushed herself up. She left the dog chewing on fresh meat in an increasing pool of gore and moved to the window. The trail of blood led outside and into the distance, but there was no sign of life.

Grace's howl of anguish forced her towards the rear of the house.

She stumbled beyond the feeding dog and into the back room, where she found the other hound, with Grace cradling Manny's head in her arms. The large hole in his chest was hard to miss. She moved past them and checked outside, which was as empty as the front. There wasn't one part of her which didn't throb, but she ignored it all.

Grace held on to Manny and wiped away her tears. 'I've called for an ambulance.'

Astrid could tell from the look on their faces that it was a forlorn hope. She left them and returned to the living room, where the dog sat on its hind legs and looked pleased with itself. She went to the front porch as the roar of an aeroplane shattered the silence. She stepped down onto the path and followed the drip of red from the cabin. She tracked it back to their car, where it disappeared into dust and a set of tyre tracks.

Then she returned to the house and waited. It was forty-five minutes before the ambulance and the police arrived.

Five minutes later, Manny Burns died in Grace's arms.

There were so many officers crawling through the cabin Astrid wondered if the town's criminals were having a field day everywhere else. Even Police Chief Roscoe Tanner arrived, quizzing Grace while Cope and Wylie peered at the dead thugs on the floor.

'Death by dog,' Dr Brianna Jones said to the two grim-looking Detectives as she finished examining the bodies. Astrid joined them as Grace pulled away from her boss, the look on her face as unpleasant as the corpses at their feet. 'But the most interesting thing is,' Dr Jones paused for effect, 'these men have no fingerprints.'

All four of them looked at her with a mixture of surprise and astonishment.

'Burnt off?'

'Indeed, Ms Snow.' The glint in Jones's eyes sparkled like a shooting star. 'The skin was removed with acid by the look of it.'

Astrid resisted the urge to peer into a dead man's mouth. 'There might be dental records on the database or identifying markers in the blood or DNA.'

'You're a suspect here, Snow, not an investigator.' Detective Wylie pushed a stray hair from his bloodshot eyes and scowled at her.

Astrid watched the hackles rise on the back of Grace's neck. 'They attacked us, Wylie. Why is she a suspect?'

Detective Peter Wylie stepped towards her. 'It's Detective Wylie to you, Crowley, so watch your mouth.'

He jabbed his finger an inch from her face, but she never flinched. His partner placed her hand on Wylie's shoulder.

'What Pete is trying to articulate in his ham-fisted way is we need to know more about why you two were here.' Julie Cope was the opposite of her partner, all sweetness and light. She gave Astrid the warmest of smiles. 'Is all of this destruction to do with your search for Alex Sanchez?'

Grace was about to reply when Astrid stopped her. 'We haven't found any leads. I thought Burns might have seen the girl in these woods. That's why we are here. And then someone started shooting at us.'

'Well, you only have one day left, Officer Crowley, before you return to your normal duties.' Chief Tanner joined them around the bodies. 'Maybe this unfortunate incident has something to do with Ms Snow's life before she arrived in town.' He stared directly at Astrid. 'I don't see why else a group of assassins with no fingerprints would be here if there wasn't a connection to the British Secret Service. What about you, Ms Snow?'

'One day and one night,' Astrid said to him.

He removed his hat and scratched at his bulbous forehead. 'What?'

'Grace still has tonight and tomorrow with me, according to our agreement, Chief.'

He squashed the hat back on to his head. 'And what if

my Detectives want to spend tonight questioning the two of you about this debacle?'

Astrid smiled at him and stepped over the closest body. 'We already gave statements to your uniformed officers before you arrived. Now I have to get cleaned up before exploring the rest of this lovely town of yours.' She moved past Dr Jones and the Detectives and headed towards the door, watching the Coroner grin at her.

Grace followed her outside. 'We need to go to the hospital. You can't do anything in your condition.'

The laugh burst from Astrid's ribs like one of those creatures from the *Aliens* movies. She picked at the dried blood on her forehead.

'Most of this is superficial and worse than it looks.' She flexed her shoulders and stared at her partner. 'I'm more concerned about you.'

Grace narrowed her eyes. 'There's nothing wrong with me.'

'What happened with you and Manny while I was out front?'

Officer Crowley crossed her arms as she leant to the side. 'They never got inside, not with the bullets we sprayed out those windows.' Her lips trembled as she spoke. 'I don't know how he got hit.' She released her arms. 'I should have protected him.'

'It wasn't your fault, Grace.' Behind then, Dr Jones was organising the removal of the bodies. 'None of this was.'

'If we'd stayed away, if I'd stayed away, this wouldn't have happened.'

'We don't know that.' Astrid watched as a man with no throat was lowered into a vehicle. 'Until we find out who those people were, we won't know the reason for any of this.'

'Do you think Tanner is right, and there's a connection to your work with the Agency?'

Astrid shrugged. 'I doubt it, but hopefully Jones will get something from the autopsies to identify them. Now we need to head back and prepare for tonight.'

'What are we doing tonight?'

They walked from the cabin, avoiding the Forensic team checking the grounds, and towards their car.

'Have you forgotten about our rendezvous at the bar?'

Grace puffed out her cheeks. 'You think that kid can tell us something useful?'

Astrid twisted her head to the side, watching the police dismantle all of Manny's traps.

'She was hiding something from us earlier. Perhaps she'll feel more comfortable talking at the bar. I want to know if she's aware of those tunnels Manny mentioned.'

'Why didn't you tell them what he said about seeing Katie coming out of the ground and running from someone, plus the fact Alex Sanchez was at his place? He might have been the last person to see her.'

They reached the car as the temperature dropped a few degrees. Astrid's fingers tingled as she put her hand on the car; either all the pain had vanished from her, or her mind was doing its usual excellent job of hiding it.

'The less they know, the better. The only people I trust are you and me.'

Grace closed the door behind her and started the engine. 'Okay, we've got a couple of hours before hitting the bar. I don't know about you, but I need coffee and a shower. Do you have a clean change of clothes?'

Astrid peered at the blood on her shirt and trousers, none of which was her own.

'Only what I wore yesterday that you put in the wash. Are you going to lend me some of yours?'

The car skidded out of the dirt as Grace laughed. 'We'd have to take a pair of scissors to them first. No, we'll stop at the store and buy you some new ones, and then I'll make sure the others are dry.'

'Are you trying to get me out of my clothes, Officer Crowley?'

Grace ignored the loaded question. 'We can go to the bar early and have something to eat there. How does that sound?'

Astrid leant into the seat and contemplated a hot shower, fresh clothes, junk food, and a few drinks. She didn't give a thought to who had attacked them. That would come later.

'That sounds great, partner,' she said as they sped out of the woods.

TWO HOURS LATER, they sat in one of the worst bars Astrid had ever visited, and she'd been in a few. Grubby posters advertising groups with terrible names, lurid strip shows and karaoke nights covered the walls. She was wearing the tightest jeans she could find in the shop, a fine Paisley shirt from a discounted rail, and a black leather jacket. Grace had paid for everything.

They hadn't spoken about what had happened. There was so much for Grace to process, with the revelation of the events at the well, her parents' death, and then the attack and Manny's passing, that Astrid didn't want to create an emotional overload in her. She'd decided the best thing to do was focus on finding Alex and checking out the Valhalla bar, hoping Polly turned up or it would all be for nothing.

She swept the sawdust from the table and glanced around the establishment. The place was pretty full when they got there, and it was only Grace's towering presence that helped them get a spot.

Grace scanned the room.

'It bothers me to see so many underage kids in here.'

'But not the one we came for,' Astrid said as a doe-eyed waitress brought them the food they'd ordered twenty minutes ago.

A giant burger and fries sat on a plate far too small for them. Astrid didn't care; her stomach roared, and she fed it as quickly as possible. Grace only picked at her steak. In the mirror opposite, Astrid glanced at the scar on her forehead and considered who it was that had attacked Manny's cabin: had they been there for him or them? Could Chief Tanner have been right about a connection to the Agency? She didn't think so. Her only friend in the UK, perhaps the world, was in charge of the Agency, and he'd promised to keep her whereabouts known only to him.

She turned from her reflection as the girl approached the table.

'Can I have some of those?' She took the empty seat and scooped half of Grace's fries into her mouth.

Grace frowned. 'I need to have a word with the owners of this place.'

Polly spat bits of food on to the dirty floor as she spoke. 'Don't bother. They won't serve alcohol to kids, no matter how much we try and get it.' She reached out for a bottle of beer, but Astrid snatched it from her. 'It's easier and cheaper to buy booze in town anyway. We only come here for the music, and it's safer than anywhere else for people like us.'

'What do you mean by that?' Astrid said as a group of scowling youths clambered up on to the stage with their instruments.

'All the misfits and the freaks the respectable peeps don't like have to find their community somewhere. It might as well be here.' Polly finished speaking and chewed through the steak Grace had left. Astrid stared at them and wondered if this was the start of a beautiful friendship. 'I thought you two would know something about that.'

'What?' Grace said.

Polly spoke through a mouthful of food. 'You must have been bullied all your life, being so tall. And I heard about what happened to you as a kid, falling down that well. I guess all the kids had a right go at you after that.' She picked a piece of meat from between her teeth. 'And English here, I don't know what it is, but there's something about her which I'm sure gets up people's noses. I bet she's taken plenty of grief in her time, and I can see why.'

Astrid emptied the bottle and signalled the bartender for another. Grace glared at her as she clung to her orange juice.

'Was Alex Sanchez one of those people, one of those freaks, or Katie Spencer?'

Polly chewed on a fry. 'Lots of peeps come here. I can't keep track of everyone, especially when the band is playing.'

As she said that, Riversludge started: two skinny kids on guitars and an even thinner girl bashing the drums as if her life depended on it. They played like a freight train crashing through a wall, combining the Ramones and Husker Du. The first song lasted no more than sixty seconds, and there was no gap as they blasted straight into the next one.

Grace screwed down her eyes and put her hands over her ears. 'Is it always this loud?'

Polly bobbed her head up and down and ignored the oldies. Astrid pushed against the seat, focused on the show, and let her mind drift back to her teenage years and plenty of other bars not too dissimilar to this one, but a world away. The kids shouted about kicking against the status quo and starting a revolution. About forty people in front of the stage, both young and old, bounced around on the floor. There was no sense of aggression, no threat of violence, and she understood why some would feel safe and connected there. Even the stink of sweat and stale beer put a smile on her face.

She leant into Polly so she could hear her over the din.

'Did you ever see Alex or Katie in here?'

Noise washed over them as the girl thrashed through the drums as if she was a bear on a rampage, while the two on guitars thrust against the strings so much, they dripped blood on to the stage.

'Katie loved it here,' Polly replied above the racket. 'She was always talking about starting her own group. I never saw Sanchez here. I guess she was too busy trying to change the world.'

She said it without malice as if it was an afterthought. On the stage, one of the girls dropped her guitar to the floor and knelt in front of her bandmate, pretending to lick the strings on the bass.

'Did that bother the other kids, Alex's activism?'

Polly's mouth creased into laughter, but Astrid couldn't hear it above the music, which reached an ear-piercing crescendo. It lasted for a minute before the band collapsed, including the drummer who threw her sweaty body onto her colleagues. Astrid reckoned they must have played twenty songs in fifteen minutes.

She asked Polly the question again.

'Why would any of us care about that stuff? She kept out of our way, so we left her alone.'

She had her fingers around the bottle of beer before Astrid realised and snatched it from her.

'What about the adults in the town? Did she bother any of them with her protests and videos?'

Polly projected a sneer worthy of Sid Vicious at his best; or worst. 'Maybe some of them did, I don't know, but I always felt Sanchez was more concerned with what effect she was having in New York than what she was doing here.' A spontaneous round of applause erupted around the bar as the group tumbled off the stage.

'What do you mean about New York?' Astrid said as Grace moved closer to her.

'She went there every weekend, sometimes during the week, that's what I heard. So she could meet up with other Social Justice Warriors and make her videos and internet posts. Angel Falls wasn't big enough for her, and she made that clear to everyone she met. It doesn't surprise me she ran away from this dump. I think you might be looking in the wrong place for her, English.' Polly slipped out of her chair, ready to leave them and head back to people her age. 'And anyway, there are worse things here for kids than whatever Sanchez was mixed up in. Just ask your friend over there.' She pointed towards the bar and the woman staring at them.

Astrid was both surprised and pleased to see Detective Julie Cope smiling at her.

17   SHE FLOATED AWAY

Grace buried her face in her hands, producing a long moan before coming up for air. 'Tanner must have sent her to spy on us. Can you see Wylie anywhere?'

'Stay calm, and I'll get you a drink.'

Astrid stood and walked towards the bar, picking a spot near Julie Cope. The night's second musical act was on stage, a middle-aged woman with blue hair and an electronic synthesiser stolen from Kraftwerk.

Detective Cope raised her glass to her, and Astrid got a whiff of bourbon. 'I see Officer Crowley is showing you all the best watering holes.'

It was clear she'd already had more than one drink. Astrid nodded towards the bartender.

'Whatever she's drinking for both of us.' She plopped her empty bottle onto the bar. 'Do you come here often?'

Julie Cope ran her finger around the top of the glass. 'Why, Ms Snow, do I detect a flirtation in the offing?'

She finished her drink as the next ones arrived. Astrid took her bourbon and downed half of it, the ice chilling her insides.

'Unless you're going to tell me you're working under-cover to arrest all these underage kids.'

Cope grabbed the bottle in front of her and snaffled a swig before returning to the bourbon. The static sound of the keyboard cut through the air.

'I don't care who comes here as long as they keep stocking my favourite booze. As terrible as this dump looks and smells, it is without a shadow of a doubt the best watering hole outside of New York.'

Astrid glanced over to see Grace glaring at her while talking to Polly. 'Do your superiors know you frequent this place?'

Cope shrugged. 'Apart from a few fundamentalists, nobody cares what anyone else gets up to in Angel Springs. We might be a town of wide roads, but not of narrow minds.' She nodded into the space behind Astrid. 'Though, from the look on her long face, I'd say your giraffe is none too happy about you chatting to me.'

A waft of cannabis drifted through the air as Astrid drank. The bourbon's caramel taste increased the volume of her thoughts and drowned out the music.

'I wonder why she's not too fond of you and your part-ner, Detective.'

Julie Cope raised her eyebrows. 'Perhaps she realises that in a couple of days, Tanner will have her stuck on traffic duty and the Saturday night drunk squad down at the hospital. That's the best she can hope for now. And she won't have your shoulder to lean on when you're gone.'

Astrid finished the bourbon and pushed the beer bottle to her mouth, letting the chill of the glass caress her lips.

'I won't be going anywhere until I find Alex and catch a serial killer.'

Cope blinked like butterfly wings in the wind. 'What

are you talking about? We'd know if there was a serial killer in Angel Springs.' Her narrow eyes burnt into Astrid. 'Where are the bodies?'

Astrid moved closer to Cope, brushing her leg against the Detective. 'Whoever's taking these missing kids is hiding the bodies. Katie Spencer's escape and unfortunate death was an accident in more ways than one.'

That's why you and Wylie were at the river. There's a serial killer in Angel Springs, and the police are keeping it quiet.

Cope ordered more drinks for them. 'How have you come up with this fantastical theory?'

Astrid pushed her skin-tight jeans into Cope's legs. 'I've seen something like this before, during a case I worked in the French countryside. A farmer kidnapped children from across the country, and then took them to a set of underground rooms he'd constructed beneath the farm. Once he'd finished with them, he fed the bodies to the pigs and cooked the rest.'

Even as she sipped on the whiskey, she smelt the aroma of burnt human flesh lingering in the back of her brain. Fascination consumed Julie Cope's face. Her eyes sparked into life as she casually placed a hand on Astrid's knee.

'How did you catch him?'

'It was pure luck.' Astrid let the hand linger there. 'One of the girls escaped from her prison and crawled out of the ground as I drove past. I thought I was seeing things, her head appearing from nowhere like a rabbit pulled from a hat. I put her into my car and tracked his route through the tunnels. Manny Burns told us he'd seen Katie come up from the dirt, and then sprint down the river as if the Devil chased her. That's what reminded me of France.'

'And you think she fell, hit her head, and then tumbled into the water?'

'It seems the likeliest scenario. Grace and I will check along the bank tomorrow.'

Cope squeezed Astrid's leg and whistled. 'That's some ground you'll have to cover, maybe five miles or so. I could ask Tanner to spare some uniformed officers to help you.'

Without realising it, Astrid took hold of Cope's hand. 'You believe what I've just told you?'

'I'd need to see more evidence there's a serial killer in Angel Springs, but what you said about Spencer being held against her will makes sense. The girl was missing for nearly two months, yet she was clean and recently fed when we found her. She hadn't been living wild. And there were those marks on her body.'

The ache returned to Astrid as she remembered Katie's wounds. 'Dr Jones thought they were self-inflicted.'

'Perhaps some of them were, but others could have been inflicted on her and masked inside those scars. There was no sign of sexual interference, but she might have been tortured and forced to do other things.' Anguish crossed Cope's face, and Astrid knew how she felt.

There was a tap on Astrid's shoulder, and she turned to see Grace frowning at her. 'Are we done here?' She didn't look at Cope.

Julie leant into Astrid and whispered in her ear. 'We could finish this conversation at my place. And I've got an unopened bottle of bourbon.'

Astrid slipped off the stool and took Grace to one side. 'What happened to Polly?'

'She's down the front, dancing with the other kids.'

'Are you not enjoying the atmosphere?'

Grace scowled. 'It's been a long day, and we got what

we wanted. Plus, this music is annoying me, and I don't drink, so I've never liked being in a bar and...'

The shadows engulfed them as Astrid pulled Grace further from Detective Cope. She held on to her arms and felt the tension in her partner's muscles.

'You're right. It's been a difficult day, especially with what happened to Manny. We need some rest because it will be another long one tomorrow, but being here, having a few drinks and flirting with the wrong people, is the best way for me to relax. So you head home, and I'll meet you later. Is that okay?'

She let go of Grace.

'Sure, Astrid, no problem.' Weariness seeped out of her. 'Is there anything you want me to do tonight?'

'We're going to case the Senator's mansion tomorrow, remember. Before that, we need to check along the river for any abandoned or hidden tunnels. If you can dig out any plans of the old mines, it would be a big help.'

'I'm on it, partner.'

Grace flicked her a mock salute as she left. Astrid returned to her new friend as another round of beer and bourbon waited for her. She squeezed next to the Detective once more.

'Did you manage to identify those who attacked us at the cabin?'

Cope lifted a hand to her chin and massaged her face as if contemplating one of the great mysteries of the universe. 'We checked their DNA, blood, teeth and ran facial recognition scans, but came up empty. Someone doesn't want you to know who is coming for you.'

'What makes you think the attack was about me and not for Manny?'

Cope's mouth popped open like a spring flower

grasping for the sun. 'You're a British Spook, right?' Astrid didn't reply. She never volunteered information unless it was unavoidable. 'So what do you believe is more likely, an untraceable hit squad goes into those woods to get you or an ancient Vietnam vet who struggles to remember his name most days?' Cope let her hand drift onto her leg again, and Astrid didn't complain. 'Who have you upset recently?'

'Fuck,' Astrid said.

'Now?' Cope replied with a mischievous grin.

'In this country, I can only think of one person who'd want to kill me: Daniel Gideon.'

A miniature version of Astrid ran around inside her skull and punched at the sides of her head. She didn't know which one of them had been the more stupid, her or Gideon.

'Daniel Gideon, the multi-millionaire media tycoon; why's he after you?'

'I kicked him in the balls when he tried to seduce me.'

'Ouch,' Cope grimaced. 'Good job I don't have any balls.'

The last band of the night appeared on stage as the two women continued to gaze at each other. Astrid grabbed Cope's hand and dragged her from the bar.

'Let's go and find this unopened bottle of bourbon of yours.'

They stumbled through the crowd like teenagers on a first date, pushed past the bouncers on the door and sprawled into the night.

'My car's over there.' Cope pointed towards a beat-up Honda Accord. Astrid pulled her through the dirt and into the side of the building, their bodies crashing and sticking like glue.

'You need to get some of that booze out of your system before you can drive, Officer.'

She pushed her face into Cope's neck, her tongue tasting perfume and alcohol. Her fingers were inside Cope's, the two of them thrusting against each other as the wood creaked behind them. They fell down the steps, laughing and tripping into the bushes opposite the bar. A branch stabbed Astrid in her side, but she didn't care, her mouth finding Cope's as she bit down on to her bottom lip. The blood tasted of burnt metal in her mouth. Their tongues twisted together like snakes wriggling on the floor. Two pairs of hands grabbed at hair, pulling and pushing, legs pinned against each other as one.

After an undetermined age, they separated and came up for air.

Julie Cope had a massive grin on her face.

'I think I've sobered up now.'

'I feel dizzy.' Astrid staggered back towards the other woman. 'I've forgotten how long it is since I've done this.' She wrapped her trembling hands around Cope's waist.

'Well, we can't have that, can we?' Cope ran her hand through Astrid's hair. A stray dog chased a feral cat near them, the animals barking and squealing into the night. 'Do you want to continue here or back at mine?'

Astrid had her fingers inside Cope's shirt, touching warm skin and feeling her flesh tingle in anticipation.

'How far is your place?'

Cope's chest moved slowly in and out, her breathing coming in gasps as Astrid's hands drifted north and south.

'About twenty minutes in the car if I put my foot down.'

'I don't think I can wait that long; how about you?'

'Absolutely not.'

Cope pulled her to the ground, the two of them plummeting into hard dirt. They tore at buttons and zips, rolling across the mud and into the bushes. A dog ran around and sniffed at their feet until Astrid kicked it away. They fumbled at each other, for once Astrid cursing she'd bought such tight trousers. But they came off eventually.

It was cold and dark in the night, but even inside the undergrowth, Cope smelt of lemon and tasted of life. Astrid forgot about everything else in the heat: no thought for Alex Sanchez or Katie Spencer; no concern for Daniel Gideon and his hired goons; no lingering yearning to get back home and see her niece.

SOMETIME LATER, she was exhausted and dressed. Detective Cope had a bigger grin than a stand-up comedian on steroids as she offered Astrid a lit cigarette. She took it and sucked the smoke deep into her lungs. She held it there, trapped, thinking how much of her life it would eventually erode. She let it out in a long blow, watching it drift into the air and rush towards the inky gloom.

Cope stared at her through curious eyes, satisfaction dripping from her face. 'Do you still want to go to my place?'

Astrid detected a hint of desperation in her voice, and it excited her even more. She took one more rasp on the cigarette before flicking it into the bushes, grabbed Cope's hand and dragged her towards the car.

'You just try and stop me, copper.'

THEIR CONTINUED FUMBLING and groping meant they didn't reach Cope's apartment for another forty minutes. Once inside, they ripped their clothes off again and rushed into the bedroom. It was two hours before Astrid slunk out and searched for the unopened bottle of bourbon. The place was a tip: dusty magazines and books stacked everywhere, a sofa which was coming apart at the seams and a bunch of ugly-looking ornaments straight out of a horror museum, figurines with twisted faces and broken limbs.

She stepped over the debris and went to the kitchen, the smell of unwashed pots and plates hitting her as she entered. The bourbon stared at her from the top of the fridge. She couldn't find any clean glasses, so she settled for the freshest cups she found, tipping a spider out of one of them. She returned to the bedroom and handed that particular cup to Cope, opening the bottle and letting the aroma drift up to her nose as she poured two measures.

'Why is your place such a mess, copper?'

She slid back on to the bed next to Cope. The Detective downed the drink and poured another one.

'Do you know how much free time you get working for the police in this town? I'm lucky if I can squeeze in any sleep most nights.'

Astrid dropped her cup on to the floor and sipped from the bottle. 'You can't afford a cleaner?'

'I had a cleaner. I think you might find her under some of those books in the living room.'

They drank together and laughed. Underneath the cobwebs on the digital clock, Astrid noticed it was four in the morning, and she still hadn't had any sleep. Her mobile vibrated somewhere on the floor. She reached down from the bed, sorting through the discarded clothes until she found the device. It was a message from Grace, asking if she was okay.

Cope wiped a smile and alcohol from her face. 'Is your mother looking for you?'

'My mother hated me. She died a long time ago.' Astrid tossed the phone on to the bedside table, displacing the mound of dust there. She slipped off the bed and grabbed her trousers.

Cope reached for her arm. 'I'm sorry. Do you want to talk about it, or perhaps do something else?'

Astrid stood with every sinew and muscle in her body throbbing like a space shuttle about to take off.

'Maybe next time. I need to return to Grace's and get some sleep before we trawl down the riverside. Can you phone me a taxi?'

She picked up the rest of her clothes and headed into the other room, peering at the books and magazines scattered everywhere as she got dressed: volumes on criminology, psychology, behavioural science, serial killers, true crime, and many other police-related works covered the carpet.

Once she'd squeezed into her trousers, Astrid stepped past the mess on the floor. She peered out of the window as Julie Cope came behind and threw her arms around her waist. As the Detective hugged her, Astrid wondered if they'd find Alex Sanchez in one of those abandoned mines later that morning.

18   DOWN BY THE RIVER

When Astrid returned to Grace's house, she slumped on to the sofa, hoping her partner was asleep in the bedroom. She drifted off to the smell of Julie still attached to her, and pulled the blanket over her aching form. Images of Katie Spencer rising from the ground raced through her head, a vision of the teenage girl fleeing from something which terrified her, so scared she stumbled into the river. The sensation of water engulfing her sent Astrid into a deep sleep, the type of slumber she rarely got.

When she woke, the kettle was screeching in the kitchen. Grace sat opposite her, flicking through the channels on a muted TV. Piles of A4 paper lay scattered across the carpet.

'While you were out gallivanting, I spent hours researching the town's mines. You've cost me a fortune in ink.'

Astrid couldn't tell if the disappointment in Grace's voice was because of the hard work she'd put in or the fact she'd come home alone last night. Astrid swung her legs over the sofa and picked up the closest bits of paper, covered with diagrams and maps dating from the late nineteenth century. She stretched out her arms and tried to shake the glue from her brain.

'I'm impressed with your diligence, Officer Crowley.' The back of her head thumped like an over-heated disco ball.

'I don't think they're going to be much help.' Grace squeezed next to her on the sofa. 'Most of the mines closed down after World War Two, and I can't find any near the river.'

Astrid let Grace's body heat warm her up, her memories of that early morning fun with Detective Cope evaporating as she dropped the papers on to the floor. She scanned through some others, but found only one valuable piece of information.

'It says the construction of the first mine started in 1880, but the town had already been here since the 1820s. Do you know what the economy was before that?'

Grace shook her head. 'I was never taught that in school.' She sipped at her coffee before grabbing her laptop and starting a search.

Astrid had already beaten her to it on her phone. 'The initial settlers traded pelts and food, using temporary lodgings they built on the riverside. Then they constructed more permanent dwellings, and the residents used the river to trade along its waters.'

'This is fascinating, but I don't see how it helps us.'

Astrid scanned through the data, and then handed it to her partner. 'Look at this.'

Grace wiped the drink from her lips and read aloud. 'The small community grew into a town, with population numbers swelling overnight. This brought prosperity to many of the early settlers, but also attracted greed and criminality. Homes were raided and people murdered before the hardiest of the traders banded together to protect themselves.'

She stopped reading as Astrid wiped the sleep from her eyes. She was in desperate need of a shower, and the throbbing plagued the back of her skull as she nodded at her partner.

'Keep going.'

Grace continued. 'They protected their goods by building storage facilities underneath the buildings erected along the riverside. Eventually, they used a series of tunnels to connect the different rooms.' She turned to Astrid. 'I wonder why this wasn't taught at school.'

Astrid swivelled her head to try to shake the ache from her neck. 'If you read further, you'll see those tunnels and rooms were used to imprison slaves. After the Civil War, the locals tried to forget about it and keep it quiet. Once the mining companies moved in, the town had a new way to prosper. Those earlier events were kept secret for more than a century. That post you're reading, the uncovering of hidden history, was only made five years ago. Most of the townspeople probably still don't know about it. But someone found out.'

'You believe they're using the original tunnels to abduct, hide, torture and kill some of the missing kids?' Grace grimaced through every word.

Astrid stood and stretched her legs. 'I think we should go and find out.'

Grace frowned at her. 'What are those marks on your neck?'

Astrid lifted her hand to her chin and ran two fingers down her skin. The flesh was harsh and sore as she remembered her early morning activities.

'Detective Cope is quite aggressive in the bedroom. I never took her to be a biter, but she does like to get her teeth and nails into you.'

Grace moved back from her. 'While you slept, I rang the station about our mystery corpses with no fingerprints. There's no record of them in any database we have, including those used by the FBI and Homeland Security. Facial recognition scans also drew a blank.'

'Cope told me the same thing last night.'

'What aren't you telling me, Astrid?'

'Those men that attacked us at the cabin; I think I know why.' She explained the situation with Daniel Gideon.

'I've heard of Gideon. I didn't know he had a daughter.'

'He likes to keep his personal life quiet, including how badly he treated Chloe's mother when he lived in England. I thought I'd warned him off, but I must be slipping.'

'He'll continue coming for you. What are we going to do about it?'

Astrid flexed her arms and cracked her knuckles. 'For now, we do nothing. We need to check those tunnels first. Finding Alex is my priority. I'll deal with Gideon later.'

She stepped over the papers and headed to the bathroom, aware that Grace still seemed unhappy. Astrid closed the door, undressed and took a shower. If it were Gideon's men who attacked the cabin, then she'd have to make good the promise she made to him; the thought of it didn't give her any pleasure. The warm water washed her clean. Closing her eyes and remembering the night she spent with Cope, she caressed the marks on her neck, let the memories linger and prepared for the day ahead.

TWENTY-FIVE MINUTES LATER, they were in the car and heading for the river. Grace had been quiet since Astrid stepped into the living room wearing the clothes smelling of alcohol and sex. She wanted to lighten the mood but couldn't think of any way to do that, so she changed the subject from missing kids to lonely ones.

'Have you given more thought to being a foster mother?'

Grace's face was unmoving. 'What makes you believe I'd be a good parent?'

The window was down and the breeze was blowing Astrid's hair across her face. An aroma of freshwater drifted off the river and into the car.

'You care about others, Grace; that's all that matters. Give it a month and see how you feel.'

Astrid was focusing on Alex Sanchez, but at the back of her mind was the memory of the last time she'd spoken to Olivia. She took out her mobile and went through the contacts for her sister's number. There'd been no reply to the last two texts she'd sent, but she tried again.

How is Olivia?

She didn't know what else to say. Astrid put her phone away as Grace parked the car near the spot where Burns had found Katie.

'There's about a five-mile walk from here to the end of the river. That will cover all the possible points were Manny could have seen Katie come out of the ground.'

'There's no way to cross the river over that distance, no bridge or anything?' Astrid glanced across the other side, considering if Katie could have crossed the water.

'I'm not sure,' Grace said. 'He never mentioned which side he saw her on, but I'm assuming it was the one near his cabin.'

'We might have to check both.'

Astrid inched from the water's edge and stepped into the grass, scanning the environment for signs of those buildings built along the river nearly two centuries ago. Grace picked up a large stick and used it to sweep through leaves and mud. Birds scattered from the ground as they moved forward.

'This will be the longest walk I've had here,' Grace said. 'I wasn't allowed to come here after what happened.'

Astrid walked with her, resisting the idea of mentioning the well again. 'How long have your family lived in Angel Springs?'

Grace strode through branches and wayward grass. 'My grandparents moved here from New York after the Great Depression, getting farm work or labouring jobs. My father was a foreman in a metal box factory.'

'Metal box?'

'It made tins for the rest of America.'

'Why did you want to be a police officer?'

Grace laughed loud enough to bother some small creatures in the grass ahead of them. 'You mean instead of being a basketball player? I used to watch repeats of 1970s cop shows all the time, so I think it came from there.'

'So, you're a *Starsky and Hutch* fan?'

'That and *Kojak*, *Police Woman*, and *Columbo*, but it was a show called *Get Christie Love!* which got me hooked on being a cop. Did you have that in Britain?'

Astrid shook her head. 'I've never heard of it.'

'The main character is an undercover female detective. I figured I could do that and escape from my real life.' She laughed. 'Imagine someone looking like me working undercover. It just goes to show you how watching videos on the internet is not good for teenagers.' Astrid frowned as the dirt clung to her shoes and the bottom of her trousers. 'What made you want to become a spy?'

Astrid picked up a stone and threw it into the river, watching it skim and bounce but not quite reaching the other side. 'Calling me a spy is far too glamorous. Working within the intelligence services is not like a Bond or Bourne movie. A lot of it is repetitive, tedious and boring.'

Grace smiled and waited for her to catch up. 'A bit like what we're doing now?'

Astrid grinned. She was no closer to finding Alex, was convinced a serial killer was in the town, and still hadn't heard from her sister or Olivia, but at that moment, watching Grace smile at her, she felt as happy as she'd been in a long time.

The only thing to dampen that newfound joy was the sudden smell of fire. She saw the wisps coming out of the earth before Grace put her foot on them. She grabbed her partner by the arm and pulled her backwards.

'What?' Grace said as Astrid pointed towards the smoke drifting from the soil.

She took the stick from Grace and pushed at the leaves covering the ground, surprised when they didn't move. She dropped the branch and knelt. The heat was there, but not strong enough to burn her fingers as she pulled at the greenery; none of it came away.

'There's a ridge here which goes into a rectangle. I think it's an entrance with leaves fixed across it to cover it up.' She grabbed the stick again, pushing it into the gap between the hatch and the earth. Smouldering air drifted everywhere as she stood and tried to get leverage in the gap, surprised at how easily it popped open.

The air smouldered around them as they placed their

hands over their faces and coughed. They moved back and waited for the smoke to escape into the sky.

Grace handed Astrid a torch. 'I think we've found one of those underground storage rooms.'

Astrid nodded. 'Did you bring a gun?'

Grace pulled the weapon from her jacket. 'Does that mean you want me to go first?'

Astrid stepped forward. 'How many searches through smoke-filled tunnels have you done before?'

'None.'

'Then I'll go before you; I've got experience of this.' She waved her arm one last time to remove the smoke, shining the torch into the gap. There were steps cut into the side of the ground. She went down with her body twisted sideways, following the light with her eyes. She counted fifty steps before she hit the bottom. 'The tunnel turns into the left.'

Grace was only a few rungs above her. 'Can you see anything?'

The space was about six feet wide. 'Not yet.' The heat was dissipating. 'The fire must have started hours ago.'

'If someone closes that hatch, we could be trapped in here.'

Astrid shone the torch on the wall. 'Do you want to go back up?'

Grace had a phone in her hand. 'No, I've got a signal if anything happens. Let's see what's here.'

They crept down the tunnel, taking great care about what was on the ground. The smoke irritated Astrid's throat and bit at her eyes. Even with the torches, there was more gloom than light, making it hard to see much, but to her, it looked more modern than something built two centuries ago. She ran her fingers across the wall, a slight warming tingle running through her skin.

'I think somebody modified the original foundations, perhaps dug it out a little wider and added a layer of concrete to these walls.'

'How did they manage to do that without anyone in the town noticing?'

'Maybe someone did,' Astrid said.

They found a door at the end of the tunnel. Grace had the gun in her hand as Astrid put her fingers on the handle. She pulled it down and pushed the door open. The stench of gasoline hit her first. Their torches flickered around the space, picking out parts of the room: two chairs on the left, a sink and taps on the right, and a large table ahead of them. Astrid made sure the place was empty before moving forward.

'Stay here,' she said to Grace in the doorway. 'And keep the light on me.'

She embraced the smell of smoke and gasoline, preferring it to the lingering one she detected underneath it: human blood. Apart from the remnants of the blaze, the floor was clean, as if someone had swept through it before setting everything alight.

Astrid winced when she reached the table, seeing evidence people had been strapped down and bled across it. She glanced around the rest of the room. There was nothing they could do now; it was time to get Forensics there.

She turned to Grace.

'Call your colleagues and get them here.'

She was striding towards the exit with a heavy heart, her torch pointed at the ground when she noticed something there.

'I'll call them now,' Grace said.

'Wait,' Astrid shouted. She shone the light at the bottom of the door, staring at the letters carved into the wood. There were four sets, and she read them out. 'KS, DP, MM, and AS.'

They looked at each other before Grace placed a hand on Astrid's arm. 'I recognise two sets of initials.'

So did Astrid: KS was Katie Spencer, and AS meant Alex Sanchez.

19 NEIGHBOURHOOD THREAT

Astrid brushed the smoke from her eyes. The smell of death lingered on her as she moved towards the river. Grace called her colleagues before checking those initials against a list on her screen.

'No names are matching DP and MM on those recorded as missing, but I do have a Diane Pearson and a Melody Monitor next to those described as runaways from the care system; both disappeared six months ago.'

Running away from home was the thing that saved Astrid's life, if not her soul. She peered at the hole in the ground they'd climbed out of, her mind full of images of Katie Spencer crawling out of there and others who didn't. The kid had escaped from one horror, only to find another below the water.

Perhaps that's what all any of us get from this life, running from one threat to another, searching for distractions to quell the silent terror ever-present in our minds.

A chill wind bit her face as she decided on her next course of action. 'I'm going to check the rest of this side for other tunnels while you wait for reinforcements.'

She put a foot forward as Grace grabbed her arm. 'Shouldn't we stay here until more officers arrive?'

'I can't do that. What if there are more kids stuck underground further along the river?'

Grace nodded as she let go of Astrid. 'Be careful.'

Astrid shook the past from her head and set off. The river ran deep and blue, catching her shadow and stretching it out until it twisted into a deformed replica of her. At times, as she walked and thought about the torture chamber, she imagined her reflection mocking her for this continuous failure, this inability to find Alex. Her mind played tricks on her, transforming her shadow into a much younger version of herself, with her face contorted into discomfort. She stopped and wondered where this memory was coming from; it was new, not one of the usual frames from her childhood, but something unseen for two decades.

She bent her knees and placed her hand into the river. She ran her fingers through it in an attempt to wipe away the vision of her younger self, happy when she succeeded, but then distraught to see it replaced with a shimmering sight of her niece, of Olivia slipping below the ripples and not returning.

Astrid staggered up with a jolt, her chest beating faster than it should. She took a deep breath and allowed nature to calm her racing heart. Trees lined the water, with their withered branches reaching for her, while a whisper on the wind told her things she didn't want to hear.

'You failed Olivia, and now you've failed Alex. Just like you failed all the others. And how you failed yourself.'

She inhaled, but all she felt was the smoke from underground attacking her lungs. The sky had vanished almost entirely, with only a few fragments of blue remaining. The air was rich with the fragrance of leaves and damp. After yesterday's storm, the soil remained wet, slowly releasing its milky white mist. The sound of running water in the river had a relaxing, hypnotic quality. She wanted to stop and stay there and let time stand still.

But then the smoke stroked the back of her throat, and she remembered the initials on that door. And she started moving again.

It took her forty minutes to get to where the land curved upwards into a small hill with a road at the top. The journey was nearly four miles long, and she'd found nothing but a couple of dead dogs a hundred yards apart; no signs of other underground rooms or anything pointing to Katie Spencer or anyone else spending time along that part of the river.

On the return, she rechecked the canine corpses, finding no wounds or bruises on them. Both hounds had irritated red skin with blisters on their bodies. She'd never seen evidence of poison in animals before, but this reminded her of what she'd witnessed in humans.

When she got back, the police were sealing the area. Detective Cope finished speaking to Grace and turned to Astrid.

'You've been busy this morning, Snow.'

She observed the professionals at work. 'I'm running out of time. Where's your partner?'

'Pete was feeling unwell yesterday, so he's having a rest day to be fighting fit for tonight.'

'What's happening tonight?' Grace said.

Cope scrunched up her face in amusement. 'We'll be at Senator Brady's fundraising party. Pete doesn't want to miss his favourite cause.'

'The more time I spend around you, the more you surprise me,' Astrid said.

Julie Cope slipped a thick pair of protective gloves on

her hands, and then did the same over her shoes. 'Did you touch anything while you were down there?'

'I didn't,' Grace said.

'I touched the wall once and the handle of the door,' Astrid said.

'You might end up solving all the serious crime in the town, Snow,' Cope said as she descended into the tunnel. 'Perhaps I'll speak to Tanner about getting you a job with the Angel Springs Police Department.'

Astrid and Grace headed back to their car.

'I gave her a statement,' Grace said. 'Did you discover anything along the river?'

Astrid told her about the dogs. 'Maybe someone poisoned them to shut them up and get them from that hatch.'

They reached the car and got in. 'Shouldn't we tell Cope about the dogs?' Grace said.

'Let her find out for herself. I need something to eat before we continue.'

'I'll take you to the town's best diner.' Grace floored the accelerator, and they headed from the river and the trees. 'Where are we going after that?'

'We need to let Christina Sanchez know where we are in the search for her daughter.'

'And then?'

There was despair in Grace's tone, and Astrid knew why. They were no closer to finding Alex, they had a serial killer on the loose, and Grace had to return to her regular job tomorrow.

'We get ready for Brady's big party.' Astrid pointed at her. 'You're going to distract him with your charm while I poke around the mansion. The Senator is hiding something, and I intend to find out what it is.'

Officer Grace Crowley scowled at her as she drove to the diner.

DURING THEIR LUNCH, Astrid ignored all Grace's attempts to talk about the plans for the party, instead questioning her temporary partner about what she was going to do when she returned to her regular police work. Grace poked at the fries on her plate, her appetite waxing and waning as she contemplated her immediate future.

'This time tomorrow, I'll be typing up traffic reports and making cups of coffee.'

Astrid sipped at her hot drink. She'd been surprised to find the diner supplied green tea with mint. It reminded her of England.

'You're only young, Grace; the old men controlling the police department will have to move on eventually. A bit of patience might get you what you want in a few years.'

Over the last two days, she'd discovered the town wasn't as rigid as she first believed. There were good people in Angel Springs, and she hoped it would be only a matter of time for Grace to achieve what her hard work deserved.

Grace reached out to touch Astrid's arm. 'You know I'll continue helping you even after tonight.'

'I appreciate the gesture, but I'm confident we'll have solved everything when we leave that party.'

A fat fry hung from Grace's mouth. 'You think we'll find Alex and discover a serial killer before the clock strikes midnight?'

Astrid lifted her hand to Grace's face, removing the fry and eating it herself. The taste of fatty food between her lips warmed her soul. 'All the answers are in that house, Grace; I'm sure of it.'

'And what about Daniel Gideon and the thugs hired to kill you?'

Astrid leant into the uncomfortable plastic booth and kicked out her feet. 'They weren't trying to kill me yesterday; that would've been too quick for Gideon. He wants to see me suffer. Those men are here to snatch me, and then take me somewhere so he can torture me. His fragile masculinity won't allow for anything else.'

'So you're just going to wait for them to come for you?'

'They'll make a mistake.' Astrid was convinced of it, though she didn't want others being put at risk because of her. 'People like that always do.'

Grace finished her drink and left the rest of her food. 'I love your self-assurance, but I have doubts.'

Astrid stood. 'Don't worry about it, partner; we'll see them soon enough. Now we have to go and give Christina Sanchez what news we have.'

'Do you think Alex is still alive?'

'She's been missing for more than a week; the chances of us finding her alive are slim. But I'm not giving up until I know what happened to her.'

The smell of the murder dungeon filled her head, the image of those four sets of initials stamped on to her brain.

Grace paid the bill, and they headed to the collection of mobile homes. Outside the trailer park were several women looking suspiciously like nightclub bouncers. Astrid registered something she'd missed the first time she was there.

'What do you notice most about this place?' she said as they parked and got out of the car.

Grace scanned the area. 'You can't miss the large number of random dogs running around.'

As she spoke, a skinny greyhound ran up to them. Astrid stuck her tongue out at the animal, and it scampered away.

'That and the fact there are no men here,' Astrid said. 'Young lads and teenage boys, I remember from the other day, but no adult males. I'm surprised I didn't notice it last time. It must be a refuge. Do you know who owns this place?'

'I don't. I always assumed it was some private company charging exorbitant monthly rentals. It's the American way.'

Astrid strode through the middle, staring at the mobile homes rooted into the ground. Pots, plants, ornaments and other miscellanea were propped up against the wheels and around the sides of the vehicles, embedding them into their environment as if they were living things with deep roots far down into the concrete. There was colour and vibrancy everywhere she looked, something she'd been oblivious to before. Even without speaking to any of the residents, she felt this was a real community.

She sensed people scrutinising them as they strode towards the Sanchez home, watching the curtains twitching as they went. Up ahead, a group of women sat outside the trailer, chairs and boards pushed up against the front so you couldn't see the bottom of it. A grill was cooking in the middle, a sweet aroma of barbecue wafting through the air. Christina turned to them as they got there.

'You've come to give me bad news about that torture room they discovered this morning.'

'We found that place, Ms Sanchez,' Grace said.

'And Alex?' Sanchez poked bits of meat around on the grill, no tremor or motion in her voice.

'It was empty,' Astrid said. 'We came here to tell you

what led us there and why we think someone has been snatching kids in this town for a long time.'

Christina Sanchez continued to cook and hand out food to her friends as Astrid recounted what they'd discovered, including the events at the youth centre and Alex's appearance at Manny's cabin. Christina was stoic and unemotional, apart from the occasional twitch in her eyes. Astrid had observed many people dealing with upsetting news over the years; most broke down and wept, but a few, mainly men trying to appear brave, kept their emotions in check. Alex's mother was doing her best to hold everything in, but Astrid assumed the tears would flow once she was away from friends and neighbours.

'I promise you, Christina, I'll know what happened to Alex by the end of tonight.'

Grace stared at Astrid in amazement, but Christina was like a blank space as she spoke.

'One day, it seems like you have forever; the next, you wonder where it all went. The hands have fallen off the clock, and there's a huge gaping piece of eternity waiting to swallow you up.' Smoke drifted from the barbecue, and resignation seeped out of her. 'I tried to stop her from doing those things she did, the protests and the activism. I even encouraged her to behave as other teenagers, to smoke and drink and mess around with boys or girls. It didn't matter to me as long as she was having a good time: as long as she was acting like a kid and not an adult.' She stared straight into Astrid's eyes. 'Why do they have to be the ones to right all of our mistakes?'

Grace stepped forward. 'We still don't know what happened to Alex, Ms Sanchez; so, don't give up hope.' With a faint smile, she dragged Astrid from the women who were speaking to Christina. Perhaps Alex's mother would open up to them.

Grace's nails dug into Astrid's arms.

Astrid frowned at her.

'Have you been taking lessons from Cope?'

Grace stopped walking and pulled her to one side. 'Why did you promise her you'd know what happened to Alex by the end of tonight? Getting her hopes up like that will only make things worse for her.'

'What do you think happened to Alex after Manny's place?'

Grace pulled in her chest and rose to her full, magnificent height. 'I'd guess she left his cabin through the back and went out of the woods the other side.'

'She went there looking for a phone and didn't find one.' Astrid peered at Grace. 'Wouldn't she have continued with that search?'

'There are no other houses or buildings in that area.'

It was Astrid's turn to pull Grace forward, this time in the direction of their car. 'Of course there are; she must have returned to the spot where she was harassed.'

Grace stopped as they got to the car, her face a bundle of confusion. 'Why would she go back to the youth centre after what they did to her?'

'Think about it, Grace. She needed to call somebody, and there was only one other place to get a phone outside of town. I don't think she felt safe on her own in those woods, and she's got enough sass to double back and get through that fence. Those people didn't break her spirit; they just reinforced it. She went there, snuck in, found a phone, then waited for someone to come and pick her up. Did you see all the security cameras dotted around when we were there? They'll have all their video stored on the computer. All I need to do is find out where it is and go through the records; then we'll have something to tell Christina.'

Grace climbed into the car. 'You're making a lot of assumptions, Astrid.'

'This will be solved when we walk out of Brady's mansion tonight, trust me.'

Grace drove away, but didn't look convinced. 'What about the initials on the door?'

'We'll see what your Forensic colleagues come up with.'

A pack of dogs barked at them as they pulled out of the trailer park.

'So, what's next for us?'

Astrid smiled at her friend. 'Now, we have to get you dressed for the ball.'

'I'm not wearing a dress.'

The shout was loud enough to rattle the cups in the kitchen. It shook Astrid from her thoughts as Grace barged into the living room.

'You're going naked, Grace? I don't think my heart could take that.'

Grace's eyes flashed like lightning in the night. 'You know what I mean. Why do you get to go to the party like that, and I have to dress up?' She pointed at Astrid's jeans and leather jacket. 'I'm not a show pony.'

Astrid glanced over, the corners of her lips fighting a smile, her eyebrows raised. 'Well, first of all, I don't have a dress with me, and I doubt any of yours would fit me; and second, you're the best distraction I can have in that mansion when I sneak off to find the video surveillance and anything else which might help us.'

Grace slumped into the chair, the ocean blue dress crawling above her knees; she dragged it down and shook her head.

'That's nice, calling me a distraction.'

Astrid stared at her. 'Well, you're distracting me now.'

The frustration seeped out of Grace. 'I can't remember the last time I had a night out.' She appeared to have got over her irritation.

'Are you booking us a taxi?'

Grace tried to cross her legs, but failed, then pulled at her dress to make it longer. 'It's okay; I'll drive. It will be easier to leave Brady's mansion if we have transport.'

Grace grabbed the keys and they left. Astrid watched her struggle to get comfortable in the dress as they got into the car, which amused her no end. Grace turned on the radio and settled for a jazz station. Something sounding like it was written for elevators screeched out of the speakers, a loud wailing cacophony which could only have been played on instruments dug up from Satan's basement.

Astrid furrowed her brow and grimaced. 'You don't really care for music, do you?'

'I know enough to recognise when someone is quoting Leonard Cohen to me.' Grace reached over and flicked through the stations. 'What would you prefer, Ms Snow?'

She bounced through rock, soul and country before Astrid stopped her on a channel playing eighties pop. The Go-Go's sang about having the beat as they headed out of town.

'This is why you need someone younger to teach you about good music, Grace.'

She ignored the jab. 'What's the plan once we get inside the mansion?'

'Did you notice all the cameras when we were on the estate the other day?' Grace nodded. 'That much surveillance means there's a control room in the building. Hopefully, they'll have a digital record of everything they've filmed in the last week, and I can search through it for when Alex was there.'

'Won't that be dangerous?'

'It is what it is. We won't discover what happened to Alex without taking risks.'

'As long as nobody gets hurt.'

They didn't argue about it, travelling through Angel Springs as Astrid noticed the billboards promoting Bob Brady's re-election had increased in number overnight. They drove past a large photo of him smiling over the town, his shining white teeth putting her in mind of someone who wanted to eat baby birds right out of the nest.

'How come I haven't seen any publicity for whoever Brady is running against?'

Grace stopped whistling to Bruce Springsteen to answer the question. 'Brady is a shoo-in, so no pretender to his throne will waste money on ads when they know they're going to lose, especially when he can outspend them ten to one.'

Astrid scanned the internet on her phone as the Boss gave way to Prince. 'I guess his popularity knows no bounds in Angel Springs.'

Grace laughed. 'Well, I've never voted for him.' Their destination was no more than five minutes away. 'I worked the police security details at one of his rallies a few years ago and saw what he was like backstage.'

'Seeing a politician in the wild is never a pretty sight.'

'I only got close to him for two minutes, but that was enough. When he didn't have to put on a show for the public, being with him was like a trip through a sewer in a glass-bottomed boat.'

Grace approached the Brady estate while Morrissey sang about running down to the safety of the town. The car slowed as they acknowledged the security outside the grounds. It was easier getting into the compound the second time; no scowling youths waited for them as the iron gates opened and they entered. They parked in a different spot because of the circus attractions the Senator had organised to entertain his guests.

Stilt walkers garbed as flappers and Gatsby rejects lined the entrance as acrobats perched on the building's railings, occasionally tumbling and falling between floors. An adult carousel was to the right, and servers attired as clowns wandered everywhere, handing out drinks and canapés. A group of teenagers dressed as cheerleaders led four baby elephants around the grounds.

Grace whistled as they stood and admired the spectacle. 'The Senator spared no expense for this.'

Astrid gritted her teeth. 'I've always hated circuses.'

And she had good reason. Her parents had organised a trip to a visiting circus for Courtney's tenth birthday. Her sister was unusually friendly towards Astrid that night, holding her hand as their mother and father ushered them between the attractions. Astrid remembered it being the last time she'd believed her family was doing something nice for her, even though it was for Courtney. She'd enjoyed watching the Cirque du Soleil on TV, but this wasn't that: it was all clowns and animals.

After the horse dressage and acrobats, Courtney sneaked Astrid away from their parents, and they ducked into a small tent for what her sister described as a special present for Astrid. It turned out to be a group of jokers with painted-on evil faces and fake axes covered in blood. They jumped out and howled at her. She fell to the floor, her screaming only stopping when her mother picked her up and laughed at her. That's when she discovered it was her parents who'd set the whole thing up as a gift for Courtney. All her sister had wanted was to humiliate and terrify Astrid, and her parents were all too willing to organise it.

She pushed the memory into the shadows as they strolled into the mansion. A wall of glass hid the grand hallway, not ordinary mirrors, but ones that twisted and distorted your appearance. She lifted her hands towards them, the reflection altering her fingers so they looked like long, withered branches on a skeletal tree. As she stared at herself, it reminded her of what she'd witnessed in the river earlier, when her shadow had transformed into a mangled, painful vision of Olivia. She stuck a fingernail into her palm to get rid of it.

The distorting glass hypnotised Grace, her body shrinking inside it. 'I guess I finally look normal.'

Astrid stood at her side, so they resembled a human salt and pepper set. 'There's no such thing as normal in this world, partner. People who think like that, who adhere to outdated societal modes of what's acceptable and what isn't, are too vanilla to appreciate the real beauty of life.'

Grace held a finger to her face, the two of them watching it twist like liquid flesh until it didn't appear to be part of her anymore.

'What do you mean by vanilla?'

Astrid took Grace's hand. 'Vanilla is boring and bland.' She squeezed her partner's arm. 'It's better to be exotic and unusual rather than that.'

As Grace laughed and her face contorted in the mirror to resemble something from Picasso, other guests followed in behind them, the mirrors becoming one heaving mass of warped human beings. Up ahead, the wall of glass parted into the banqueting area of the mansion. A great banner proclaiming the re-election of Senator Brady stretched across the ceiling. He stepped out and addressed the gathering crowd.

'Welcome, friends, to my humble home.' He extended his arms like Christ on the cross. 'Please eat and drink until you can eat and drink no more.' Out from behind him sprang a glitterati of costumed performers, jumping and tumbling into the room and between the startled masses: grim-faced clowns, agile acrobats, scantily clad females and muscular he-men, and many others. 'Follow and enjoy my entertainers and make sure you contribute to my campaign wholeheartedly.'

As he grinned, streamers burst from above, and party music blasted through the mansion. Astrid watched the people behind her disappear in the twisted mirrors, replaced with the family she wished she'd never known. Lawrence pointed at her while holding a whip, slapping it against his leg, each whack increasing the width of his smile until it threatened to slip from his face. Her mother, Gloria, sucked on a bottle of booze as if it was an umbilical cord as she wrapped herself in a Union Jack. Courtney stood between them, cradling a baby who could only have been Olivia. She ogled Astrid, her eyes telling her sister she had something she'd never have.

As Astrid continued to stare at them, Grace whispered to her.

'This is great; you've got an excuse to go in every room now if you say you were only following one of these performers.'

Astrid gazed at a distorted version of Courtney sneering at her, transferred from her memory and into the mirror.

'I need alcohol first.' She seized a glass of champagne from a server dressed as a southern belle of the Civil War.

Worry lines appeared across Grace's face. 'We have to keep a clear head, remember.'

'I have to blend in, partner.'

She downed the drink and grabbed another one, the warmth of the booze chipping away at her hallucination until her family disappeared. She strode towards the table of food, grabbing a sandwich that wouldn't have satisfied a tiny bird.

More people came into the mansion as the piped music dissipated and a band struck up some terrible jazz fusion. Astrid devoured the sarnie in a gulp before sticking a finger into one ear. She scanned the area, watching Brady shake hands and grin his way to adding more money to his re-election fund.

Grace tapped her on the shoulder. 'Your friend and her partner are observing from the shadows.' She pointed at Cope and Wylie, standing like grim statues in the far corner.

'You distract them while I go upstairs.' Astrid slipped away before Grace protested.

She dodged a couple of harlequins loping towards her and stepped into the room opposite, an impressive-looking library with entertainers dressed as famous fictional characters serving refreshments. She took a glass from Hamlet and turned on her heels. Further down the corridor, she peered into the rest of the rooms, ignoring the punters and the costumed servants.

A crowd surrounded an Egyptian sarcophagus, from which an exotic princess popped out as Astrid went upstairs to the first floor. It was more of the same, with staff in fancy dress and guests gazing at handsome men or scantily clad women. The surveillance room couldn't be there; it had to be away from everyone and would probably be locked, so she searched for anywhere that was off-limits.

Astrid continued upwards and on to the next level. Gilded frames hung from the walls, unsmiling characters with a resemblance to Brady glared at her. Opulent soft furnishings lined the corridor, leading to the only room there. She marched towards it and tried the door, happy to find it locked.

She removed a paper clip from her pocket, bending it out of shape so it was stretched and pointed with small indents along the length. Astrid pressed it into the handle and wiggled the metal on metal for thirty seconds before the lock clicked open. She pushed at the door and stepped inside.

Apart from the humming computers and the barrage of screens exhibiting the building's current events, the room was empty. She checked every monitor, ignoring most of them and settling on the sight of Grace speaking to the Detectives. Grace's lips twisted upwards and there was a fire in her eyes as she appeared to be arguing with Pete Wylie. Cope stood there impassively and sipped on her drink. Astrid peered at the screen and raised one finger to her neck, touching the mark Julie had left there.

She was about to move away and search for the video footage when something caught her attention behind Cope. A man stared at Grace, the cut of his hair, his physique and his movement marking him out as ex-military. But he wasn't just staring at her; he was scrutinising her as if she was the most important person there. The intensity of his gaze, even through the screen, made Astrid uneasy. Was he Brady's security?

No, she'd seen them around the mansion, all of them dressed the same with earpieces and microphones, a physical presence for all the guests to see. This man was different; he was trying to be normal. There was something familiar about him, but she couldn't place what it was.

Astrid checked all the cameras, looking through the other rooms, and found three men of a similar disposition. If they weren't Brady's private security, perhaps they were secret service operatives. Whoever they were, they just added to her problems if she got caught poking around the mansion.

She turned from the screens and headed for the closest computer.

Let's see how lucky I am.

She clicked on the keyboard, and the screen lit up. She was fortunate; no password required, and there was a prominent folder named SURVEILLANCE VIDEOS on the desktop. She opened it, flicking through the files to find the date she wanted. She was blessed again because each clip was divided into hours, with twenty-four segments for each day.

Astrid located the clips for the morning Alex was supposedly set free from the compound, fast-forwarding through one before watching the teenager walk out of the gates just after nine. Alex strode into the woods, her movement telling Astrid what she'd already surmised: the girl hadn't been broken by what these people did to her; she was defiant and determined.

She calculated the time it would have taken Alex to get to Manny's place, linger there, and then return to the compound. Astrid went through every video taken from eleven until midnight, getting more and more frustrated with each one. There was no sign of Alex or a vehicle to pick her up on any of them. Could she have been wrong about the teenager returning to the mansion for a phone?

Astrid was about to go through the clips from after midnight when the wood creaked behind her. She twisted around in time for a fist to brush her head and thump into the desk. She fell to the floor and rolled into the wall, her shoulder throbbing as she hit the concrete. From downstairs came the sounds of laughter and music, of people shouting and enjoying themselves.

She stood and looked into the face of a giant.

'You shouldn't be in here.'

Blood dripped from his knuckles as he towered over her. He was taller than Grace, with a body packed full of sinew and muscle. His forehead was almost square, large and imposing, crisscrossed with lines. He might have come straight from the circus if he hadn't been wearing an expensive suit adorned with a prominent RE-ELECT BRADY button.

Astrid touched the side of her head. 'I got lost coming up the stairs.' He'd missed in his attempt to punch her, but she faked a grimace as if in pain. 'Did the Senator tell you to hit his guests?'

'Don't lie to me, English. I know who you are.' He flexed both hands. 'My orders are to bring you downstairs, but you don't have to be in one piece.'

As he reached to grab her, she punched him in the chest. It was like throwing her arm into a brick wall. Pain shot through her fingers and wrist, but he didn't move.

'Fuck!' she shouted as he dug his hand into her, dragging Astrid across the room and tossing her onto the floor.

Dust swirled over her face and into her eyes, her hands scrambling for anything to use as a weapon. He seized her foot and pulled again as electricity shot up her leg.

'Stop struggling,' he said as they reached the door. 'Or I'll drag you like this all the way downstairs.'

Astrid found some leverage and kicked him in the groin with her free foot. He screamed, digging his nail into her ankle and throwing her into a desk. A laptop tumbled from it and fell into her stomach. A small table lamp followed and landed on her neck, the bulb catching the marks Cope had left there earlier.

She lay there, wondering how she'd gone from rolling around on the floor with the copper to pushing bits of electric equipment from her damaged body a few hours later.

Astrid grabbed the lamp and stood, the computer slipping from her gut as she watched the tall man clutch at his groin as he staggered up. She recognised the hatred in his eyes.

Hate is power, and he's bursting with it.

She moved back towards the far end of the room, seeing the surveillance screens flickering as she went, noticing performers dressed as Charlie Chaplin and Wonder Woman entertaining Brady's guests. She couldn't see Grace or the Senator as her assailant growled and stumbled at her.

There was murder in his eyes as she dodged to the side, kicking the laptop so it slid into his foot. His grin was crooked, his head lopsided as if the weight of the world was in his shoulder as he bent to pick up the computer. It seemed small to her in his massive grasp; and then he hurled it at her.

She ducked as it smacked into the wall, bits of the screen splintering near her hands. She grabbed the largest piece as he sprinted forward. Her reflexes were quicker than his, and she pushed the broken glass towards his foot. He stepped on to it and twisted his ankle, stumbling and crashing into a table. As his bulk thumped into the ground, she reached over and seized the lamp. He tried to push up, but she smashed the light into his head. The porcelain crashed apart, the bulb splitting into pieces as he crumbled.

She stood over him as he rolled on the floor. Astrid thrust her hand down so quickly he had no chance of stopping her jabbing her fingers into his throat, hitting the precise spot she knew would render him unconscious.

She hobbled out and down the stairs, dodging over-excited clowns and flappers, and headed for the main room. Grace was nowhere around, but Julie Cope waved at her from the far end of the corridor. Astrid limped forward as Wylie scowled at her.

'Too much to drink, Snow?' Cope's smile wasn't as attractive as she remembered.

'Do you know where Grace is?'

Cope shrugged. 'Probably preening herself somewhere before signing up for the circus.'

An elephant trumpeted outside the window as Detective Wylie leered at Astrid. 'You've missed the boat, English.'

She grabbed a glass of champagne from a waiter and downed it in one. 'I am the boat, mate.' Then she turned to Cope. 'What's going on, Jules?'

'Brady wants to see you in the drawing room,' she said. 'You need to follow me.'

Astrid did so while trying to shake the pain from her leg. 'Are you acting in a Cluedo recreation, Jules?'

They strode into the corridor past guests and entertainers. The Detective moved towards the room and opened the door. 'I want you to know this isn't personal, Snow.'

The reply was strangled in Astrid's mouth by the sight of Grace held by two men. She pushed beyond the pain and strode forward, with Cope closing the door behind her. Brady stood in front of the fireplace, flanked by two of his security guards. The thugs holding Grace were not his goons, but similar types to the ex-military bloke she'd seen on the screen earlier. He was also in the room, with one other.

'How bad are your secrets, Senator, that you'd assault a Police Officer?'

Astrid was halfway between him and Grace when his men stepped forward. Even in pain and hobbling, she was in no doubt she could deal with them, but the six others were a different matter.

'Follow me, Ms Snow.'

Brady moved past the grand piano, with a goon in front and another behind. The front one grabbed the edge of an ornate cloth hanging from the wall and pulled it to the side. Another door was behind it, Brady walking through it and indicating she should as well. She glanced over at Grace to see she was okay. The goons had let go of her, but stood by her side; close enough, she wouldn't be able to get away without a fight. Astrid rubbed at her bruised stomach and knew it was too soon for that.

'How far into the labyrinth are you taking me, Senator?'

Was this some elaborate extension of the secret tunnel they'd found near the river? Was he connected to the missing children, after all?

Am I walking deeper into a trap, one I'll never get out of?

'I thought it was time I showed you my collection, Ms Snow.'

She trailed him inside, unmoving when the second thug

brushed by her to close the door. The Senator smelt of cheap aftershave, moving as if he'd had too much to drink. Astrid strode inside and scanned the surroundings, identifying where the dangers and escape points might be.

The room was unlike the others, more modern as if added as an afterthought. There was a giant screen at the back, with portraits of old movie stars covering the walls: Valentino, Garbo, Harlow, Swanson, Chaplin, Brooks, and Pickford. As a child, locked up physically and mentally at home, Astrid had escaped into other worlds via the internet and television, dreaming of a life she might have had in different black and white days. History and fiction had been her only friends then, but now there was one upstairs, a real, live friend whose life depended upon her.

She ignored Brady and his goons and strode towards the paintings of faces she hadn't seen for a long time.

'All this so you can show me pictures of dead people?'

Brady's eyes narrowed as he peered at her. 'The first time I met you, once I got past the annoyance of someone intruding into my business, I knew you'd appreciate what I have here.' He moved by her side and pointed at a painting. 'Do you know who this is?'

She scrutinised the canvas while struggling to create an escape map out of the building. Hypnotic eyes stared from the frame underneath thick curls covering the top of the subject's face. She clasped her hands together as if they contained some dark secret.

'That's Norma Shearer,' Astrid said. 'The portrait on her right is Kay Francis; the one on her left is Ann Harding.' She turned to him. 'So, you have a fixation for little known 1930s movie stars.'

He stepped from her and reached into his pocket. He removed a remote control and switched on the large screen.

'They're not just from the thirties; I watch their movies and the best of the silent age. I like to escape into their worlds when mine doesn't satisfy me.' He stared at her. 'I think you know how that feels.'

'Does your world include kidnapping children?'

The cinema whirred into life, electricity charging the air. Brady's eyes shrank into his face as he shook his head. 'It was only the one time with Alex Sanchez, and that was a mistake. I listened to bad advice and learnt a valuable lesson from it. We let her go, and her mother was well rewarded.'

Astrid flinched at his words. 'You gave Christina money?'

He laughed at her. 'It was nothing so vulgar, Ms Snow. One of my businesses bought the land she and her community live on, made some adjustments to it, and let them run it as a co-op for the rest of their lives.' He sank into a chair as the titles came up on a movie over a hundred years old.

Astrid moved to the side of the screen, still processing what he'd told her. 'Why would you do that?'

Brady muted the sound. 'My mother's heritage was one of backwoods trailer trash. She was fourteen when she married her cousin, a violent man twice her age who thought he was Jerry Lee Lewis's reincarnation, even though the Killer wasn't dead. He had none of Jerry Lee's musical talent, but all of his rage and anger.

'I was born the day before her fifteenth birthday. When my father died, I was five, standing in the wings as he was electrocuted on stage while trying to tune a guitar he couldn't play. If only someone had told him Jerry Lee was a piano player.'

Astrid tried to shake the confusion from her head. 'What's your sordid life story got to do with this?'

'Our childhood experiences are what forge the whole of

our existence, don't you think, Ms Snow? Some use the terrible things that happen to them to become terrible people; I used mine as real-life education.'

'You're an inspiration to us all, Brady.' She glanced around the room. 'It must be difficult for you, having to live in such splendour.'

He waved his hand in the air. 'This is all spectacle; size and grandeur to draw the masses in, but the thing that hooks them, the thing that creates the connection, is intimacy. Give them something which fills the four chambers of their hearts, and you'll have them for life. There are several ways you can achieve this: generosity, love, sacrifice, tragedy.'

'Is that what you're giving to the people?'

'The world is a prison, and we can either be its inmates or its governor. I choose the latter.'

He was different now to when they'd first met. There was hypnotic power in his voice: the tone, the resonance, the way it rose and fell; she imagined it had a powerful effect on all who heard it.

'Is that why you're keen to lead the nation's youth into a better world?'

'You mean the Future Youth Project?' He reached into his pocket, removed a photograph and handed it to her. She stared at the image of a teenage girl with long blonde hair and the same sparkling blue eyes as him. 'That's my sister, Jocelyn. She died of cancer when she was twelve; I was sixteen.' He took the photo from her and placed it on the table near them. 'To survive that trauma, I convinced myself her death was the best thing for her, considering our circumstances.'

'Your circumstances?'

'My parents lived in poverty, Ms Snow. Jocelyn and I barely had enough to eat or adequate clothes to wear. We were the butt of everyone's jokes, ridiculed at school and everywhere we went. It toughened me up, but it was a struggle for her. At home, we knelt around dilapidated chairs every night to say our prayers, asking God for release from our burdens.' He glanced across the large room. 'And perhaps he did.'

'So, you worked your way up from poverty into the most powerful man in the state, and now you want to give something back to the youth of the nation?' Astrid tried to rein in her sarcasm.

'Good God, no. These kids are scenery, that's all; background figures in my story, insignificant actors to a drama they don't understand.' A sneer slithered across his face like a fat slug. 'Handing things to people for free only makes them lazy and ungrateful; everyone needs to work for what they get. There's no sense of achievement if everything gets handed to you on a plate.'

She watched the snake oil veneer slip from him. Quite why he was so keen to parade his ignorance was a mystery to her; she'd have thought he'd have preferred to leave room for doubt.

'You're no different from every other slime ball eager to exploit others for their own ends, and while I'd love to spend some time explaining the error of your ways, I've got more pressing things to do. And you need to let Grace go.'

He shook his head. 'My upbringing taught me that if I didn't think and act big, I'd get swept up amongst all the human debris in life. Unfortunately, it means I have to make deals with some unsavoury characters, which is why I have to apologise to you, Ms Snow.'

He increased the sound from the speakers, and a giant gorilla howled from the screen.

'What do you mean?' Tension rippled through her fingers.

'You need to leave here and return opposite if you want your friend the policewoman to remain unharmed.' Brady turned from her and concentrated on the movie. She ran past him and out of the door as Fay Wray grimaced in fear.

She burst into the other room. Grace stood at the back, perspiration dripping from her. Astrid marched across to see if she was okay, only realising they weren't alone when she was halfway there. She stopped and turned: six men peered at her, only one of them smiling.

Daniel Gideon's grin chilled her heart.

The grin dripped from his mouth like dirty water from a leaky pipe.

'You don't have me at a disadvantage anymore, Snow.'

She peered at the man standing behind him, the ex-military she'd observed on the camera upstairs. Astrid glanced to the side as her partner flexed her arms and joined her; at least Grace was free.

Grace gritted her teeth. 'You won't get away with this, Gideon. It doesn't matter how rich you are, you can't assault a police officer and abduct people without serious consequences.'

Astrid scrutinised the room and what they faced: five hired goons and Gideon against her and Grace. She searched through the escape maps in her mind, calculated the odds of getting out unscathed and didn't like the results.

Even if we get out in one piece, if Brady set this up, his security is all over this building.

Gideon dismissed Grace with barely a flicker of emotion. 'I don't care about you, Ms Crowley; your unfortunate situation was necessary to attract Snow's attention. You're free to leave at any time.'

He moved towards them, unconcerned about anything in the world, a master of his universe. Astrid was glad of his arrogance.

Grace swatted his confidence back at him. 'We're leaving together.'

He ignored her words. 'I've learnt a lot about you in the last twenty-four hours, Ms Snow, all thanks to my new friend.'

He glanced behind him at the man with the piercing blue eyes. She could have grabbed Gideon then, pulled him towards her and used him as a hostage. But she didn't, willing to let it play out a bit more.

'You must have a pretty boring life to focus on me so much. I'm only a visitor in this vast country of yours.'

The smirk grew bigger, threatening to consume all of him. 'Is that why you attacked me in New York and kidnapped my daughter? Because it was one of your tourist activities?'

Tension shimmered through the air. 'Well, it was more of a rescue than anything else, but it was more exciting than going to the Statue of Liberty.'

She stared at the blue-eyed man. She didn't know him, but there was something familiar about his manner.

Gideon's smile faded into nothing. 'None of that matters now. You'll tell me where my daughter is, or the two of you will suffer.'

Astrid mapped out the room's contents: the writing desk behind her, bookcases along the walls, and a single chair to her right. A thin layer of dust clung to the carpet. An aroma of violence to come lingered in the air, the atmosphere heightened as if a tiger waited to pounce on an unsuspecting antelope, and she was unsure which animal she was in that scenario.

She rubbed at the fading love bite on her neck.

'Even if I did know where she was, I wouldn't tell you.'

Gideon clenched his fists. 'Are you a good woman, Ms Snow?'

A deep curve on Astrid's lips made the world stop around her. 'Not very.'

He was close enough, she smelt his expensive cologne. 'You think your Agency training will save you against these five?'

She ignored his question and turned to the blue-eyed man. 'You're from the Agency?' They'd promised to leave her alone, so what was this?

'I'm on a break,' he said.

'They'll know you're here.' The Agency didn't let their agents out of their sight.

He seemed unconcerned and held up his arm. 'Things have changed since you left, Snow. All field agents have a tracker implanted in them. They're aware I'm here, but they won't know what goes on inside this room Mr Gideon bought from Senator Brady.'

Gideon strode to the closest bookcase and removed a copy of *Live and Let Die*. 'This place was purchased at a considerable price, but it will be worth it to spend some quality time with you, Snow.'

Astrid stared into his eyes, so black and deep, like a bottomless well. They dragged her in; she was sinking into his arrogance and drowning in his egotism. The others matched his smugness. If the blue-eyed guy were from the Agency, then this would be harder than she'd thought.

'I read all your Agency files before taking this job.'

'Did they keep you up at night?'

His laugh made the whole of his face vibrate. 'You're admired, but not well-liked is the consensus: a one-woman Terminator whose systems are riddled with malware, hell-bent on destroying everything around her. That's my favourite quote about you from your colleagues.'

He kept her talking, and she knew he was trying to distract her before they attacked together. She had to wrest the initiative from him. In her head, there was only one map that would work.

She stepped forward before anyone could react, grabbed Gideon by the wrist and twisted it back. He dropped the book onto the floor and screamed as she pulled him to her.

'I can break his arm and poke his eyes out before any of you reach me.' She increased the pressure on his fingers as he fell to his knees.

'We get paid even if he dies,' blue eyes said.

'How much are you getting?'

'A million dollars,' he replied.

She laughed. 'A million dollars between five of you? That's hardly retirement money. Though I guess it won't be between five of you once I've finished.'

One of the others finally spoke, the bald guy standing opposite Grace. 'What do you mean?'

Astrid flexed her shoulders. 'You and the hipster beard next to you,' she nodded at baldy, 'will have to deal with Grace, and that leaves the other three for me: blue eyes, nervous twitch and you with the trembling fingers. Only blue won't come for me; he'll let you two suffer first. I don't know what he told you about me, but I'm guessing it wasn't everything.'

She squeezed Gideon's fingers and he squealed. She pulled him to the side and stood behind the large sofa.

'You can't stop three of us at once,' nervous twitch said.

Astrid shook her head. 'I told you, old blue eyes there will step back and let you two do the heavy lifting. I'll throw Gideon at the closer of you. The other will have one eye on me and the other on this chair in the way. A split focus is a recipe for distraction. If you look at me, I'll push the furniture into you; if you glance at the sofa to avoid it, I'll punch you in the throat. Then I'll do the same to whoever is unfortunate enough to be struggling with Gideon.' With her free hand, she removed the pencil from her jacket. 'Then I'll stick this in one of those blue eyes and help Grace finish the rest of you.'

'You've just told us your whole plan, you stupid woman.' Hipster beard wasn't as woke as he appeared.

'I told you one plan. There's plenty more where that came from.'

She scanned their faces, trying to work out how desperate they were. Blue eyes gave nothing away.

'We don't care about the cop,' said the hipster. 'You can't deal with five of us at once.'

Astrid laughed at him. 'How long have you boys been together? Less than twenty-four hours, I'd guess. Gideon must have recruited my friend from the Agency after I visited New York, so it's strange he wasn't involved in the debacle in the woods. You lot haven't worked together, probably too reliant on using guns which you don't have, thanks to Brady's reluctance to allow unauthorised weapons in his home. Do you trust each other? Do you have a plan other than all rushing me at once? If you do that, I'll blind the first bloke and squash the balls of the next. While that happens, Grace will get behind you and crack one of the Senator's vases over someone's skull. That'll leave two of you against two of us; I like those odds.'

Gideon coughed as blue eyes spoke. 'Make your offer, Snow.'

She grinned at him. 'You said he guaranteed you a million dollars, regardless of what transpires here. I'll give you five million, a million each, if you go now.'

Grace exhaled loudly as the men glanced at each other. Furrowed brows greeted Astrid's proposal of financial reward, their frowns as dark as their clothes. The room turned fridge cold, the goons looking like something left over from the night before.

'Don't listen to her,' Gideon squeaked. She increased the pressure on his wrist.

'How will you get us the money?' said blue eyes.

Astrid slipped the pencil behind her ear and took hold of her phone. 'I'll transfer it from my bank into an account of your choosing. Then you can split it between you.'

Grace looked as confused as the thugs. She whispered to Astrid, 'Where did you get so much cash from?'

Astrid eased up on Gideon, holding his hand as if he was about to propose to her. 'I'm a woman of many talents, Grace; acquiring cash is only one of them.'

Gideon's goons gathered together, speaking in hushed tones. Mr Blue Eyes was the only one to keep his gaze on her. Gideon coughed up half a lung and stared at her.

'This won't work, Snow; those men are loyal to me.'

She couldn't control her laughter. 'Their only loyalty is to themselves and what they earn. Your pain is about to get much worse.'

Blue eyes pulled away and spoke for the mercenaries. 'We want ten million. Then you can do what you want with him.'

Astrid turned to Grace. 'Will you hold Gideon's hand for me?'

She dragged his complaining bulk to Grace and handed him over before switching her focus to blue eyes. He held out a slip of paper to her.

'Transfer the payment into this account.'

'What put you into the Agency's bad books?'

He peered deep into her face. 'I didn't complete a mission as expected. Now I have to wait to find out the consequences.' There was a slight tremble in his fingers as she took the number from him. 'But I'd rather get my retirement pension now and forget about the Agency.'

'Do you think Gideon's wealth and influence will protect you from them? No amount of money will help you, Mr Blue Eyes. They'll scour the planet for you, and when they find you, which they will, they'll make you an example so no agent will do anything like this ever again.'

He didn't appear too concerned. 'You escaped from their clutches.'

'I'm a special case.' She moved from him and used her phone to find the correct bank account.

'Once you've transferred the money, what's to stop us from taking you away as well?'

She typed two levels of password security into the screen as she spoke.

'Is that their idea?' She nodded at the others. 'I don't think you're stupid enough to take that risk. Go back to the Agency and face your punishment. If you're good enough, they won't want to waste you. What was it you failed to do for them?'

She hit send on the screen. Thirty seconds later, a phone vibrated in his pocket.

'I was supposed to kill someone, and I refused.'

He removed the cell and checked it. He shot a brief look to Gideon before going to the others and giving them the news. She watched him speak to them like a leader instructing his soldiers what to do. They shuffled out of the room without a second glance at Astrid or Grace. Only Mr Blue Eyes remained.

'You should forget all this nonsense and take your punishment like a good little agent.'

'People still talk about you in hushed tones at the Agency, Snow. Some of those higher up the food chain would have you back, maybe even as the Director.'

Her lips trembled as she laughed. 'Now I know you're messing with me, Mr Blue. Who was it you refused to kill?'

He moved towards the exit. 'I loved him, but he was a double agent.' Sadness bled out of him. 'Sometimes, deception is so close to you, it's impossible to see it.'

With that, he left. Now she had to decide what to do with Gideon. Grace let go of him, and he collapsed onto the floor.

'I don't think I'm happy with you giving them all that money, even if it did get us out of a tight spot.'

Astrid stood over Gideon as he squirmed on the carpet. 'Don't worry about it. If I don't send the bank a confirmation code in the next hour, the cash reverts to me.'

It was Grace's turn to laugh. 'They won't be happy when they find out.'

'Which means we haven't got a lot of time to find our serial killer and discover where Alex is.' She bent and grabbed Gideon by the collar. 'But I need to deal with this specimen first.' She dragged him across the floor and dumped him in front of the empty fireplace. 'How do you see this ending, this situation between you and me?'

He pushed his back into the wall, wiping sweat from his forehead. His face was a picture of despair, eyes narrowing and teeth bared. She guessed it must have been a long time since anyone treated him as badly as this.

He spat the words at her.

'There's plenty more mercenaries in the world. I'll find the right ones and make you suffer for what you've done. It doesn't matter how many times you escape from me; I have the resources to get you someday.'

Astrid sighed. 'You're not even a pale imitation of a man, Gideon; you're something scraped from the bottom of my shoe. I don't think you care about your daughter at all; you just want to punish her mother. And you're upset with me because I've embarrassed you twice, and your self-respect is in the toilet right now. Pride will make you keep coming for me, and that's a problem which needs a dramatic solution to end this.'

She removed the pencil from behind her ear and rolled it between her fingers. Grace grabbed her by the arm and pulled her to the side.

'What are you going to do?'

'Well, I could stick this into his eye and perforate his brain. What do you think?' Her grin was infectious, but Grace wasn't happy.

'I can't let you do that.'

Astrid snapped the pencil in half and dropped the pieces onto the floor. 'There's only one thing important to Gideon, and that's what I'll destroy if he doesn't back off.'

She returned to him as he staggered to his feet. He'd regained his arrogance and a smirk, his injured wrist hanging at his side.

'You can't beat me, Snow.'

'What did Mr Blue tell you about me?'

He twisted some movement into his broken fingers, grimacing as he did so. 'He wasn't the first to spill the beans about your career in the Agency, but he gave me the fascinating details. There's nowhere for you to hide from me.'

'I've no intention of hiding from you or anyone else. I'm going to ruin your life, Gideon. I'll destroy your reputation and drain your wealth from every bank account you have.'

He slid backwards across the wall. 'You're not capable of such a thing.'

She stared at him, but it was something else she saw: someone else; someone hiding in plain sight.

Astrid pushed her face into his. 'I'm going to set up a time-delayed internet post addressed to the major news sites in this country and YouTube, Twitter and all the other social media outlets. It will provide evidence linking you to a white supremacist paedophile ring.'

He clutched at his chest while she pressed her fingers into the marks on her neck.

'All lies,' he said.

'All of it will be convincing, genuine enough to ruin you completely. If I don't input a delay password every day, it will be posted immediately. If you do anything to harm me or your daughter and her mother, the information will be online within minutes.'

She moved from him and headed for the door. Grace scrambled after her and out of the room as Gideon howled behind them.

'Can you do that?'

Astrid left the question unanswered. It was close to midnight, and most of the guests had filtered away. Tired-looking staff wandered around like drunks at a wedding.

As they neared the exit, Brady was standing by the door. He held his hand out to her.

'You're a woman of constant surprises, Ms Snow. Are you sure you don't want to work for me?'

They brushed past him and stepped into the night air. A row of cars waited for patrons with less money than when they'd arrived.

'You take the car home, and I'll get a taxi,' Astrid said.

Grace narrowed her eyes in surprise. 'And why would I do that?'

'I have to give Christina Sanchez some bad news.' She told Grace about what she'd found on the surveillance videos; or rather, what she hadn't discovered.

'Won't it be better if both of us are there?'

Astrid stepped towards the closest empty cab. 'By the time I get there, it will be gone midnight, and our partnership will be officially over. You've already got someone keeping tabs on you.' She nodded at Tanner, who was glaring at them through the haze of cigarette smoke as he strode from the mansion.

Astrid opened the car door. 'Don't wait up for me.'

She gave the driver the address, but it wasn't for the Sanchez home.

23   SECRET LOVE

It was a new day when she knocked on the door.
'This is a pleasant surprise, Snow.'
Cope dragged her inside and pushed her against the
wall. A stack of books tumbled onto the carpet as the Detec-
tive thrust her tongue into Astrid's mouth. Cope's nails dug
into her palms and drew blood. When they separated,
Astrid was breathing heavily. She stepped over the mess
and into the room.
'I'm not here for that.'
The place was as she remembered it: a tip covered with
mountains of books stacked in no particular order or system.
She picked one up and studied the cover.
Cope removed a cigarette from her pocket and lit it.
'Are you breaking up with me?'
'How old were you when you realised you enjoyed
inflicting pain on others?'
Smoke circled the room, creating a nicotine haze and
irritating Astrid's lungs. The Detective pursed her lips and
pondered the question.
'I never took you for a prude, Snow.' Her eyes sparkled

as she peered at Astrid. 'Didn't you know sadomasochistic sex is the new normal? Millions of women have discovered their inner hidden pleasures and aren't afraid to show them to the world.' She dragged on the cigarette. 'Or are you here to tell me you regret what happened between us and you're consumed by shame?'

'That's not what I'm talking about, Jules. I want to know when you realised you enjoyed killing people.'

Cope sucked on the cigarette as if it was the last she'd ever have. 'Did they hurt you at the Brady mansion, Snow? Maybe one of the Senator's thugs knocked you on the head and scrambled your brains because you're speaking nonsense now.'

Astrid pressed her fingers into the mark on her neck. 'Lying to me is a waste of time, Jules, so I'll ask you again: how old were you when you recognised you enjoyed inflicting pain on others?'

Detective Julie Cope continued to blow smoke around the room. She took a long, hard look at Astrid before she replied.

'It was about the same point I realised if I didn't keep my proclivities hidden, I'd end up in serious trouble.'

'So you thought the best way to do that was in plain sight and became a cop.'

'If paedophiles can join the Church, then surely the perfect place for a sadist is in the Police Force? It made sense to me.'

'My desire stopped me recognising what you are straight away.'

Cope finished her cigarette and stubbed it on her hand. 'Don't fret it, Snow; we all make mistakes, and that wasn't your only one.'

As Astrid lunged for her, something thick and heavy hit

the side of her face. The last thing she saw was the carpet rushing towards her.

––––––––

TINY BUILDERS WERE HAMMERING into her jaw when she woke. Half-light dripped through her flickering eyes.

'He's never been the same since he got trapped inside a shabby movie house watching *The Incredible Shrinking Man* while on a bad acid trip.'

Cope's words made no sense to her. Who was she talking about? And who had punched her? She tried to stand, but her body failed to do as she asked; or perhaps it was because she was strapped to a chair and, for once, it wasn't for pleasure.

'I think I broke my fingers on her face.'

The voice sounded familiar, but the howling of wolves in her ears didn't help. Astrid shook her head so her vision and hearing returned to normal. She wiggled her jaw. It ached, but she could speak.

'That was a kiss with a fist. You must be the junior partner in this murderous duo.'

Detective Pete Wylie glared at her, stepping forward as if to strike again.

'You'll get used to the discomfort.' Cope approached Astrid and ran her fingers across their captive's face. 'I wonder, though, how much pain you can take.' She stroked Astrid's cheek before dropping down to the bite marks she'd inflicted on the neck the other night. 'You've had some experience of this, haven't you?'

Astrid snapped her head backwards, the tight constraints of the rope cutting into her arms and legs.

'You two make a terrible couple. I predict trouble on the horizon for both of you.'

Cope pushed out her cheeks and pulled a chair close to her. Their knees touched as she sat.

'You're getting desperate, Snow, and it's sad to see. I'd hoped you were made of sterner stuff than our usual playdates.'

She placed her hand on Astrid's knee and squeezed hard. Astrid resisted the urge to spit in her face. Inside her head, she searched for an escape map but came up with nothing. She needed more time; she had to keep them talking.

'All these books you have about serial killers and profiling; are they just a front so you could blend into the background of law enforcement?' As she spoke, she pushed out her shoulders, flexing her arms and legs in the hope of loosening her bonds.

Cope sank into her chair. 'They're educational.' She grabbed one about the Hillside Stranglers. 'We needed to learn from other people's mistakes. Being cops didn't guarantee our safety; we had to be smarter than everyone else. And we were until you arrived.'

Astrid forced a smile from her dry lips. 'I'm flattered.'

Wylie lit a cigarette and filled the room with smoke. 'You're giving her too much credit, Jules. Just because you rolled around in the hay for a few hours doesn't mean you should be blind to what she is.'

Cope turned to her partner. 'I know exactly what she is; she's like us. I recognised it as soon as I saw her; the other night only confirmed it.'

Painful laughter sputtered out of Astrid. 'Psychopaths are always deluded, and you two are no different. I'm nothing like you.'

If she could stand, she might be able to throw herself into the wall and smash her way out of the chair; but she couldn't get up.

Julie Cope patted Astrid's knee. 'You're exactly like me, Snow. You find meaning in your life wherever you want to, and you don't let anyone stop you from doing that, regardless of who they are. You may blend into society's conformist rules every once in a while, but it's just a façade as you pursue your wants and needs as they dictate.'

'You're delusional. I don't hurt people to satisfy my desires.'

Cope smirked at her. 'Come now, you know that's not true. You told me you tortured and killed while working for the Agency. Would you have done that if it made you feel terrible?' She got out of the chair and went to Wylie as he held up his damaged hand. 'I bet you'd enjoy killing both of us right now.'

Cope put her lips on his and they shared the smoke from the cigarette, sucking it in before exhaling. Astrid's palms were turned upwards, the rope cutting into her wrists as she flexed her fingers.

'You're damn right I would.' She bared her teeth and glared at them, but it was a fake show of anger designed to keep them off guard. 'What did you do to Alex Sanchez?'

Wylie grimaced as Cope let go of his hand.

'We didn't do anything to her. If you're trying to maintain a low profile, you don't snatch the most famous teenager in the town. We only take those who won't be missed, even by their own families, some of which are glad not to have another mouth to feed and clothe.'

Astrid was about to argue the point when she remembered how much her family hated her.

'I saw Alex's initials on the door of your torture dungeon.'

Wylie laughed at her. 'I did that as a joke, to wind you up, and it looks like it worked.'

Cope glared at him. 'I wasn't happy about it. We need to reduce the risks we take, but he won't listen.'

She stepped from him, and for the first time since she woke, Astrid recognised the tension between her captors. She had to work with that and increase it; divide and conquer was her only way out alive.

'Wasn't it dangerous, using that old tunnel in the woods?'

As she observed them, she managed to twist her ankles against the rope and wriggle them free a little. A bit more and perhaps she could stand.

'It was safer than the other places we've used,' Cope said. 'I only knew it was there because my father told me about it when I was a kid. He was a local amateur historian, but nobody ever listened to him.'

'Enough of this chattering. I need a release.' Wylie didn't attempt to hide his frustration. 'You know what happens if I don't get it.'

Cope's shoulders shrank as she sighed. 'Okay, Pete; it won't be long now.' She sat opposite Astrid again and removed a screwdriver from her pocket. 'He gets frustrated if he doesn't have a sexual fix regularly.'

Astrid turned to him. 'Don't mind me if you want to yank that small cock of yours in here, Pete.'

She smiled as he glared at her. Cope shook her head.

'If it were that simple, we'd never have met in the first place.'

Astrid pictured the meeting. 'Let me guess: you two fell in love over stained leather at a fetish club.'

Cope grimaced. 'I hate leather, but you're not far from the truth. The strangest thing was we were both already cops, but in different towns. The club was in New York, but Pete transferred here soon after.' She turned to him. 'How long ago was it, partner?'

He continued spitting smoke into the air. 'Five years, Jules.'

The tension between them had dissipated, and Astrid wasn't happy about it. 'So, you came up with a plan to snatch vulnerable kids off the streets, targeting ones you thought wouldn't be missed, and torturing and killing them for sexual pleasure?'

Cope glanced at her partner, continuing to roll the screwdriver between her fingers. 'Yes, that's about the gist of it. And everything was fine until you arrived.'

'I might not have known anything if that girl hadn't turned up dead near the river.'

'Yes, the ill-starred Katie,' said Cope.

'It was unfortunate for her, and you. How did she get away from your torture chamber?'

'Are we doing this now?' Wylie growled.

'I'm not going to kill her here,' Cope replied. 'What do I keep telling you? No more risks.' She glared at him. 'We wouldn't have had to torch the tunnel if you hadn't let the girl escape.'

'We don't have to kill her. You know what I need.'

Cope leant into her chair and laughed out loud. 'Pete, she'll bite it off if you dangle it anywhere near her.'

'Not if we remove her teeth first. We've done it before.'

She considered his words. 'You'll have to put plastic sheets over the floor and the furniture. I'm not getting blood all over the place.'

'That's okay; I have some in the car.'

It was his fault Katie escaped. She's the one in charge, so he has to be the weak link.

Wylie moved close to Astrid, his face resembling a manic clown. Cope sighed loudly.

'He'd been visiting her on his own when he knows that's forbidden.' He stepped back from Cope's stern glare. 'He thought she was his Patty Hearst. I think the poor girl had Stockholm Syndrome.'

'It was an accident, Jules. I told you.'

She stood and glared at him. 'You didn't tie her up properly, so she escaped, and that's why we're in this fucking mess now.'

She thrust her hand down and pushed the screwdriver through Astrid's palm. Before she could scream, Cope had her other hand over Astrid's mouth. Pain surged through her as she struggled to breathe through her nose.

'It won't happen again.' Wylie towered over her. 'Can I get the plastic from the car?'

Cope nodded as Astrid bit into her hand, her teeth going deep into the Detective's flesh. Cope never blinked or moved.

'Now, isn't this fun?' Cope said as Wylie stepped out.

She let go of Astrid and went into the kitchen, returning with a towel to clean the blood from her hand and mop up that which seeped from Astrid's wound. She removed the screwdriver, and Astrid winced.

'He's becoming a liability to you, Jules. You'll get caught because of him.' She spoke through gritted teeth. 'If I can find you because of his mistake, then others will as well.'

Cope wiped the blood from the tool. 'You could be right, but what's a girl like me to do in a situation like this?'

'Get professional help.'

Cope sank into her seat and laughed again. 'Oh, I will

miss you, Snow. We could've had so much more fun together.'

'Are you going to pull all my teeth out?'

'Pete can do it; I like you too much.' She grinned at her. 'I guess I do have a soft spot after all.'

'I'll scream while he does it. If you don't want the neighbours to hear, you'll have to cut my tongue out first.'

Her smile was brighter than the sun. 'You've done this type of thing before, haven't you?' Cope slapped her leg like a cowgirl at a rodeo. 'See, I told you we're very much alike.'

'There's one big difference between us, Jules.' The blood turned cold in Astrid's palm.

'And what's that?'

'You're going to prison, and I'm not.'

Cope laughed again. 'Oh, I do love the balls on you. Will you still be this arrogant when you're missing a tongue and all your teeth while Pete's wangling his dong in your face? And, I have to tell you, he's quite a big boy down there, so you might want to flex the muscles in your jaw as preparation.'

'The thing which annoys me the most, Jules, is I think you'll enjoy yourself in prison.'

Detective Julie Cope was about to fashion a reply when a hand pushed cold steel into the back of her neck.

Officer Grace Crowley gripped on to her gun. 'Did you get lost on the way to the Sanchez place, Astrid?'

'I had to take a slight detour. What have you done with Wylie?'

Confusion furrowed Grace's brow. 'Detective Wylie? I haven't seen him since the Senator's party.'

Then pandemonium broke out in the apartment.

Wylie threw the plastic over Grace's head and dragged her backwards. When the gun disappeared from Cope's neck, she bolted up. Astrid had leveraged her feet away from the tape binding her and pushed forward. She barrelled her head into Cope's gut, and they tumbled into the others. All four of them crashed into the back wall. Electricity surged through Astrid's body.

'Fuck!' Cope shouted as she swung the screwdriver at Astrid's face. Astrid threw herself backwards and on to the floor. The chair hit the ground hard and splintered apart as she rolled to the side as Cope lunged at her. She was on her feet in seconds, bits of wood hanging from her wrists like mittens. She swung one up as Cope went for her again, catching the Detective across the head and sending her reeling.

Astrid glanced around to find Grace, but she and Wylie were nowhere. She refocused just in time to see the screwdriver heading for her. It clipped her cheek as she twisted away. It clattered into the wall behind her.

She wiped the blood from her face. 'How good is your hand to hand combat, Jules?'

Fire flashed through Cope's eyes. 'You know Pete will break your little friend's neck.'

A tiny laugh escaped from Astrid's hard-working lungs. 'My not so little friend will have his balls on a plate, and I'm going to smash this piece of chair into your nose.'

She held up the splintered wood as books lay scattered around them. For the first time, she witnessed confusion in Julie Cope's eyes.

'You're out of condition, Snow; too used to looking for children to handle someone like me. I do this for a living; you're just an amateur now.'

The Agency had taught Astrid patience was the key: let your enemy make the initial mistake because the first was usually the last. But there was Grace to consider. Was she confident her partner could deal with Wylie? She couldn't wait around and take that risk.

'I'll give you a farewell kiss to remember me by.'

She moved towards Cope, placing her foot next to a pile of books when the Detective stepped to the side. Astrid got her shoe underneath the closest hardback and kicked it forward. As Cope tried to dodge an attack, the book landed in the middle of her face.

She groaned and tumbled to the floor. 'You broke my fucking nose!' Cope screamed as she threw Ted Bundy's biography down, her blood slipping across the front cover. She struggled to get up as Astrid leapt forward and planted her knee in the Detective's chest.

'This reminds me of the other morning,' she said as Cope thrashed beneath her.

Then footsteps entered the room.

Astrid turned Cope on to her stomach and pulled the Detective's hands behind her back. Then Grace slapped the cuffs on her colleague.

'Do we have time for a threesome?' Cope laughed. 'Or are you going to read me my rights, Officer Crowley?'

Astrid hauled Cope to the side and threw her on to the sofa. She kept one eye on her as she spoke to Grace.

'Where's Wylie?'

'He's unconscious and chained to a railing outside.'

'How did you know where I was?'

'I followed you here.' She looked sheepish. 'After we found nothing at Brady's mansion, I thought you'd given up. I sat there and called you all the names under the sun, ready to quit this job, forget about becoming a foster parent and leave this town forever. My brain was frazzled'

'You were imaging all kinds of weird sex games going on, weren't you?'

'I didn't know what to think.' She coughed and scratched at her throat. 'I was about to knock on the door when I heard her talking to you. That's when I came in and saw what was happening. It's a good job I had a weapon with me.'

Astrid agreed. 'What happened with you and Wylie?'

'He pulled me outside, but I guess he wasn't used to dealing with someone as tall as me.'

'He's a pervert and a coward, but still a big bloke. How did you overcome him?'

Grace puffed out her cheeks. 'It was pure luck. As he struggled to get hold of me, he lost his footing at the top of the stairs and fell. Once I'd cuffed him to the radiator in the hall, I came back up for you.' She checked the damage in the room. 'What happened here?'

Astrid peered at the hole in the palm of her hand. 'Wylie and Cope are our serial killers. They've been taking kids they know won't be missed or those who the police won't look too closely into where they went.' As she spoke, Cope grinned. The wound in Astrid's palm throbbed as she flexed her fingers. 'They worked as a murder team in the town, but I'd guess both of them killed on their own before they arrived in Angel Springs.'

Grace gasped. 'Fuck me.'

Cope leant forward, her back arched, and her grin sparkled like the stars. 'I'm game, Officer Crowley. Perhaps Astrid is keen for a threesome.'

'I should call this in.' Grace removed her phone.

Astrid stopped her. 'I need to talk to her first.'

'We can do that at the station.'

'No, I have to get her alone, away from your superiors and her former colleagues. Who's to say other police aren't involved in these crimes?'

Grace was ashen, her lips almost blue. 'That's hard to believe.'

'Before tonight, would you have imagined them as serial killers?'

She shook her head. 'No, but surely it's only the two of them. We would have known otherwise.'

'I wouldn't count on it, Grace. I've known serial killers who worked in groups. It's rare, but not unknown.'

'What are you whispering about?' Cope's confidence hadn't vanished, even with her current predicament. 'Are you arguing about who will be in charge?'

She'd made herself comfortable on the sofa, legs crossed as if waiting to be served in a restaurant.

'Where's Alex?' Astrid said.

Cope arched her eyebrows. 'Alex, Alex.' She licked her bottom lip. 'I don't know anyone by that name.'

Astrid balled her fingers into a fist. 'I could kill you right now, Jules. I'd torture you first if I didn't think you'd enjoy it, but I will finish you, and no one will ever know.'

'You're wrong, Astrid. Officer Crowley would know. And I don't think it would sit well on her conscience.' Cope smirked at her colleague. 'Would it, Grace?'

'Smile all you want, Cope, but you'll be behind bars soon enough.'

'What will you charge me with?'

'Kidnapping, torture, murder. There'll be plenty to choose from.'

'On what evidence? You have nothing apart from my skirmish with Snow. And that was only a lover's tiff, wasn't it, Astrid?'

Astrid reached down and dragged Cope up by her shirt before forcing her into the wall. The strength of it knocked a framed Klimt print onto the floor. The glass cracked and scattered at her feet.

'Tell me what you did to Alex and the others, Jules.'

Grace grabbed Astrid's shoulder and pulled her off the Detective. 'Let's get her to the station, and we'll interrogate her.'

Astrid shrugged her off and glared at Cope, her hackles raised by that constant grin.

'I won't say anything, either here or at the station. But I'll show you.'

'What?' Astrid and Grace said together.

'I can take you where she is, but only Astrid; not you, Crowley.'

Grace shook her head. 'There's no chance of that. You and Wylie will tell us everything in an interrogation room.'

The laughter came from Cope's eyes first, in the way they expanded and her pupils sparkled, before travelling down her cheeks and exploding from her mouth.

'As I said earlier, girls, you have no evidence against either me or Pete. But I'm feeling sorry for Snow, so I'll show her what she's looking for, but only her.'

Astrid placed her hand on Grace's arm. 'Even if we do get something from them at the station, it might take too long. They could have Alex restrained somewhere, in pain and suffering.' She stared at Cope. 'Is Alex alive?'

Cope used her handcuffed hands to straighten her shirt. 'As far as I know, she is.' She twisted the manacles to glance at her watch. 'But time is ticking.'

Grace clutched the phone in her fingers, peering at her partner as Astrid waited for a response.

'You can't trust her.'

'I know, but it's the only option we have of finding Alex. We owe it to her mother and her, and all the others these two psychos hurt and killed. If they have Alex imprisoned somewhere, other kids could be there, and evidence of Cope and Wylie's crimes in Angel Springs.'

Those words were all it took to convince Grace. 'Okay, but I don't like it.' She shook her phone at Astrid. 'You need to keep in touch with me and make sure you stay safe.'

'I promise to do both.' Astrid stepped across the room and opened the top drawer near the TV. She removed Detective Cope's police revolver and checked it was loaded. 'This will suffice.' She grabbed Cope by the arm and lugged her towards the door. 'You get Wylie in a cell, and I'll see you soon.'

The night bit at her as she shoved Cope into the street. It was the type of cold that gets under the skin and reaches into the bones.

Cope rattled the cuffs as she shivered. 'Would you like me to drive?'

Astrid pushed her forward. 'Where's your car?'

She nodded across the road at a blue Toyota. 'The keys are in my right trouser pocket, but I can't reach them.' She held up her cuffed hands. Astrid strode towards her, Cope's gun in one hand as she used the other to get the keys. Cope squirmed as she did so. 'Oh, Astrid, this brings back so many happy memories.'

Astrid clutched on to the keys and shoved Cope forward. They got into the front seat, with Astrid behind the wheel.

'Tell me where Alex is, Jules, or I'll drive into the woods and blow your brains out.'

There was no emotion in her voice or expression, just cold determination filling her eyes. Cope rubbed at the palm of her hand through the cuffs.

'Can you remember how to get to Jed Fowler's place?'

Astrid slammed the brakes on, the car screeching to a halt on an empty street.

'Senator Brady's nephew?'

'That's the guy. You've met him, right?' Cope gave an exaggerated shiver. 'He even gives me the creeps.' She raised her eyebrows. 'And that house he lives in.'

'That's where Alex is?'

'You know what happened to her at Brady's place, with those Future Youth nut-jobs?'

'I've seen the video of what they did to her. What's your involvement in this?'

'Fowler followed her after they let her go from the mansion. Then he snatched Alex as she left Manny's cabin and took her back to his house.'

I'd stared into Fowler's eyes and believed what he told me, convinced he had nothing to do with Alex's disappearance. Were my instincts wrong from the start?

'How do you know this?'

'You know Fowler is into S&M, right?' Astrid nodded. 'I met him in a club one night in New York, recognising him as Brady's nephew, so I cultivated a friendship with him and discovered how similar our interests are.'

'Sado-masochistic sex?'

She pursed her lips. 'Torture and killing. Inflicting pain on others purely for pleasure is quite a bonding agent in the right circumstances. I recognised that in you as well.'

'We've nothing in common, and you know it. If you knew Fowler had imprisoned Alex, why didn't you do something about it?'

Cope rolled her eyes. 'What did I care about the girl? I only wanted leverage on Jed.'

'Why, so you could blackmail Brady?'

'I learnt a long time ago the only way for someone like me to survive is to influence those in power. Once I discovered what Fowler was up to, I knew I could use it to control the Senator if I needed to. The missing Sanchez girl only became an issue when you came looking for her. As much as I like you, Astrid, I'd hoped Gideon's men would deal with you, but they turned out to be as useless as I expected.'

'Did you tell him I was here?'

She shook her head. 'That had nothing to do with me. I knew they were in Angel Springs, but I didn't know why until they attacked the cabin.'

Astrid stared at her, wondering if her instincts were still wonky and processing what she'd heard.

'Were you involved in that nonsense with Gideon at Brady's mansion?'

Cope sighed. 'All I know is Gideon contacted Brady and set everything in motion. The first people he hired messed things up at the cabin, so they laid that trap for you at the fundraiser. Brady got well paid, and Gideon got what he wanted: you on a plate.' She formed cow eyes at Astrid. 'I wasn't happy about it, but it was obvious you'd become more trouble than it would be worth to me at some point. And Pete was glad. I'm not sure who he hates the most, you or Crowley. But they fucked the whole thing up, and then you ended up at my place with your crazy story.'

Against her better judgement, Astrid laughed. 'Are you still denying you're a serial killer?'

Cope grinned at her. 'Are you?'

'You're desperate, Jules, with that lame track again. You and I are nothing alike. Yes, I've killed people, but not for pleasure. But you, well, you need to kill to live, don't you? You're no different from every other psychopath I've met. Playing games with me won't change that one bit.'

'Oh please, Ms High and Mighty Astrid Snow. You killed for Crown and Country and never for enjoyment, is that what you're going to say?'

'It'll do for now.'

A vast belly laugh erupted from Cope. 'You're claiming not once did you get any tingle of delight from killing?' She shook her head. 'I don't believe you.'

'It doesn't matter what you believe, Jules. But if I don't find Alex at Fowler's place, then I'll enjoy snuffing out your life.'

She started the car and headed for Jed Fowler's house. Cope tapped her fingers on her leg.

'Well, this will be fun.'

Astrid pushed her foot down. 'Does Fowler know about you and Wylie?'

The town slipped by outside, the night bringing unrelenting darkness which wrapped around them, burying them beneath a starless sky. Astrid had her window down, and the air thickened as the temperature dropped, silence consuming everything. She kept her eye on the road, but her focus was making sure Cope didn't do anything stupid.

'Fowler? The man's an idiot; he's lucky he can find his feet when putting shoes on. No wonder the army kicked him out.' She smiled at Astrid. 'Only you were clever enough to work it out, my English rose. How did you do that?'

Astrid drove into Fowler's street and parked outside his house. She didn't need to drag Cope from the car, the Detective stepping out without hesitation.

'You make a wrong move, Jules, and I'll shoot.'

Cope feigned innocence. 'So, what's the plan, partner? Are you going to burst in with my gun blazing?'

Astrid pointed the revolver at her. 'Take the path which leads to the rear of the house.'

Astrid followed Cope at a close distance. She kept the revolver aimed at her back as they pushed through the bushes. They strode up the hill and reached the entrance.

She removed a nail file from her jacket to pick the lock, but Cope tutted.

'You don't need that, partner. Fowler keeps a spare key under the brown flower pot near the door.'

'You get it.' Astrid kept the gun on her. 'And don't try anything stupid.'

Cope bent and picked up the pot. 'You mean like throwing this at you?' She grabbed the key and tossed the container into the garden. 'As if I'd do something as silly as that.'

She pushed the key into the lock and opened the door. They entered the house, the smell of unwashed plates and fried food smothering everything. Astrid thrust the revolver into Cope's back and shoved her forward.

'Move into the corridor and head to the stairs; there's a hidden basement there.'

'I know where it is.'

Cope did as instructed as they left the kitchen. The Detective needed no prompting to go to the cloth covering the entrance and pull it away; there was no padlock this time. She opened it, and Astrid pushed her inside, switching the light on as they went down the stairs. The bondage gear and the bed were still there, but there was no sign of Fowler or the girl she'd come to find.

There was no sound in the house apart from the thunder booming around Astrid's skull. Her mouth was drier than the desert, the wound in her palm throbbing as if plugged into an electric socket.

'Where's Alex, Jules?'

Cope shrugged as they reached the bottom. 'I don't know what Jed's done with her.' She held her cuffed hands to her nose. 'But it certainly stinks in here. The man needs to clean up after he's played his games.'

Astrid grabbed Cope and shoved her on to the bed. 'Don't move from there.'

The computer equipment was gone, and the stains had vanished from the floor. She scanned the room while watching Cope. There was no sign of anywhere a person could be hidden: if Alex was in the house, it wasn't there.

Cope sat on the bed, her legs hanging over the edge like an innocent schoolgirl.

'Perhaps we're too late, and he's gotten rid of her already.'

Astrid took a deep breath, pushing the frustration into her gut. Had this all been for nothing? She was contemplating what to do when the basement door opened. She turned to see Fowler coming down the steps, taking her eyes from Cope for only a second.

But that was enough.

The Detective sprang from the bed, her hands free from the cuffs, and lunged at Astrid. She knocked the weapon from her and swung the metal dangling from her wrists into Astrid's face. It caught her in the cheek, and she staggered backwards. Cope thrust a twisted elongated paper clip into Astrid's skin as her side hit a bench. Pain surged through her as she dropped the gun. She scrambled for balance as Cope snatched up the weapon.

Then she shot Jed Fowler.

'I always keep a paper clip in my pocket in case I have to pick a lock, don't you?'

Cope pointed the revolver at Astrid as Jed Fowler lay bleeding on the floor. He let out a low moan as his fingers twitched. Astrid rubbed at the wound in her cheek, her pride hurting more than her body.

'Alex was never here, was she?'

She focused on the gun, but her mind darted all over the place. Could she use Fowler as a distraction? Would she reach Cope in time before she fired? How likely was it she'd get up the stairs and out of the house without being shot?

'I honestly didn't think you'd fall for it, but I was desperate. And then I saw it was even worse for you, that desperation eating at you. You need to save this kid because it means something to you.' The gun shook in her hand as she laughed. 'That hope burning behind your eyes, I've seen it before, and I know how it weakens people. My mother had it all her life, but it never did her any good. And now it's the same for you, but you had a choice of taking me in or believing what I said. You like the risk, and that's why you're on the floor with me looming over you.' Her finger caressed the trigger. 'I think you're here for that as much as hoping to find the girl, aren't you, my English rose?'

Astrid squeezed her back into the bench. 'I want to save lives and help people, Jules; you know, the job you're employed to do.' Fowler groaned next to her. 'How are you going to explain this?'

'It's simple. I was following a lead and came here.' She inched closer to Astrid. 'Some planted evidence in Jed's bedroom connected to missing girls will corroborate that, and when I got here, I discovered you two fighting. I tried to intervene, but you grabbed my gun and shot him twice.' She stopped to stare at him. 'Or perhaps it was three times, and he stabbed you in the gut with one of the knives he has here.'

Astrid laughed. 'You forget Grace has Wylie at the station. She'll tell Tanner what happened at your place, and that you were leading me here to find Alex. And then your partner will spill the beans about your crimes.'

It was Cope's turn to laugh. 'Pete's as loyal as a dog; he'd rather take the blame himself than snitch on me. And then it's only my word against Crowley's, and who do you think Tanner will believe when the Giraffe has no evidence?' She grinned like a demented circus clown. 'I'll admit you came close, and you've taught me a few things I must implement going forward, with or without Pete, but you still failed.' She pointed the gun at Astrid while reaching for a knife on the table next to her. 'And the worst thing for you is I have no idea where Alex Sanchez is.'

'There's no need to lie anymore, Jules; not when you've won. So tell me what happened to Alex.'

Cope twisted her head and arm to grab the blade. As she did so, Astrid found the bent paper clip which had cut into her face on the ground, and threw herself at the Detective. Her shoulder slammed into the gun, the two of them falling on top of Fowler. He whimpered as Astrid rolled to the side and reached for the weapon. Her fingers were on the handle when Cope plunged the knife through Astrid's palm. It went straight through flesh and bone and pinned her to the floor.

Cope jumped up, her eyes scanning everywhere for the revolver, seeing it in Astrid's other hand.

'I don't want to shoot you, Jules, but I will if I have to.'

'Perhaps you should.' Cope stood next to the bed. 'With your fingerprints on the gun and bullets in Fowler and me, it'll only add credence to the story I'll tell of finding you two fighting here.'

Every part of Astrid throbbed, her hands aching as if they'd been trapped inside a washing machine all night. She'd have matching scars on both palms now.

'And what about the evidence you were going to plant here? There's no time for that.'

Cope shrugged. 'No plan is perfect.'

'Or I could kill you now.'

'Do you think Fowler saw who blasted him as he came down the stairs? Because I don't believe he did. You took my gun and shot us both. Who knows why, but regardless of what happens to me, you'll never get the chance to find Alex Sanchez from inside a cell.'

Astrid ignored the taunts, kept the gun aimed at her and lifted her other hand, taking the knife with it. Her blood seeped onto the floor as the blade sat uncomfortably through the middle of her flesh. She took the pain and reached into her jacket for the phone, grabbing it so it was cradled next to the knife.

'Let's see what your colleagues think about this.'

She used her aching fingers to find Grace's number and hit dial. Then she waited and watched Detective Julie Cope smile at her without saying another word.

———————

'GET THIS INSIDE YOU.' Grace offered Astrid a coffee, but she refused. Both her hands ached as if they were about to drop off. She stared at the bandages covering her palms and wondered if she deserved all the pain.

'How's Fowler?'

'He's doing fine in hospital, which is where you should be.'

'The paramedics said there's no need; both wounds were clean and went straight through without causing much damage.' She held her bandaged hands up and flexed her fingers, not showing Grace how agonising such a simple movement was. 'All I needed was stitches. Did Fowler say who shot him?'

'He didn't see who it was, and he can't remember anything after falling.'

Astrid let out a long sigh. 'What happened with Wylie?'

'I brought him here and told Tanner what happened at Cope's place. My colleagues took him away and have been interviewing him ever since.'

'You've had no news on what he's said?'

'That's well below my pay grade. I'm just glad the Chief didn't laugh at me and set Wylie free.'

Astrid remembered the things Julie had said to her in that basement. 'Maybe they still will.'

Her heart sank as she rubbed her finger. They may have stopped Wylie and Cope's killing spree, but she still had to find Alex. She'd failed, and she didn't know what to do about it.

Grace must have read her mind.

'Cope didn't give you any clue as to what happened to Sanchez?'

A smaller version of Astrid stomped around inside her head and karate kicked the sides of her skull. 'It was all a trick, and I was too desperate and gullible to realise it until it was too late.'

'It's not your fault. You had to try everything to find her.'

The way Grace spoke, it was as if she'd given up on the girl. As Astrid touched the phone inside her jacket, her mind wandered to thoughts of Olivia and England.

I'm too dangerous to be around, so how can I expose my niece to that? Courtney was right all along.

The door opened as that thought burnt into her brain, and Chief Tanner entered. He nodded at Astrid while holding an evidence bag towards Grace: it contained a phone.

'We found a dozen of these in Wylie's house. Can you guess what's on them?' His lips curled upwards in an imper-sonation of Jack Nicholson on his most manic days.

Julie Cope's voice lingered inside Astrid's head. 'He took videos of their victims. Cope said he was taking more and more risks.'

'You're correct, Ms Snow. I've only had a brief look at this one, the material is far too distressing for extended viewing, but Forensics and Cybercrime say there's enough evidence on this device alone to put him behind bars for the rest of his life.'

Grace wiped coffee from her trembling lips. 'What about Cope? Is she in any of the videos?'

Tanner's smile vanished in a blink of an eye. 'We haven't gone through every phone yet, so I don't know, but there's nothing to incriminate Cope so far. The good news is Wylie is singing like a bird as we speak, so I have no doubt he'll implicate his partner in all their crimes. But I thought you could interrogate Cope and get her side of the story, Detective Crowley.'

Astrid observed the shock sweep through Grace's body as her eyes threatened to bulge out of her head like an over-excited frog's.

'What?' Grace stammered.

'A promotion is long overdue, Crowley, and with what you did bringing them in, there's no time like the present. Plus, the department is two detectives short at the moment. You'll get your new badge in the morning.' He pushed the evidence bag closer to her. 'So, are you ready to interrogate Cope?'

Grace turned to Astrid as she took the phone from Tanner. 'My first official decision is to ask you to join me in the interview room, Astrid Snow, if you want to.'

Astrid watched Cope through the window, studying her relaxed manner and the massive smile on her face. The Detective's confidence was unwavering, regardless of the circumstances she found herself in.

Was she lying to me in Fowler's house, saying she didn't know what happened to Alex? She might be the last chance I have of finding the girl. And we did have a connection, no matter how brief it was.

'After you, Detective Crowley.'

Grace led Astrid into the room and stopped across the table from their suspect. The smile never left Cope's face, and she looked at them as if preparing for a night out.

'I assume my lawyer is on the way.'

Astrid sat first, waiting for Grace to start the recording equipment, but she didn't, addressing Cope instead.

'This isn't a formal interview, Detective. We'll begin that when your legal representation arrives. We want a word with you before that.'

'Let me guess, ladies; you're going to offer me a deal if I tell you where Alex Sanchez is.'

Astrid's knuckles cracked as she placed her arms on the table. 'Were you lying to me before; do you know where she is?'

Cope's smirk increased the irritation wriggling underneath Astrid's skin. 'I'll keep saying it until the cows come home or it finally gets into your skull: I have no knowledge of what happened to Alex Sanchez or any missing kids from this town or any other.' Her eyes sparkled. 'I had one night of lust with Ms Snow, and that was enough for me. She appears to have taken the rejection personally and has cooked up this ridiculous story of me as a sadomasochistic serial killer.' Cope glanced towards the glass where Tanner observed her from the other side. 'There's no proof for any of her fantasies, and I'm surprised, and not a little offended, that people in this station are falling for it.' She rubbed her hands and leant into the chair. 'And that's all I'm going to say until my lawyer arrives.'

It was Grace's turn to smile as she placed the bag containing one of Wylie's phones on the table. 'There's video evidence on here and on other devices Wylie used, incriminating him and you in numerous crimes, including but not limited to the following: abduction and kidnapping, torture, rape, and murder.' Grace clasped her hands together. 'What do you say to that, Detective Cope?'

Julie Cope lost her grin, replacing it with a blank expression. 'Why isn't Tanner or one of the other Detectives interviewing me?' She appeared offended by the assumed slight. 'I don't answer to you, Officer Crowley.'

'Grace was promoted, Jules; she's Detective Crowley now.' Astrid grinned at her. 'And you and Wylie, with the help of all the videos he made, are going to make her famous.'

Cope crossed her arms and scrutinised Astrid. 'This is just for you, Snow; once the lawyer arrives, I'll be saying nothing until I know what you get from Wylie.'

Tension rippled through Astrid's shoulders. 'Thank you, Jules.'

Her stomach was in knots as she spoke, but she knew she couldn't antagonise Cope if she wanted the truth.

Cope pushed the chair back and stretched her legs.

'Alex Sanchez's disappearance is nothing to do with me, and I don't know where she is.' She looked at Astrid. 'Sorry, love.' Then she turned to Crowley. 'Since the day I met Detective Wylie, he manipulated and groomed me into doing everything he desired. He used emotional and physical means to control me, and if I questioned him or refused to do what he wanted, he would beat me violently. He also sexually assaulted me on many occasions.' She sighed loudly. 'This has gone on for at least five years, and I've had to switch off emotionally at times to live with the horror he's put me through.'

Astrid shook her head. 'You're saying none of your criminal actions has been your own, that Detective Wylie forced you to kidnap, torture, rape, and kill several teenagers?'

Julie Cope's lips trembled as she moved closer to the table, holding her hand towards Astrid. 'It's all true; whatever you find on his videos, he made me do.' A single tear trickled down her face. 'Look at him compared to me; he's six foot three, two hundred and twenty pounds of muscle.'

She wiped at her cheek. 'How could I fight back against someone like that?'

Astrid had sat across from many expert liars in her time, but Julie Cope was one of the best. She already had an image of her convincing the toughest of juries of her innocence.

'You could have gone to your superiors, Jules; there are plenty of people you might have spoken to about Wylie's actions.'

'This tough exterior I portray is only a façade.' She unfolded her fingers towards Astrid like a blossoming flower. 'This is why we connected so quickly because I recognised the same thing in you.' She placed her other hand on her heart. 'Inside, I'm weak and vulnerable, and Wylie took that and exploited me.'

She pulled her hands back and buried her head in them. Grace and Astrid glanced at each other.

'We should postpone this conversation until your lawyer arrives, Detective Cope,' Grace said.

Cope lifted her head and wiped her shaking fingers across her face. 'The day our home burnt down, I was in my room watching TV. It was two in the morning, and my younger sister and parents were sound asleep. It was the heat I felt first, my skin burning when I tried to open my bedroom door.' She held up her hand. 'My flesh healed years ago, but the scars are still there.'

Astrid studied her face, impressed by the mask Julie had managed to pull on so quickly. She wondered if she'd constructed this story a long time ago for a moment such as this.

'I'd fallen asleep watching Buffy, my mind full of images of me killing monsters. I'm not sure how the fire started, but later, the police told me they thought it was in the wiring. The house was old, passed on from my grand-parents to my parents. I woke up to an inferno and jumped for the door. When I fell back from the heat, the smoke billowed black across the room, filling my lungs with dark fingers, clawing at my heart. I don't know how I climbed out of the window, but I did, falling twenty feet into the garden and breaking a leg and arm. I lay and waited for the sirens to arrive, peering into the flames and knowing the rest of my family had died.' She gazed into Astrid's eyes. 'I was never the same after that, always weak on the inside.'

Cope sat back and folded her arms. Astrid was lost for words. She stood, and Grace followed her out of the room.

Chief Tanner was outside waiting for them.

'Wow, she knows how to weave a tale. All the years I've known Julie, and it's the first I've heard of this.'

Astrid couldn't help but admire the woman, no matter how monstrous she was. 'It was a witchery of fiction at the highest level. Imagine how a jury will respond to that when you get her in court and on the stand.' She looked at Tanner. 'Have you found any video evidence of her in Wylie's collection?'

He held out his hands. 'My officers continue to sift through the material, but, from the little I've viewed, there's some terrible stuff there, and even for hardened profession-als, it's not an easy thing to do.' He peered at Cope through the glass. 'She must know there's video incriminating her to make up a story like that.'

Astrid thought the same, watching Julie on the other side of the room, happy she'd managed to end the woman's terrible crimes. But a tremendous ache continued to punch at her heart.

Now she had to tell Christina Sanchez she believed her daughter was dead.

'Do you want to continue when her lawyer turns up?'

Astrid considered what she'd heard in the other room. 'You stick with her, Grace. I have to see Christina Sanchez.'

Bad news follows me around until it gets ahead of me.

Grace edged closer to her. 'There's something I need to tell you.'

Astrid recognised the invisible weight on her friend's shoulders, guessing it was there to mirror the despair in her heart because they hadn't found Alex.

'I'm listening, Grace.'

Detective Crowley took a deep breath. 'I didn't tell you the whole truth about what happened at the well.' She glanced through the glass at Cope examining her nails. 'I said Manny saw the girls drop me down, and then came and rescued me, but it wasn't like that.' She took another deep breath. 'He didn't see what happened; he only found me because I was crying for so long.'

'How long were you in there?'

Grace shook her head. 'I don't know, more than an hour

at least. I thought the girls would come back for me, but they never did. I sat in the dark, jumping every time something crawled over me or I heard a noise. I was a wreck by the time Manny got me out.'

'Did you tell your grandmother this?'

'No, I couldn't, but deep down, I think she knew I'd kept something from her. The nightmares came each night until my teenage years. She said it was all in my mind, and there was nothing to scare me in the dark.' She turned and stared at Cope through the glass. 'But I knew she was wrong.'

Astrid did something unusual for her: she pulled Grace close and hugged her. They stood in silence until she let go.

'Are you going to be okay if I go and talk to Christina?'

Grace nodded and gave her the car keys. 'Take these. I'll see you at my place.'

Astrid took a last look at Julie Cope through the glass before she left. Cope's eyes had frozen over like the surface of a winter lake, robbing them of her intensity. The real Jules was in there, Astrid knew it, but now she'd retreated into a shell, into a façade to show the rest of the world. Perhaps it was only one of many masks she'd projected in her life, all to hide that person who enjoyed inflicting suffering and death on to others. She didn't know why, maybe it had something to do with what Grace had told her, but she had the urge to reach inside and tell Cope it was better to release her pain, to open up instead of burying it behind falsehood, cruelty, and murder.

The story Cope had told them was a detailed construction proving how manipulative she was. Had she and Wylie lied about Alex and the initials on the bottom of the door to their murder chamber? The image of the events in that room made her hands ache even more. As she left the building, she hoped there were no clips of Alex in Wylie's collection. It was terrible to think she might never find the girl, but she couldn't bear the thought of seeing her on video if it was to watch her suffer and die.

As she drove to the trailer park, she ran through the things she'd say to Christina; none of them made her feel any good. The early morning sun flickered across the sky as she entered the gates. The streets were quiet as she got out of the car; even the dogs slept, snoozing outside the trailers. She flexed her fingers, but the pain wouldn't go away. It wasn't from the damage Cope had done but from her inability to discover the girl she'd been tasked to find.

This time, Astrid paid more attention to the homes as she went, admiring how each was personalised to stand out from the rest. Some were painted with exotic dragons or brightly feathered birds, while vibrant colours stretching from the top to the gap between the bottom and the ground covered the others.

She wondered how none of this had grabbed her attention before, realising her focus on finding Alex had distracted her from things that were right in front of her face.

Astrid reached the Sanchez home and paused. Initially, it was to gather her thoughts, taking no account of the time and how her presence would inconvenience Christina, but then a realisation froze her mind as well as her legs. There was something different about the trailer compared to all the rest. She'd noticed it before, but it hadn't meant anything significant to her then.

The gap between the bottom and the ground was obscured by ornaments placed in front of it. She moved closer, glancing at the other homes, and then back to Christina's: it was smaller in height than the others. She double-checked; perhaps it was just a different model, a shorter one.

No, it wasn't that.

She ran towards it, dropping to the ground and pushing the Disney figures and potted plants out of the way. The trailer had no legs, no support; it stood on the cement, no gap to separate it. Astrid turned away and sprinted up the steps, hand out to bang on the door; it creaked open without her touching it.

'Christina, are you here?' The place was a mess, with magazines strewn everywhere, a table broken in half and the television on its side. 'Christina?'

Her feet crunched through the smashed glass, and then she saw the lump in the carpet. She reached down and pulled the material away, revealing the hatch which hadn't been closed properly. Astrid got her fingers into the gap and dragged it open. Her hands throbbed as she touched the ladder built into the side.

What is it about this town and underground rooms?

She removed the phone from her pocket and turned on the torch, her memory flashing back to the recent excursion below the earth near the river.

'Christina, are you there?' she shouted with one hand shining light into the dark and the other on the first rung of the ladder.

She ignored any concern for her safety and lowered herself into the space; it was roomy, half the trailer's length and the same width. It had been dug into the concrete below the motorhome, hidden beneath the vehicle. She couldn't tell if it was a recent construction or not, but it wasn't as old as Cope and Wylie's underground torture chamber.

She moved the torch across the space: there was no

damage, only an unmade bed, a small bookshelf crammed with items, and a laptop humming on the floor.

Astrid sat on the bed and picked up the computer; it was still warm and had twenty minutes of battery left. She touched the screen, and it sprang to life, static electricity penetrating her flesh.

The background picture was an image of Alex and Christina smiling into the camera, but it wasn't that which attracted her attention. Down the side was a stack of digital folders, named for things Alex was interested in or attended: protests, demonstrations, charity events, fundraisers, and on it went until the very last one and a name she instantly recognised.

Roger Taylor. What are you doing on a teenage girl's computer?

She moved the pointer on to the yellow icon and opened it. Inside were pictures and videos. Astrid selected all the images, right-clicked on them, and picked the photo gallery option.

'Fuck!' She closed them all just as quickly. She didn't need to go through a dozen or so naked photos of Taylor; one was enough. Were these sent to Christina, and Alex had found them?

The first video answered that question in the negative.

'You have a beautiful body, Alex,' Taylor said on the clip.

Vitriol shot through Astrid's stomach and up her throat. Forcing herself to watch five seconds of the two of them having sex, she switched it off and spat on to the floor.

You perverted scumbag.

'I love that video; it's my favourite of them all.'

Astrid turned to see Taylor pointing a gun at her. 'What

did you do to her?' Wrath and venom were a heady mixture in her mouth.

'I loved her, and she loved me; that's all there is to it.'

Astrid dug her fingers into the bed. 'She's seventeen, a child; you're a forty-year-old failed human being. Is this why you sent me to find her?' Sickness swelled inside her gut like an inflatable balloon.

He waved the gun at her. 'I didn't realise she had those until I went through that computer. No, I'm looking for something else she stole from me. Do you know where she is?' A flush of irritation brightened his skin. 'I can't believe it took me so long to understand her mother had hidden her here all this time. But Christina won't tell me anything, no matter how much I beat her. So I'm guessing the great Astrid Snow knows where the girl is.'

'I knew you were a piece of shit, Taylor, but this is something else.'

He raised the gun and brought it down on to the side of her face. The metal cut into Astrid's flesh and knocked her into the bed. He pressed the barrel into her skull.

'Tell me where she is, or I'll splatter your brains over this room.'

Anger and frustration oozed out of him as blood dripped from her cheek. She rubbed at the wound in her palm.

'Okay, Roge; I'll tell you where she is if you tell me what it is you want.'

Astrid considered the options if she grabbed the pistol; they weren't good. She was fast, but not like lightning, which she'd need to be to get the weapon before he made a significant hole in her head.

He moved back, the gun still directed at her. 'She stole

some digital files from me. They're not on that computer, so she must have them on a portable drive.'

Astrid lifted and sat on the edge of the bed. 'So, you've given up grooming and abusing the girl for some memory stick she took from you.' She brushed cold blood from her cheek. 'These must be some important documents she has.' A mischievous grin crawled over her face. 'Something worse than the video I watched? What have you been doing, Roge?'

'It doesn't matter, Snow. Now tell me where she is.'

He moved a step closer to her. She had one hand on the pillow; if she brought it across her head, would it be enough to soften the impact? Did she have any other choice?

As she prepared to lie to him, the floor creaked above her. It was sufficient for Taylor to flinch upwards and distract his attention. She grabbed the cushion and threw it at him.

The gun went off near her head, his fingers diverted by the pillow, a movement just enough for the bullet to scrape past her cheek. Her ears exploded, her skull ringing like drunken church bells. She had matching scars on both sides of her face now. Her fingers were on his wrist, twisting it before he pulled the trigger again. Astrid's head throbbed, smoke drifting up to her nose, as she pushed him against the wall.

Taylor brought his knee up into her groin and knocked her across the bed. Her back hit the side, and she flopped on to the floor. He moved forward and glared at her.

'I guess I'll have to find her myself.'

He caressed the trigger. She was about to throw herself into his legs when something large dropped down the hatch and landed on his head. Taylor crumbled to the ground before he could fire, the microwave crashing into his spent form.

Astrid grabbed the gun and watched the figure coming down the steps.

'That's him cooked,' Alex Sanchez said as she grinned. She peered at Astrid. 'Are you okay?'

Astrid didn't know whether to hug her, shake her hand, or do nothing. She did nothing.

'I'm fine.' Blood trickled down her cheek. 'It's only a nick.' She stared at Alex, impressed with the girl's maturity until she recognised it was a forced maturity she knew only too well.

Alex gazed at Taylor on the floor. 'Is he dead?' The cracked microwave lay next to him. Astrid didn't care either way, but she checked his pulse and examined his head.

'He'll live.' She took out her phone. 'We need to find your mother. God knows what he did to her.'

'She's fine,' Alex replied. 'I found her tied up at the back of the motorhome. Our neighbours are looking after her.' The girl was seventeen going on fifty. 'I saw him creep into here and followed; then I heard the two of you fighting in my room.'

'Are you all right?'

Alex looked older than her age, her eyes filled with things most people never experience. 'I am now Mum's okay, and he's out cold.'

'What did you take from him?'

She reached into her pocket and removed a memory stick. She handed it to Astrid.

'This.'

'What happened to you after you left the Future Youth compound?'

'I found a cabin in the woods, and the old man who

lived there helped me. I stayed until it got dark and walked home, making sure no one saw me. I told Mum everything, and she kept me hidden in here.'

Astrid admired her coolness. 'She didn't dig a hole in the ground for you, then?'

Alex grinned. 'No, it's been here for years. There are a few of these in the park. If you hadn't already guessed, this place is part of a refuge and rooms like this are used for safety if any unwanted visitors arrive.'

Astrid glanced at Taylor as he moaned on the floor. 'Like him.'

'And worse than him.'

'Did he force you into a relationship?'

Her eyes darkened. 'I was fifteen, and he made me feel like the most important, most beautiful girl in the world.' She clenched her fists. 'But I woke up eventually.'

Astrid didn't want to push Alex any further on what had happened between her and Taylor. She held up the memory stick. 'Do you know what's on this?'

Alex nodded. 'It's why I hid from him. I didn't know what to do about its contents, but I knew he'd come looking for it, and me.'

'Let's have a look at them.'

They went through the files together on the laptop; then Astrid called Grace and the British Embassy in New York. She peered at Taylor's slumbering body again before phoning for an ambulance. By the time the police and the medics arrived, she knew Roger Taylor would be going to prison for a long time.

CHRISTINA SANCHEZ WAS DRINKING coffee with her daughter at the police station when Grace strode into the room.

'Are you all okay?'

Astrid nodded. 'There are only a few bruises for Christina where he tied her up.' She'd confirmed that Taylor hadn't laid a finger on her otherwise, with his claims of violence only a bluff. 'Alex is in good health considering how much time she's spent underground.'

'What about the cut on your face?'

'It's just a scratch. Where's Taylor now?'

'The Feds have him downstairs. They're not telling Tanner much. What was on the memory stick Alex gave you?'

Astrid took Grace to one side. 'He groomed her when he was seeing the mother, starting when she was fifteen. Christina didn't know what was going on when Alex went to New York for demonstrations and stayed with Taylor.'

'What a scumbag.'

'Thankfully, Alex eventually realised that.' Astrid glanced at the girl, pleased to see her smiling, but knowing from experience it wouldn't be something she could quickly shake off. 'Then she secretly videoed him handing documents over to a Russian contact.'

Grace let out a low whistle. 'His employers won't be happy with that.'

'They won't be the only ones. There were files on the memory stick from the US State Department. I don't know how Taylor acquired them, but he passed them to the Russians as well.' She let go of Grace's arm. 'What happened with Cope?'

'She wouldn't give anything away, said it was all Wylie's

doing, and she was trying to save you from him when I arrived.'

Astrid shook her head. 'She certainly knows how to lie.'

'It won't help her. Wylie is spilling the beans about their crimes, and he has plenty of videos incriminating Cope.' Grace relaxed her shoulders. 'He's given us evidence she knew nothing about. She'll be an old woman if she ever gets out of jail. I'd say this has been a successful day all round. What will you do now?'

Astrid touched the wounds in both her hands. She wasn't comfortable with goodbyes, taking a final look at the reunited Sanchez family and hugging Grace.

'I expect to get regular updates on your new life as a detective.' Then she let go. 'And what it's like to be a foster mother.'

Chief Tanner called Crowley away before she could reply, the American giving her English friend one last grin.

Astrid strode through the station and stepped outside. It was time to move on, but to where? Return to England or perhaps keep travelling through the States?

There's still so much to see.

As she contemplated the options, the phone vibrated in her pocket with a new message. She removed it, her heart fluttering as she saw who the sender was: her sister. This would help her decide what to do.

Astrid opened it with shaky fingers.

ABOUT THE AUTHOR

Andrew French lives amongst faded seaside glamour on the North East coast of England. He likes gin and cats but not together, new music and old movies, curry and ice cream. Slow bike rides and long walks to the pub are his usual exercise, as well as flicking through the pages of good books and the memoirs of bad people.

Find out more at www.andrewsfrench.com

Facebook:

https://www.facebook.com/A-S-French-Author-150145625006018

Twitter:

www.twitter.com/andrewfrench100

Instagram:

www.instagram.com/andrewfrench100

And replies to all his email at mail@andrewsfrench.com

If you have the time, please leave a review at Amazon or Goodreads

Thank you!

ACKNOWLEDGMENTS

Many thanks to my wonderful wife for all her support and patience.

The Killing Moon edited by Alison Jack.

Cover design by James, GoOnWrite.com